D1293166

The Road to the Sea

The Road to the Sea

ciara hegarty

Macmillan New Writing

First published 2010 by Macmillan New Writing
an imprint of Pan Macmillan, a division of Macmillan Publishers Limited
Pan Macmillan, 20 New Wharf Road, London N1 9RR
Basingstoke and Oxford
Associated companies throughout the world
www.panmacmillan.com

ISBN 978-0-230-74426-4

Typeset by Ellipsis Books Limited, Glasgow
Printed and bound in the UK by CPI Mackays, Chatham ME5 8TD

Visit **www.panmacmillan.com** to read more about all our books
and to buy them. You will also find features, author interviews and
news of any author events, and you can sign up for e-newsletters
so that you're always first to hear about our new releases.

For my Grandma

Acknowledgements

I would like to thank my parents and children for their unwavering support and patience. Special thanks also to Maria Rejt, Will Atkins, Mary Chamberlain and Amy Cunnah.

ONE

Kathleen Steele watched her feet walking the path they had been walking, Monday to Saturday, since she was out of the double pram. The pram was still used by her brother and sisters – they had made a small wagon out of it, in which they pushed each other down the hill at terrifying speeds. Kathleen often enviously watched them at their play from the window of a bedroom. Her brother Tomás shared it with her sisters, Molly and Laura. Their parents shared the other room with Paddy, the baby, who was transported about the village in another pram, a grand blue one on loan from Crowley's over in the town – but they'd be expecting it back any day now, the size of Catherine Crowley. Kathleen hoped that she would never have the misfortune to marry, to become a vehicle for child after child to enter the world, only to be run ragged. Although she enjoyed the numerous tasks she dutifully carried out, with her father out working the fields and her mother still mourning the loss of Nuala, Kathleen rarely had a moment to herself. She felt for the children as their mother was daily so visibly dipped in grief, so she entertained them, and patched the knees and legs of Tomás – who never walked but always ran – and laundered the baby's things. She told fairy stories to the girls and brushed their stubborn hair and made sure their teeth were cleaned. But Kathleen did not feel sorry for herself. People in the village saw this, and it endeared her to them all the more. She barely seemed to notice that she had sacrificed play in the years since her sister's death.

As she walked, and as she looked, she saw beneath her feet the familiar little pebbles embedded in the road. She felt she knew the pattern and placement of them as surely as she knew the lines on her own hand. How many times, she wondered, had she placed a foot over a certain selection of the stones as they looked up at her over the years on her messages down in the village?

The morning was nearly broken. Little Paddy would be waking again soon and she should be back for warming up his milk, but Kathleen had stopped walking. She decided to linger a little, to just take in the breath of the air, the gentle heave of the land, as the sky and the sea drew breath as one with her. In and out. She could stop for a moment or two. There to her right was the little wall she used to sit on with Nuala. A tangle of brambles had grown there with such possessiveness that, each year, less and less of the wall could be seen.

She walked over to it now. If she crouched down a little – not all the way, but a half-crouch – it brought her eyes into line with what the two sisters would have seen. It was as though Nuala were still there beside her sometimes. She could almost hear their laughter and taste the purple juice of the berries. With their noses reaching up to the wall's top, through the brambles, they could see all the way down past the bottom field to the sea. But sometimes, if it was a thick fog, even as far in as the dairy would be completely hidden. They used to squeal with a half-pretend fear when the foghorn would sound, echoing through the valley, and the red light of the lighthouse was swallowed up by the thick blankets of mist. The two girls would crouch down behind the wall and pretend they were on a ship in dangerous waters, waiting for the good pirates to come and rescue them. There was not a day that went by when Kathleen did not miss her sister, and she worried sometimes whether it was wrong to hope that this day would never come.

Kathleen had the small room to herself of course but, rather than being a haven away from the bustle of the house, it made her feel isolated from the rest of the family. The way the family interacted would change periodically, but Kathleen remained static, slightly apart. The little girls spent a good few months shadowing their father, silent as he worked. Tomás played alone at this time, or with Brendan Reilly. Occasionally, one of them came to their mother's side to watch the baby feed, or to express a hug from her when he was sleeping. But, as their affection was generally met with a blank look from their grey-faced mother, they had all begun to play out together, finding a comfort in their childish imaginations that could take them out of this world and into another, where there was no sad mother, no lost sister. She marvelled at their imagination, and understood that God did not want them to have the money to be spoiled with toys from the department store in town, and trips and the like. His mission for the Steele family was clearly to let children be children, and for family love to be enough. And that is the thought Kathleen, thin but beautiful, took with her to Mass on a Sunday.

As dawn's first light began to give feature to the scene in front of him, Joseph Foley lifted his eyes to watch. He rose up a little, his left elbow bearing the uneven load of his torso, and he cocked his head upright, so that the view before him was as God intended. It was always a cool, watery blue, this very first light, the darkness reluctantly fading, and then pinky – not pink like on a small child's hairband or a bouncing ball, but dusty pink, like behind the ear of a young pig, or the colour of the skin of a mother's hand after baking something of which a main ingredient is flour. Each time Joseph's dry, leaden lids reopened there were whole new patches filled in – different hues of the same colour, all monochrome still, but the change was perceptible to him, as if he were secretly watching an unwitting God painting by numbers.

At night it was different, he had noticed. Dusk and dawn, although performing exactly the same synchrony of moves, behaved so differently. Even if he concentrated with all his mind, the colours just slipped away without warning, without an indication of the speed or the deftness with which it would happen. He could not sense the changes. God did it with less stealth than dawn. Joseph had come to feel uneasy by the onset of evening, and he would turn his back on the red and gold fire of cloud that sat on the horizon until the stars began to appear.

He needed a distraction from the thoughts and images always in his head. If only he had a book beside him. As a boy, he would read one of his father's old books to relieve the frac-

tious boredom of long sibling-less summers. They were usually
about ships and nautical adventures, in which the main character would have his own face in his imagining of the story.
And he would sit on his bed and read the hours away, innocent
of what lay ahead of him as a man. It seemed so long ago now,
his childhood self a stranger after all that he had seen.

Each time Joseph Foley did or thought something, he
reminded himself of the futility, and really the audaciousness,
of the doing or the thinking, and would remind himself of why
he was here. Why he was the dot on this enormous landscape,
and why really this dot should leave, and yet he was beginning
to feel like a permanent fixture, an old oak that has been there
for a hundred years. Joseph knew the sounds and smells –
particularly the smells – of the field. The air smelled different
according to the time of day and, naturally, according to which
way the wind was blowing. If it blew from the west it brought
with it the sweet odour of the neighbouring field of cattle, and
from the east the smell of leather saddles after being scrubbed
and shined and laid out in the sun. If there was no wind, just
the slightest breath of warmth that stroked at his nose and lips
as he lay there, Joseph could taste the salt of the sea and, if he
inhaled as deeply as he could, right at the end of that breath
he would recognize the honey-like scent of a woman. He drank
in these simplicities with the passion of a man who has been
exposed to nothing but mud and dirt and decay, as though it
were his first experience of them.

They had sat in the same order, in the same row, at Mass each
Sunday for as long as she could remember – their father by the

aisle on the left, the children in descending height order, with their mother on the right-hand end, to keep the young ones in order. But now it was Kathleen on the far right, in between her mother and the pram; trying not to notice the gap on the bench that Nuala left, trying to concentrate on Father Nolan's sermons as she attended to her mother, with one hand ready to rock in case the baby hollered – which he invariably did as soon as Father began. Little Paddy – it was as if he was objecting where his mother could not. Kathleen could see her turning away from God. She had watched it happening slowly over time, unnoticed by anybody else, even her father, she thought, but little by little, Kathleen could see it. Further from God and closer to nothing.

Kathleen looked at her mother often. Sometimes, at home, she thought that she could pull her chair right up to her mother's so that their knees were touching, and look her right in the eyes for a whole minute, and Nora Steele would barely blink. When she had watched her mother breastfeeding Paddy at the beginning she thought how awful it was that she barely registered the beautiful miracle propped up against her, expressing sustenance as she sat staring out the window.

For the first while, after Nuala's death, Mrs Steele deliberately avoided looking at Kathleen. They had been identical. When Kathleen noticed this tendency, she began making simple changes, for her mother's sake – ceasing to wear the colour blue, Nuala's favourite, and wearing her hair up, as Nuala's had always flowed long and wild after her. But still her mother would not look at her. It had soon become automatic, and the aggrieved woman did not need to try to avert her gaze; her eyes simply never came to rest upon her daughter. Kathleen presumed this was why she was never part of the ever-changing dynamics within the household. They all, knowingly or not, kept her to their periphery to spare them the pain of being reminded of Nuala's absence. It was understandable, she supposed. But recently, she had noticed that the younger girls, too, were excluded from their mother's attention, although they did not especially resemble Nuala, and were younger than she had been when she died. They had sensed it too, but instead of moving towards Kathleen or their father as their mother moved away from them, they stuck together and, in their way, supported each other through it. Kathleen longed to speak to her twin, for guidance – she would have the answers. For while everyone else in the family, and in the village, remembered her only as a little girl, Nuala had grown with Kathleen. Kathleen still knew her and could sense Nuala within herself. She could see her smiling, just by looking in the mirror and gently lifting the corners of her own mouth. Sometimes this feeling was so strong, it made her small dark room seem less empty.

She stood up and surveyed the land over the bramble-screened wall. She had picked a handful of berries and had begun eating them when she spied the figure of a man in Murphy's Holy Cross field. From her vantage point she thought at first he was a fallen-down scarecrow, such was his posture – arms outstretched, head slightly to one side. But of course this could not be the case as Seán Murphy kept no crop or animal in that field. She watched a while and wondered for a moment was he dead. Then the scarecrow man's left arm flapped, as if at a fly, and then lay still again. Kathleen watched the man a few moments longer as she picked more blackberries for tomorrow's pie. He was a good bit away, and down a hill, but she could see that he was still young, maybe just ten years older than her. He had very dark hair, as far as she could make out, and from that she deduced that he must be some eccentric cousin of Mr Murphy's, come to stay.

On his first day, Joseph had not known quite how to behave. He felt exposed, self-conscious. Even the closest house or farm building was distant enough for him to have to strain his eyes to count the windows. In the vastness of the L-shaped field, he was acutely aware of his human form. He felt his warm blood slowly, smoothly, coursing through his body, heard it thrum in the space behind his ears. His fingertips were dry and cool, despite the weather. He assumed this was due to lack of food, but he knew the only way to endure it was to banish the mere thought of sustenance the moment it entered his mind.

He had, that first day, crossed through the grass to the centre of the field, as that would leave him most exposed to the elements, but now he headed towards the hedge lining the upper end. His plan was not working. He found himself distracted, marvelling at each small living organism. He would often be amused by his surroundings until the sun was at its highest point in the sky, which meant it was probably dinnertime. The mere fact of the field itself awed him still – the pure, undulating blanket of untouched grass, not a bit of it displaced by heavy boot or shovel.

It was on about day four or five that the unbearable, maddening ache of hunger began to ebb, and was replaced by a heavy, intimidating feeling in his gut. A resignation. It made Joseph feel weak, but he saw this as a good sign. Maybe he would grow so weak he would not notice himself slipping away.

He had feared rain on the third day, worried that it would take some days for him to go, and that he would be lying in wet clothes, shivering and pathetic. He still feared the weather and what it can do to a body when there is no means of sheltering it. But the heat endured and now, each time he saw a cloud, he sent a little message with it as it went on its way, for the rain to come. Sodden clothes and a hungry stomach were sure to speed things up. Maybe he would catch pleurisy or polio or some other awful illness. But then he worried that these would be unpleasant, unnerving, painful. He didn't want his last days to be like that. He just wanted to lie down and go peacefully, without a bother, and if there was a God up there, which he doubted, he was sure He would understand. Maybe he could discuss reincarnation, be a better person next time around, be more likeable. Or a dog.

It was a strange thought for Joseph Foley, to be wishing for rain. It had been a long time since he had had a thought on what he wished a day to bring. He had given up long ago on the childish hopings of his youth, had learned that reality is more brutal than dreams. His days were his own now, long and slow, devoid here of harsh sounds, of movement even. Life was muted, unreal. A branch that swayed in the corner of his vision caused him no alarm. But from time to time a distant pheasant would fall from the sky and he would clutch himself in anticipation of the crack that would follow.

But now that he had been here over a week, he had begun

to wake with an interest in the day ahead. It would not do. He decided today to be ruthless. The sun was urging his body to find shade, so with renewed fervour he lay down on the chosen spot and covered as much of his body as he could with his great-coat, in doing so noticing that his shoelaces had worn where they had rubbed at the holes. Soon they would break. The laces were not his, but he had needed them. The boots were his, and he was still in them, though he did not deserve to be. He lay down once again and waited to fade out.

He dreamed often, fitfully, of black, smoke-filled skies, voices gasping and crying out. Memories would become distorted and exaggerated and he would wake suddenly, with a shock, as though someone had thrown a bucket of icy water over him. Then he would sigh and lie back down and close his eyes again, willing himself to be able to forget.

It was two days later when those stones next witnessed Kathleen's feet carrying her down the road. This time she would not stop at the blackberry wall, but walk on, following the sweeping bend down the hill, and then left for the long walk into Killnarnan. She needed to go to the big store and school books were to be bought. The children had been sent out, the girls to Walsh's and Tomás up to Reilly's. Paddy was asleep in the pram next to their mother, and their father was under strict instruction by Kathleen to check in every five minutes and to 'only give him a bottle if he's hollering the house down'. If it wasn't such a long walk Kathleen would take Paddy with her, but he would only waste his sleep half the way there, and bawl for the other half through boredom and hunger. It didn't feel right to be leaving him for so long. But she would take this time to relax a little, to enjoy this rare time to herself.

While she was in town she thought she might find something in the chemist's for her mother's sleeplessness at night. Her father used to tend the baby if he woke, even though the boy's mother would be lying there, looking wide-eyed at the dark. But it was not right that he should have broken sleep before getting up at a farmer's hour, and so Kathleen had, some nights, begun to bring Paddy into her own room beneath their parents' little attic room. Besides, he settled much more quickly with her.

The day was fine, with a gentle heat dotted here and there and a breeze that was as refreshing as a cold drink. Kathleen marvelled at how pleasurable it was to find herself letting her mind wander, not having any child to instruct, scold, tickle; no one to attend to but herself, out walking on such a beautiful day.

She had wanted to leave Killnarnan at one o'clock so that Paddy's routine would not be disrupted, but had met one of her father's men's sons on her way out of the chemist. Jimmy Neely was a small man, prematurely balding, and lacked the nice demeanour of most men in the area. While he talked on about a lame pig on some neighbour's farm, Kathleen looked up at a wisp of cloud that was moving swiftly over from the direction of home, and as she did, a curl of hair fell loose from her plaited bun. She would have been self-conscious of this if she were talking to any other man, but Jimmy Neely barely looked at her face at all, never mind her hair. He had the off-putting habit of looking anywhere but at the person whom he was addressing, eyes darting this way and that. It made her uncomfortable, and she was bored with the stream of pig-related speech, but she was too polite to interrupt. Kathleen let the curl rest where it was, a dark river across the white of her cheekbone.

'. . . it wouldn't matter so much but he hadn't fixed the side of the pen up properly. It's always me who makes sure the animals are safe and sound.'

She took advantage of Neely's pause for breath and inserted quickly as she backed away, ''Twas lovely talking with you, Jimmy. Give my regards to your mother and father, and I'll surely see you at Mass.'

On the way back home, Kathleen observed the long stretch of hill road, and the land either side unblemished by houses or farm buildings, Ballinara nestled at the bottom. This stretch of road, unusually, was quite straight and it always felt foreign to her. On the rare occasions when cousins from out east came they would always complain about the windy, curvy roads that led to nowhere. But they had not stood atop this hill and surveyed the map of her home and felt that sense of belonging as she did. At its crest, such a trial to reach on the way up into Killnarnan, Kathleen stopped and stood, looking down the long length of straight road. The girls would imagine it as a slide, like the ones they see in story books; the boys, Tomás and his friend Brendan Reilly, a challenge for racing their homespun wagons. The air was mild but the wind was picking up. A gust buffeted Kathleen backwards a little and again a strand of rich brown hair fell down in front of her eyes.

She had a compulsion, then. To take the pins out, to wear her hair down, as she had not done in public for so long. Even at night, she braided two long plaits, tying them with the elastic taken from her mother's old smocks. There was nobody around; she listened hard for the sound of horses' hooves, but there was none. The wind came again, like two soft balls of warmth against her cheeks, and she reached up one pale wrist and began to take the pins out. She could feel her hair, longer than she thought it was, cascading chaotically behind her. It felt so refreshing, and free. A memory, a lovely sunny memory, came before her eyes, of the two of them, running and running and laughing down to the sea, with their identical locks, lighter then, billowing out rhythmically behind them, just as the mane of a horse slaps up and down in a bold canter.

Kathleen watched her feet gather speed, tripping happily down the descent. She could envisage her face as she ran, as youthful as Laura's or Molly's, but she didn't care. It had been so long since she had been physically away from her responsibilities, so long since she had let all of those things melt away from her even for a moment.

The foot of the hill was getting close, but Kathleen did not slow her step. She did not want to stop. She did not want to go back to the darkened room where her mother would be sitting, with the sun brightening the world outside; she did not want to sit in the big, musty chair feeding the baby, with her mother's deafening silence drumming in her ears, and her absent staring.

She took a detour then, over the hills above some stranger's farm, and marvelled at how different a field can look just because it is unfamiliar – just an empty square of land, no emotion or memory attached to it. She followed a stream south, noting the sparkling reflection of sky on it, the little darting fish beneath the surface. She picked a flower she had not seen before and smelled it. It was like an imagining, like reading a new story in which she was discovering a new world. She let her feet lead her through the new landscape that seemed to her a million miles away from home but was only just up the road.

She ran all the way to the bend in the road before the Steele boreen, and she stood panting while her heart slowed. She thought for a moment she heard her father's voice calling her from far off, but of course it couldn't be because he was at home with the baby. She located some of the pins and gathered her hair up again. She was eager to get back to Paddy now. He would be due another bottle before long.

Joseph Foley had been standing awhile, feeling as though he should perhaps do something with the day. The sea was not far off, he could walk to it in fifteen minutes or so, although not having had any food for a good few days now he might find the journey rather tiring. The walk itself, indeed, might finish him off.

Most men, Joseph supposed, did not spend much time in thought about how they would like to go, although most men would have definite ideas of how they did not want to go. But when a man has been thinking about his departure from the world for so long and as privately as Joseph, things become more significant. Like the position he was found in – that is, assuming he was ever found, of course; there had been no sign of human life near the field since Joseph had arrived. He could dig a trench under the hedge. But again, this felt like cheating and Joseph had decided he wanted to die in a natural position, with a contented expression on his face. Day eight was spent entirely testing out variations of a few 'natural' positions which, the more he concentrated on them, the more unnatural and absurd they seemed.

After much of this kind of contemplation and experimentation, Joseph had become annoyed with his stubbornly high energy levels and increasing boredom, not to mention the length of time the task was taking. He had estimated a couple of days, three or four at the very most. He had started losing track, although he knew he was definitely into his second week. Besides a dry mouth and the apparent cessation of his bowel movements, there were no physical clues that his body was shutting down, no indication of fading away at all.

And so, as Joseph stood up, feeling slightly dizzy, it was with some jubilation that he noticed a third indicator – a headache, sudden and piercing, which brought with it the idea of a further plan. He could give up his tipple of water from the stream. That would work eventually, but he could do with a little help along the way. He would take a trip to the chemist's for some Aspro. This way he would be killing two birds with one stone. He chuckled to himself and the sound he emitted was absorbed into the thick air around him. He felt as though he could scream at the top of his voice and no one in the world would hear him.

The road above was visible from where he stood, and he squinted, shielding his face from the sun to look up and see was there any old feller along the way who could give him a spin to the town, help him on his quest a little. He waited a good while, his headache worsening with the squinting and the heat, ears straining for the sound of a vehicle above. But then, as he was about to turn away, he did see somebody walking. A girl. A young woman.

He must have called out to her, because she stopped and looked around her, as though confused. She had been running and, though he could not see her features as she was almost silhouetted, a haze of afternoon sunlight around her, he knew that she would have a milky-white complexion, which would be flushed from her hurrying. The afternoon light filtered through her hair, making it shimmer. Clearly she had not seen who it was that had called to her, as she looked around once again, and then hurriedly set to pulling and gathering her swathe of dark hair. Joseph watched the girl and thought it uncanny how different her outline looked with her hair drawn back tight at the nape of her neck. He could see that she had his mother's sort of hair – not that smooth kind that the ladies in the city have, but big and wild, and beautiful because of it. He wondered what her name was. Something pretty: Orla or Rosemary.

She bent down, to pick up something she had dropped, or to fix her shoe. Then she carried along the road, walking. How strange, Joseph thought, for her to be in such a hurry a few moments ago, but to be strolling along now. He thought of calling out to her again, to ask her name, to start a conversation. But Joseph had not heard his own voice for days now. Seeing this woman – girl – though, up on the road, had triggered something in Joseph's brain: the form of a female, the shape of her shadow of a waist, the gentle sway of skirt on her hips as she moved her body along the road to or from home. The slender arms as she worked at her hair; maybe she had 'tutted' up there on the road, scolding it for having a mind of its own.

When she arrived back at the house her father had already returned from the fields. He took tea at around five every day, so that he could watch the little ones with their dinner and see them a bit before their bedtime. He would have his own evening meal late, just before his own bedtime. He would strip down, discarding the day's clothes and its toil with them, and climb with a groan into the hot bath Kathleen had poured for him, while she warmed his plate. Her father was good at seeing to his own things, assessing the level of dirt on his outer garments to see whether they needed a good soak, and putting his shirts and socks into the wash pile for Kathleen. She never found his underpants in the pile, though when it came to hanging out the washing they would be there for her to hang out with the shirts to bleach in the sun. It embarrassed her. Obviously he had felt embarrassed himself when she first took over the various domestic duties, because she was sure he had not done this when her mother was herself. If she were herself, her mother would have said something like, 'Ah now, Pat, don't be faffing, haven't we women enough to be doing without having to be waiting on your drawers?'

She could hear their giggles now, that interaction between them such a distant memory now that it seemed alien, inappropriate, somehow. Sure her father would still laugh at times with the children outside, fooling around, swinging one of the girls up in the air over the slurry pit to scare them, but more and more the farm demanded him, his time, his energy. They hadn't the money to employ another farmhand. There was only so much that Tomás could do, and both parents wanted him to go to school as much as possible. All the same, it wasn't right for the children, Kathleen thought, having a father who was not there in body and a mother not there in mind or spirit.

She felt bad then, as she walked in on the family tableau, having been absent for a good couple of hours. It was strange to Kathleen. Normally she would be part of it, working among it, filling any unbearable gaps of quiet with chatter or song. Her father was sitting at the long wooden table with his tea, his work boots still on. One leg was under the table, the other leg up on a chair, and he was scraping the mud off the boots onto a newspaper while he drank his milky tea. There were plates with scraps of food on them at the table and the ruins of an abandoned game across the kitchen floor. Miniature horses lay among scattered soldiers, frozen in their combatant stances. Who had made the children's tea? Not himself, surely? She felt terrible. She was obviously gone longer than she thought. At least he'd put the newspaper down. The girls were arranging pebbles around the shoeless feet of their mother, who sat motionless in the large green chair that faced out the window to the world outside, which beyond the haggard was obscured by a line of poplars. Paddy was asleep by the unlit fire. He would be up all the night now. He was lying atop two cushions she had herself covered with one of her old dresses that no longer fitted past her newly curved hips. Whose idea was that? If he rolled off he could have his eye out on the fireplace.

Kathleen was still standing at the door, looking in on her life, when Tomás burst in from the parlour, saying, 'I don't know how much butter she puts on your teacake, Da, but I have it here anyways.'

'S'all right, Tomás, she's here now.' Kathleen felt herself arrive back in the room. She was aware now that her father had been watching her standing at the door surveying the scene. 'Sorry, Father . . . Warm out today, isn't it? Bet those sheep'll be feeling it—'

She broke off. He was smiling at her, but his eyes weren't. His eyes looked quite vacant, like Jimmy Neely's. 'Where have you been, Kathy? Your mother's been worried sick.'

He was the only one who had ever called her anything other than Kathleen. She had always thought of her name as sounding rather formal, probably because of Sister Kathleen who lived in the next parish and who insisted on them all doing the rosary every time she came to visit. 'That's who you're going to turn into when you're older, Kathleen,' Tomás would say. 'A nun – a moody, grumpy, moany nun who won't even take a biscuit with her tea. "If God intended us to have such luxuries he would have put a biscuit tree and a cake tree in the garden of Eden too,"' he would mimic. Even as a young girl with a limited understanding of God's message, she knew that Sister Kathleen's argument made little sense, so she was content from an early age that she would not turn out to be like her, even if she did grow up to be a nun.

She liked her father calling her Kathy, but it would have felt odd if anybody else had. She was to everyone, including herself, Kathleen Steele, the sister of Nuala Steele; the sister of the girl who died.

'I'm sorry, Da. I didn't think . . . I wasn't gone all that long.

I had to go into town.' And, as if to give a further reason for her lateness, she held aloft the bag of school exercise books and pencils. The girls caught sight of it and squealed, scrabbling to get their new copy books.

'No, Kathy, you didn't think, did you?' He looked down to his plate and began buttering his teacake with the butter Tomás had placed in front of him. Tomás sat down on the cold floor by his father's boots and began picking at a large scab on his knee with a grubby nail, pretending not to be interested in what was being said above him. Kathleen was distracted by the dirty nail working away at the scab, which was not ready for picking. A little tiny point of blood issued forth from underneath the crust.

'Tomás, if you must do that, please do it with clean hands. Go on, go and scrub them, but not with the soap, mind. Mother wouldn't want to be washing with soap that has been near those grubby fellers, and neither would I.'

'Ah, Kathleen, don't be so boring!'

She glared at him, suddenly upset by the knowledge that she would always be viewed as the older sister who looked after the little ones, always scolding, playing mam, laughing inside at their jokes, but never really able to share in them. Instead of responding in the mock-annoyed tone that he had spoken to her with, she snapped at him, 'And not in here, Tomás Steele. For the love of God, amn't I only after mopping the floor this morning!'

He jumped up, the pinprick of blood now the size of a pea. She had an urge to dab it before it smeared onto the fresh, unwounded skin next to it, but she was feeling stubborn, angry even. She was angry that her father was angry with her. She was angry that her mother could not see the boy before her picking away at a scab with God-knows-what on his hands. He had probably been down the cattle field, stroking their friendly, slobbering noses. 'Go on, Tomás, I'll not tell you again nicely . . .'

Tomás did as he was told.

'You're good with the children, you are, Kathy. Very good. Everyone sees what a good mother you are to them.' Her father seemed to have forgotten that he was annoyed with her. Kathleen's body wanted to draw out a chair and sit and talk awhile at the table with him while he had his tea. She was used to rushing, to organizing various things at once, but she was not used to the physical exertion of running, or the feelings of elation and freedom that came with it. Her body was at once physically worn out and relaxed; the thrill of feeling childish and carefree had brought a moment's peace to her. Not the kind of peace that she experienced when all the little ones were tucked up at night, nor the Peace that Father Nolan told them about, but a private sensation inside her. A feeling that was hers alone. And now that her father's voice had gentled, it would be nice to make a cup of tea and share these quiet few moments with him while Paddy was sleeping and the others were at their play.

But he had aggravated her thoughts; she knew she would not be able to relax. She could not bring her legs to move towards the table, her hand to pull out the chair. Kathleen was hurt that this man thought of her as the mother of his children more than a thinking, feeling grown-up, or rather growing-up, version of the child he had created. She would tell him now how she felt. After all, if she was mature enough to be responsible for a baby, she was mature enough to tell her father how wrong he was, how cruel he could be, treating her like a child one minute and an old friend the next. She would tell him she was not their mother, that she was not yet anyone's mother. She wanted to say it loudly, to shout it at him, so that he couldn't interrupt her and cajole her with his deep, gentle voice: I am one of them, Father! I am one of the children, too, do you not remember when I was Paddy's age? And how can you say that Mother was worried sick? Worried sick! She probably didn't even notice I was gone! Did you, Mother? You wouldn't notice if I danced naked in front of you right now, would you?

But instead, her hand trembling with the intensity of her exasperation and with the effort of restraining herself from speaking, she began silently and swiftly sweeping the crumbs around her father's plate into a little mound. She lifted her skirt with the other hand and leaned in to catch the crumbs on it. The cool air of the room caressed the exposed skin of her leg. As she busied herself, her father sat motionless, watching, with his tea going cold. There was a silence in the room that she was not prepared to fill with song or humming. It seemed to Kathleen that it took her an age to tidy adequately enough to leave the room, and she wished her father would leave and she could breathe again. But he didn't. And it was only when she had washed, dried and replaced the last teaspoon in the dresser that he stood up. He had obviously sensed her mood as he watched her, and was annoyed at her lack of response. He waited, standing there, until Kathleen glanced over and he caught her eye.

'You will not get waylaid on errands again, Kathleen. And you will not be late, all right?'

Kathleen assumed that this was a rhetorical question, an order from father to daughter, and she turned around, ready to leave the room. But she sensed her father lingering. She turned to face him again.

'Well?' he said.

From the first moment she knew her help was needed she had given it graciously, uncomplaining, seamlessly switching from being a girl on the cusp of womanhood to occupying a mother's role, and she wanted to say this to him.

But she said only, 'Yes, Da, of course. I don't want to upset you, or Mother.'

The woman behind the counter was talking to him, asking him something. He was concentrating on the sounds she was making and thought it strange that he could not understand her. Maybe she was talking in Irish. He had not spoken a word of it since he was a boy at school. And all his years in England had nearly erased them altogether.

'Will you be wanting anything, mister, or will I see to Mrs O'Brien? Only I'm not actually open . . . I don't know why I don't just lock the door on a Sunday.' The woman leaned her elbows on the counter and her face moved towards him. 'Mister, are you going to . . . are you all right?'

Joseph became aware of a warm sensation on one side of his head, then the pain. His eyes were closed. Was it only a dream? He must have fallen asleep in the sun in his field. At last some real pain, and in his head too. Something was really starting to happen. He felt very strange. But then he could hear voices, several, a boy, a woman, and another woman, a shout – but no one ever came to his field. He had not accounted for madness as one of the stages. He ought to open his eyes, but they seemed sore too, and his right one was definitely wet, warm and wet.

'What was he saying?'

'Just jabbering. He wouldn't answer me . . . probably an oul' drunk from the city, or a tinker from down Carrickbrook way . . . looks like he's had a rough night or two.'

'What . . . did he trip over something?'

'Do you mind, Mrs O'Brien, you can't blame me—'

'Sorry, Caroline, but—'

'The feller just said something to me, and kind of fell forward. All by himself . . . I suppose you'll tell me my counter's too hard now, is it? In the way of my customers, is it?'

'All right, Caroline. Ah, here comes little Johnny now with Dr Fitzgerald. Well done, John, Mrs Walsh has a bar of chocolate for you for being so helpful, don't you, Caroline? Now, run on home quickly and tell your sister to put the kettle on, and Dr Fitzgerald'll be needing the parlour for this man.'

'What's happened here, then?' The doctor set down his bag and surveyed the scene in the small shop. 'Thank you for sending your boy, Breda – thank you, Johnny . . . I think we'll look at him in here. Don't want to move him too much. Is it all right to use your back room, Caroline?'

''Tis, of course, Doctor. Come on through.'

The wetness felt less warm now, and it was sticky, and Joseph wanted to ask the voices for a cloth. He opened an eye and saw two figures standing in the light of the shop doorway, and then the face of the woman from behind the counter loomed into view, very close up.

'He's all right, I think,' Caroline offered. 'He's come to, look. A strong cup of tea and, well, a good long soak, and he'll be grand. Maybe you can come back tomorrow when you remember what it is that you wanted, mister.' The woman's last sentence was spoken very slowly and very loudly. She spoke to him as if he were stupid. They thought he was simple. And there was a doctor here to look at him. Well, he couldn't have that; he would just have to explain that he had made a mistake, very sorry for any bother, and then he would return home, back to the field. It was uphill on the way back. About half an hour it took coming down, so he would have to allow almost double for the walk back up. He would explain that it would be getting dark soon. Maybe he could say he must dash back to tend his sheep. But they would know he was no farmer of this parish, and Joseph suddenly felt confused, and tired. Maybe this house would have a nice pot of soup on the stove, and a blanket, and he had definitely heard somebody mention a bath. Oh, the leap his heart made at the thought! He opened his eyes again, briefly – he was moving. But, although he was definitely moving forward, his feet were barely making steps. His toes gently scraped along the ground. He opened his eyes again; yes, his shoes were definitely being scuffed at the toes. He tried to make steps but his feet felt detached from him. And his arms were up in the air, and outstretched. Maybe this was how one was transported to heaven, in the stance of the Christ Jesus.

'Thank you, God,' he heard his voice say.

The Steeles had returned home from Mass and each was absorbed in his or her own thoughts, at his or her own tasks.

Mrs Steele had been reinstated in her position in the chair facing the window and Patrick Steele, after loosening the shawl around his wife's shoulders, took refuge from the heat and the impending onslaught of the children's noise in the outhouse, where it was always cool in the summer, and warm enough in winter. He liked this time on a Sunday. Of course he could not rest for long – there was always something waiting to be done – but it was peaceful for now.

Each Sunday, the baby would fall asleep on the last bend home from Mass, and it was always a deep sleep brought on by his trying to stay awake to watch his siblings chattering on down the road and the stimulation of all the faces at church. He loved seeing all of them together, and giggled at his brother and sisters skipping along the road, pulling faces for him. Patrick Steele knew he should make them walk in an orderly way, respectful-like, it being Sunday, but he too loved to see them so free. He supposed he enjoyed watching them so much because he, unusually, had had no brothers or sisters. There was a baby, a boy he thought, before him that hadn't survived, and his mother died soon after he himself was born. He often regretted the rather stiff and virtually silent relationship he had had with his father. There was no laughter, no life about the house, but now, as a father himself, he could look back and see that his own father did watch him, delighted in him, worried about him, but didn't let on that he did, in the same way that he himself now observed his own children. He could tell any man who bothered to ask what dream it was that woke Laura a week last Tuesday, or why Tomás flicked at his hair when he was thinking of something that worried him, or the first word that

Kathleen muttered, or the date of her first step, a day before Nuala's. Poor Nuala, always playing catch-up.

As he squeezed off a shoe, with its black, Sunday boot polish temporarily covering up the scuffs and cracks, he felt the cool of the earthen floor of the outhouse and thought of how long ago that seemed. How long ago it was when he tickled Kathleen's little toes, or smoothed her sleeping hair at night. He had noticed today, walking behind her with his wife on his arm like a half-painted presence, a mismatched shadow, that even her ankles had changed since last he looked. They were slender now and pale and looked as though they would be as smooth as marble to touch. She was a strong young woman, though, despite her gentle, compassionate nature. She had to be. And a saint, of course. He would apologize for talking to her as though she were one of the children. He would not interfere with decisions of the house or the children again. That was her domain now.

He was distracted from his thoughts by her humming outside. He leaned forwards to peer through a crack in the wooden slats of the door. She had her shawl and basket. He guessed that she was off down to Walsh's for something. She was obviously making use of the relative calm while the children were still worn out from their walk home. How thoughtful of her to leave her mother alone with the quiet, and to be back before they started misbehaving. How amazing for her to be so kind and gentle when she had lost half of herself with Nuala passing. He held his breath as she passed the tiny slit of a window and watched her till she was out of sight.

*

It was toilet paper that Kathleen had to step out for. The children could not understand how her and her father still viewed it as a luxury and they refused to grab a handful of grass if they had none in. She had scolded herself as she prepared to put the vegetables into the range. It was unlike her to be forgetful about domestic issues. She was usually meticulous. If she hurried, she would be back in time to baste the bird one last time and put the tart in. She had pulled the fireguard away from the fireplace and placed it in front of the hot stove, and arranged a few cushions around the fireplace in case Paddy awoke while she was gone and Tomás wasn't paying proper attention. He would surely give out to her about that when she got back. While wanting so much to be a carefree child, he was conscious of his role as next oldest in the Steele household, and the responsibilities that brought with it. He switched uncomfortably from role to role, one minute playing carefree with Brendan Reilly and trying to behave like an adult the next. She had bent down to kiss Paddy's damp forehead, the colour of cream, and said sorry for having to go. She had pulled his blanket down a bit, exposing two little round puffs of knees, and headed off vowing to be more diligent.

Since that day when she had that little run, certain thoughts had begun swimming softly through the routine of daily tasks. She did not notice them coming, but she would be at the darning and find that she was not seeing her father's sock, but her own bare feet patting gently through the water where it laps up to the sand, so that you cannot tell whether you are walking on sand or on water. Or she would be sponging down Molly and Laura, or rinsing their hair, with her mind not there at all;

instead it would be with those beautiful flowers she saw on the hedgerow, or with the taste of blackberry pie. She had not only visited the past as she skipped along, but actually felt just as she had when she was her carefree childhood self.

Knowing her father would be in the outhouse, having his weekly time to himself, Kathleen began humming a line of a tune as she passed his window. And, as she looked out to the field that awaited her footsteps, she realized it was a tune he used to sing to her as a child. Then, she had thought the song merely about apples growing where they shouldn't, but now she knew the song was about the fable that is unending, unrequited love, about growing old and things never remaining the same, 'and the sweetest apple is the soonest rotten ... a youth again I will never be, till apples grow on an ivy tree'. Again, she was transported back to her childhood and felt the need for another small moment of freedom. She had to restrain herself from skipping lest one of their neighbours should see.

When she arrived at the store, the closed sign swung in the window. She must have just missed Caroline, but they were friends, and she was desperate for the toilet paper for the sake of peace in the household. She pushed open the door and the bell jingled in the dust of the air, glinting in the light she brought in with her.

'Caroline, 'tis only Kathleen ... Would you believe I've run out of toilet paper already!' She was answered by the quietness of the room which was made up of the distant sea waves and the call of the children she had passed on the way. It was nice hearing other people's children out playing far off, carefree. It was when you passed close, Kathleen had noticed, that you had to close your ears. Even in the few years since she was small things had changed. Tomás was the worst for his language and his manners; she was always having to pick him up on them. But it was to be expected; they all want to be like their friends. Caroline must be up the stairs in the children's room. Kathleen walked towards the tiny doorway space behind the counter and called into the golden dust, looking up at the ceiling.

'I'll just leave the money in the jar, Caroline. Those little ones'll have me back down here for something tomorrow, no doubt.' She reached into her skirt to the little sewn-in pocket for the money, and the door opened so suddenly that the bell seemed to jump as much as she did. 'Oh, Bríd, you gave me a fright there. I'm just fetching—'

'Don't just stand there, for God's sake, girl,' Brigid responded, as Kathleen stepped around the counter again. Her neighbour was all a-fluster and, Kathleen guessed, very eager to share whatever bit of new gossip she had just heard. There was nothing Brigid Callaghan liked more than knowing other people's business and, even more than that, she took great pleasure in retelling it in her own elaborate words, to anyone she was able to catch in the road. Kathleen did not find it easy to escape her, especially now as her formidable figure was blocking her path to the door, and frequently Kathleen found herself unhappily privy to too many of the villagers' ailments, worries and wrongdoings. Often she would stop herself just in time before asking various older neighbours how their arthritis or other ailment was – it was difficult to recall whether it was Brigid or they themselves who had told her.

The unending summer sun shone outside, but because of her

angle, Kathleen could not see through the shimmering of dust that had been disturbed by the woman, who eclipsed the doorway. She suddenly felt the need for the fresh air again.

'You are nearer, girl. Go and fetch the bucket and fill it with water. Caroline will not want it to stain her floor.'

'Oh, sorry, I would have done it myself had I noticed,' said Kathleen, spotting the dark stain by her feet.

'Ah, Kathleen Steele, a living, breathing saint.' Brigid was a few years older and had looked on as Kathleen had been sweeter than her as a baby, more mild-mannered as a child, and more beautiful as a young woman. Kathleen had always had Nuala for company, and their own secrets to share; and while Brigid herself had two sisters, theirs was not what could be regarded as a close bond. And since the accident, people had doted on Kathleen all the more. 'If I had known a young feller would be coming into the shop today, ranting and raving, and falling about the place spilling his blood everywhere . . .'

'His blood? . . . Is this somebody's blood on the floor? Whatever happened, Bríd?' Kathleen stepped aside and checked the undersides of her shoes.

'Why, don't you know? I heard it from O'Brien's. Some oul' tramp. Ranting and raving so he was. Oh, and the smell off of him! Apparently. I've come in to see can I help, of course . . . Kathleen, the man must be touched. Not normal at all. Just came in here, tried to grab Caroline, and fell over! Just plain fell, straight onto the counter there and put a crack in his skull. I would say he'd been drinking only I know Pat McCarthy's been sick the past two days and the whole village is dry. Any wife will tell you her husband is not himself at all. For all their moaning about their fondness for the drink, aren't the wives all kicking themselves for not having a secret supply of poitín to calm their nerves?'

'The poor feller. Is he all right? That must have been some awkward fall to have bled from it. I suppose it is quite sharp,' said Kathleen, running her fingers along the cool edge of Caroline's counter. 'Maybe I should go and ask if I can help at all.'

'Don't you go blaming the counter for the silly man's maladies. Not right in the head, I tell you. Maybe Father Nolan should have a look at him. Fitzgerald is with up with him now.' Brigid Callaghan indicated with her eyes upwards. No wonder Caroline hadn't heard her calls.

Kathleen paid for the toilet roll and put a few extra coins in for some bread and one of the apple pies that Breda O'Brien took all the praise for even though they were baked by her mother-in-law. She knew Caroline would be needing a little extra if this young man was to be in her house for the afternoon, and it was only right that it was paid for.

'I'll go up, Bríd. 'Tis best if I go. Caroline's little ones are used to me.'

'All right, but I'm not going anywhere.' Brigid decided that she should have the more important job of minding that no more waifs and strays came into the shop, which Kathleen knew would involve her luring in any passer-by to fill them in on the drama.

When Joseph finally opened his eyes, it was quiet all around him. The air surrounding his body was still. Nothing moved. There was no hint of nature teasing at his nostrils, no breeze.

Sounds were enclosed, muted. He was indoors. He began remembering what had happened and the ache in his head became a pain on the outside of his head too. He reached up to touch the wound, to wipe away that sticky wet, but he found that someone had already done this for him. There was a bandage; it had been wrapped around under the nape of his neck. He felt that too. His hair was dishevelled there, and needed cutting. Maybe he would ask the bandage-maker if they were smart with a pair of scissors as well as a good nurse.

Joseph let his heavy hand drop back down onto the settee and his eyelids shut again. His hand was tired, his arm too. In fact his whole body felt as though he had been asleep for a year but that it still needed another two. But surely he must be an imposition on the woman of this household? And he must smell. Jesus. Joseph decided it was time to leave.

As he began to muster up the energy to move, he heard a murmuring coming from another room. A tap let out a short gush of water, metal grated against metal. A spoon dinging against a cup. Tea. A cup of tea! Maybe he could stay a little while longer. But he must have drifted off momentarily, for when he finally looked about him, two young women were suddenly there, as if by magic, attending him, and the heat and odour of his mug of tea was silkily climbing towards his nose. He wiped at it, and began to say his thank-yous for the tea and the care.

'Don't bother yourself now, mister, you've had a fair shock. In your own time, now.' The voice came from the woman whose house it clearly was. She had a tea-towel tucked into her apron and was holding a toy aeroplane and a red tin truck upside down as if in mid-tidy-up. Her voice was self-assured, strong, and her hair was smoothed and pinned in the current style. Joseph imagined her husband to be a genial man, fair-looking, slightly in awe of his fine lady, but a man capable of keeping a woman happy nevertheless.

'Are you certain you won't let me stay, Caroline? I'm sure my father won't mind.'

'No, no, God knows you've more to be getting on with than me. The children are all up at Síle's for the afternoon, thank the blessed Lord, so don't you mind me. We'll be just grand, now. A sup of tea makes the world seem right, doesn't it, mister, no matter what? And we might even find out your name after a bun or two.' The woman called Caroline smiled warmly and he opened his lips to tell her his name, but his throat was ever so dry. He must be coming down with something. Whenever he was poorly as a lad, the throat was always the first to go.

'If you're sure, Caroline. But I'll wait till Dr Fitzgerald gets back. I'll get you some water, mister, will I? The tea's still steaming.' This second voice was younger than Caroline's, softer. It had a lilt to it, as though she might actually be singing the words to him. She had been sitting by his head, just behind him, and he had not yet seen her. As she rose up and stepped into the light of the kitchen door, her skirt left a shimmer of light in her wake. He tried to get up, but found that his limbs failed him.

'Miss,' he called, although he merely heard a croak. 'It's you, I've seen you before, what is your name?' He wanted to ask her.

She stopped and turned around.

'Name?' they both repeated after him.

'Name, oh, he's going to tell us his name,' Caroline said.

'That's right. 'Twould be a help to us, if only so's we can stop calling you mister.'

But Joseph could not muster another word. He was muted by his all-enveloping tiredness and by the girl's beauty. Such milky soft skin, with that gorgeous dappling of freckles in an uneven line across the nose and atop the cheekbones. Joseph managed a smile as the kitchen door that led to the outside world opened and the doctor walked in, meaning that the girl with the freckles would leave and go home to her father.

'All right, Caroline', said the doctor, 'Pat will take him for tonight, but he says he'll need payment. You can manage to pay for a room above the pub, above McCarthy's, can't you, sir? Caroline, no tea for the moment, thank you, the man needs nothing but water for now, and a lot of it. But don't make it too cold now.'

'Of course, Diarmuid. Will you have a cup yourself?' A smooth hand with delicately rounded nails swept up the tea.

'No, no, thank you, Caroline. Kathleen, you get on home now, won't you?'

'Are you sure, Doctor? I could stay if you're busy . . .'

'Sunday is the one day I'm not busy, Kathleen . . . not supposed to be, anyway,' but Joseph detected a smile in his words and felt a little less ill at ease. When he had a bit more energy he might ask the doctor about the pain he had been having in his back for the past few days too. 'But I'll stay till Mr Walsh comes in. He won't be too long, sure, will he, Caroline?'

'Not at all, just out fixing up the—'

'Grand, that's settled then. Maybe I will have that cup so,

Caroline. Then you carry on, I'll keep my eye on him. We wouldn't want the children coming home and bearing witness to any ... unpredictable behaviour.' The doctor's last words were hushed, but Joseph heard them. Unpredictable behaviour. The man had only just met him, what on earth did he think he was going to do? But Joseph thought of his clothes, how he must look to them. They would think him unhinged, touched. He had no clean shirts with him, of course, and one of the shoelaces was missing now. He had dropped it in the stream one day and the current took it. And there was the tear in his right trouser-leg from when he fell onto some brambles after climbing through a gap in a hedge. How he must look to the girl called Kathleen! He was ashamed, then, and felt his chest move deeply with a sigh. The hairs around his jaw line prickled with the movement and he could almost feel the smell of stale sweat that clung to them. Too ashamed to attempt conversation with the doctor, Joseph kept his eyes closed and listened to the sound of the two women's cheeks touching as they kissed goodbye. They must be close, he thought. Everybody in this little village must be close to her, or if not would wish to be. He heard her say goodbye to the doctor, and ask if there was anything she could do; so kind. He heard the swish of her skirts, and the gentle tap-tap of something knocking on the window of the outside door as she left.

It would be the perfect day for doing the sheets. The fall of light from the gap in the curtain that almost perfectly aligned with the baby's bald spot, just to the left on the back of his head, was bright: too bright for this time in the morning. It had only just stopped being night. It would be another scorcher today so. The light of the next day had just begun to seep across the land, touching first O'Brien's farm to the eastern edge of the village, and was slowly, quietly lighting the different parts of their own ... then over to the other side of the village, then over to the shop and Pat McCarthy's, and the doctor's. The light would be falling on the man.

He had been in her thoughts since the day at Caroline's. She was not one usually partial to gossip, but she found herself lingering at the shop, finding excuses to bump into the awful Brigid Callaghan, so intrigued was she to find out about this stranger who had appeared in their midst. Some said he was mad, escaped from a special institution; others thought he was a drunk, a tinker. But Kathleen wondered about him, and what had brought him to Ballinara, wondered why he would just sit and sit, and be seemingly completely content with lying in that certain spot in Murphy's field.

'I don't know why Seán Murphy doesn't fling him out on his ear. Evict him ... he's no right to be here. The whole county is talking of it, sure ...' Brigid Callaghan was a wealth of information, but Kathleen wondered had anyone asked the feller what he wanted to be doing there? Maybe he hadn't any money to stay above at McCarthy's and maybe that is why Seán Murphy turned a blind eye. It was not as though the field was used for anything. But what did he do for shelter? Maybe he was a nature-observer, and he needed to be in situ to conduct his studies. Or, if it was true that he was 'a tinker who's lost his caravan', shouldn't they take pity on the poor man?

But still, it did not explain why he would lie on his back,

motionless, most of the day. He was there on the way down and on the way back every day. She would talk to her father about it. His views, his instincts, were always right. Whenever she had a problem, a doubt of faith, a low moment, he would always find a comforting way of saying the words she already knew were in her.

She had settled Paddy a while ago but hadn't felt like turning herself back into bed yet. She just sat, rocking him ever so slightly, back and forth, her lips closed and soft against the fluff of his little head. She stared at the wall, the curtains, at him, but saw nothing. It was contentment. It was sitting still and taking time to do nothing, to think of nothing, to just be. She could be the only person awake for miles around, only her and the cattle, maybe; she could not even hear the hens' gentle squawking that awakened her most mornings.

How small and warm and comforting this little body was against her. It reminded her of her old teddy she used to cuddle – one arm tightly around it, the other scooped around her sister's arm, belly or leg. Their mother had made them – two, almost matching, but one had a yellow button on an ear, and one a pink button on its tummy. Nuala's was the ear-button one – Yellow Ear was its name – but the button kept falling off and one day rolled under the range and was never replaced. Kathleen wondered now where these two vestiges of their shared childhood had gone. She could not recall putting them in her special Goodbye Nuala box and with a frown she thought of her mother's explosive clear-out that time.

When the washing was done she would search the house for them. Now that she had remembered the teddies, she needed to find them, and the thought that she might not made her hold Paddy to her all the more tightly. Before disturbing him by getting up to begin the day's chores, Kathleen inhaled deeply the sweet, milky scent of his skin.

Had she known late that morning, as she hung out the sheets to bleach in the sun, that she was being admired from afar by two men – one from the field above, concealed by a row of trees, and one from a window of a bedroom – Kathleen would have surely felt self-conscious and would have gone about her outdoor duties quickly and without singing nursery songs to herself. And, had the two men caught a glimpse of each other through the white sheets that flapped like the wings of some giant seagull, had they known that they were both thinking the same thing – one longingly, one bewildered – maybe their days would have panned out differently.

Often, when the children were all in bed and their mother had been installed in the makeshift bedroom off the kitchen, or, if it was a good day, in her own bed up the narrow stairs at the other end of the house, Kathleen and her father would share a last cup of tea or cocoa. Kathleen would throw her apron in the wash pile and hang up the next day's one on the nail by the scullery door. There used to hang holy water there, in a dish attached to a plaque with Jesus as a shepherd painted on it, but Kathleen could not think where it had gone now, or why it had been removed.

She would set out on the side the necessary items for making the bread for the next day, dust out the range and put out six bowls and spoons for the morning. Although their mother did not take breakfast with them at the table, Kathleen set a place for her anyway. It had felt wrong, the one time she thought to do her mother's separately. It had always been her job, laying the table for the dinner, while Nuala was sent out to fetch in the eggs and feed the dog. For a long time after, Kathleen would automatically set a place for Nuala and then, upon realizing that her dead sister could not possibly sit at the table with them, would never again eat next to Kathleen, their nearest legs intertwined, or her right gently knocking against her sister's left under the table, Kathleen would wail, shockingly, suddenly and silently, and run from the table. She would not allow herself to be comforted by her father for she felt that their mother's loss was far greater and more awful. Kathleen did not want to undermine her parents' grief, and so dealt with it alone in her room, in a field, in the school toilet.

Her father would call through the bedroom door, 'It is all right for you to be sad too, love. She was half of you, you knew her . . . Please come out.' The times when he did manage to grab her as she ran, or found her hidden behind a hay bale, soundlessly bawling, he would hold her till her quivering stopped and the immenseness of it passed, for now. She learned that he needed to hold her as much as she needed it, because his wife was beyond comfort at the moment, giving or receiving. The sitting, the staring; it was like embracing a cow at market, or a tree, strange and uncomfortable and utterly pointless. And so, to be able to comfort his daughter was to comfort himself, and though he did not consciously mean for it to be so, it brought him closer to his dead daughter, so similar were they in form and nature. It was as though God had planned it, as though He knew the terrible thing that was in store for this family, so He fashioned a replica, that they would not be too broken-hearted when she was gone. At least they still had Kathleen, he would tell himself. But despite this blessing, their grief could not be so easily remedied.

Kathleen would sit by the fire and sip her tea, while her father would take his at the long wooden table which, at every inch, told stories of the Steeles, from the time when they first began – the first knock against the side as he dented it on moving it to its first and final position, the promise it had held then of the heart of their home, the stories and laughter and good meals that would be had at it, happy children in every chair around. There were numerous scratches and indentations made by the children over the years; the corner where Kathleen and Nuala had practised and practised at writing their names when they were very small – you could see a K and a back-to-front N if you looked closely. Nora had painted the chairs white in order to brighten the room, but they were chipped and scuffed now, the paint almost completely worn away in places. Patrick's feelings towards his wife had dissipated to nothing, but he did not regret it, nor feel guilt over it. It was a natural result of her condition, the ways things were. And any desires he had were easily relieved in any of his solitary places in the day.

It was the empty chair in the evenings that transformed the atmosphere in that room, the absence of her. The slow crackle of the fire would soon smoulder down to gentle embers and he and Kathleen would gaze at them after speaking quietly about the day, or the children, both exhausted from their separate tasks and responsibilities, but neither complaining. Each night

Kathleen would say, 'Come and rest your bones on a comfortable chair ... come and sit by the fire.' A little ritual, an invitation, an acknowledgement of the sacrifices made in a day, which was each time returned with a simple, 'I will so.' And he would take the single candle from the table and place it between them on the floor, lighting up a small circular space around them. He would lift the kettle to top up her cup a little and with a deep sigh sit down in the opposite chair where once his own father rested his bones at the end of a day in the field.

It was a low, soft light, those evenings. They had both long given up on talking about Nora, unless Dr Fitzgerald had said something specific about her on his weekly visit. And with her in bed, her chair empty, the blanket folded neatly away, it was as though she wasn't there. It was not that they did not want her there – they wanted her to be well again, of course – but they could talk more freely and easily when it was just the two of them. And the darkness in the rest of the room, and the soundlessly sleeping children on the other side of the wall, gave them both a secret feeling that they were the only two living things for miles around. They whispered, on those nights, although there was no need to; on many occasions one or the other had had a sudden attack of laughter and not a soul had stirred.

They laughed about the time when Paddy burped so loudly at Mass that it echoed around the whole church and Father Nolan had struggled to keep a straight face. And they chuckled about when Kathleen was caught short in the middle of the night and ran outside to the toilet only to find her father in there, and suddenly the heavens had opened and they were sandwiched together in the privy, having to speak right into each other's ears over the sound of the rain clattering on the little tin roof. He privately recalled how he had to make a dash for it in the end in case she noticed him involuntarily hardening against her in that confined space. She might not have understood that these things happen to men sometimes.

And despite their tiredness, hours could go by before they said their goodnights, each being the only person the other really engaged with each day. And because they were both reluctant to part company some evenings, especially if he had been in the mood for reading aloud for them both, Kathleen sometimes found herself startled awake to find the candle burned right down, a crick in her neck, and only the merest orange glow in the grate. He would have tucked her mother's blanket around her and either headed off to bed, or stayed awhile, watching, nodding off himself.

Kathleen was glad that her dream had woken her. Although she was trying to fall back to sleep her body was as alert as if she were standing barefoot in an icy stream. She lay there listening. The familiar sounds in and around the house were interrupted by Paddy's muffled snuffling. She had thought his cheeks were looking a bit red in the day, and that the relentless crying was because his teeth were at him. He often woke in the early hours of the morning and Kathleen would stumble in the dark, afraid to light the lamp in case, in her sleepiness, she knocked it over near him. She would lift him out of his cot and sit in the chair by the puddle of moonlight at the little window just to the right of her parents' bed. They never woke at the sound of his crying, her father worn out from his day's working, and her mother entrenched in the dreams that refused to leave her, even when she was awake. Often, tired from the children's antics or the endless errands of a day, Kathleen would nod off in the chair that gently rocked with the weight of her breathing, and little Paddy would remind her it was time to return to her own room with a sudden dream movement or subconscious gurgle. It would have been easier to have the cot in her room; it would just fit next to her own bed if the small table and chair were taken out. Or else she could bring him into her bed when he woke, so the two could have a good rest. But she was afraid that her mother would be terrified at the sight of an empty cot.

But this night Kathleen heard the grumpy protestations that preceded his bawling and she leapt up so as to get him back off quickly. It is always easier to catch a baby at this stage, before the real crying has started; a little rocking and shushing and they're soon off again. And it was so nice to be going to him while she was wide awake. Instead of feeling mildly annoyed at being woken, she felt elated that this little being, alone in the dark, was calling out for her, that he needed her, and that she could comfort him in an instant. Recently he had been following her every move with his green eyes, and holding out his arms, excitedly gurgling whenever she entered the room. Of all the bodies in the house, Paddy was the one she felt most connected to. They found comfort in each other, and joy. When they were alone she could chat and goo away to him and he would respond with an enthusiasm that lifted her heart.

As she was so alert, Kathleen lit the lamp this time. The dusty wood of the floor was cool and her skin quivered under her nightgown. But it was a warm night, so she left her shawl hanging on the chair and quietly went up the little stairs to her parents' attic room. She was used to seeing the room in the bright of day when she set about changing sheets on the bed or cot, or refreshing the vase of flowers she kept on her mother's side of the bed, and in the dark of night too, when she could only just make out the outline of the sleeping couple if the moon sent its light through the window. It felt odd, then, with the lamp, seeing the room in this subdued and flickering light. In the room she had flitted happily in and out of since she was a small child, she now felt like an intruder.

Paddy had stopped grumbling and was looking from Kathleen to the moving shadows made by the lamp as it gently flickered. Embarrassed to see her parents together in the bed in this soft, yellow light, she averted her gaze and crept over to him, smiling. She set the lamp down on the little shelf above the cot. She always took extra care dusting there. He had so little, being the sixth child, that what he did have should be treasured. Looking at the porcelain oval with a painted Mary, she said a quick prayer. A picture that Laura had drawn for her baby brother on his first day in the world had slipped down, so she propped it up behind the figure of a fawn that had once been her own. Then she spoke ever so softly, and stroked the yellow tuft that was sure to grow into a mess of curls just like Molly's.

'What are you doing up in the night? There's no fun happening in the dark, everyone's asleep.'

He cooed and smiled, and stretched his arms and legs straight with a yawn. She picked him up and patted his bottom, and felt his head relax onto her shoulder.

'Are those teeth bothering you, little laddy? You'll need them, you know, when you get big, for eating all the food that I eat. And when you're bigger I'll bake you the tastiest apple pie you'll ever eat, and we can take it down the boreen to one of the fields and eat it all up. Just you and me. That'd be grand now, wouldn't it, Pad?'

The little child closed his hand over a length of her hair that had come loose and closed his eyes. Kathleen also closed her eyes and swayed to the song that was in her head, humming it ever so softly. She would put him down when his breathing was slow and loud and content.

'Will I take him for you?' Her father's whisper trickled through the dark. The bed creaked as he rose from it and he stepped towards her. 'He looks so peaceful when he sleeps.'

'Sorry, did we wake you? Paddy was getting growly. It's his teeth, I think . . . I'll pop him down in a moment.'

'No, no, I was awake. Can't seem to get off tonight.'

Kathleen turned to place Paddy back in the cot. She suddenly felt horribly self-conscious in her nightgown and bare feet in her father's bedroom.

'Sorry. The light, the light's not going to help, is it? I think he's off now, I'll leave ye in peace.'

She bent down to place Paddy in his cot and blew out the lamp as she did so, conscious that the nightie was years old, and that bending over would reveal much of her thighs. As her eyes tried to adjust, she could hear her father beside her, settling Paddy's blankets over him. She wished he would go back to his bed so that she could reach the door, but she sensed him still near. She turned around, her eyes searching the darkness, but she could see nothing. It must have been a cloudy night.

Kathleen felt for Paddy's forehead and bent over briefly to kiss him. Then, she stood up and said goodnight in the direction of her father's bed.

'Goodnight, Kathleen. You're a picture with him, you know. He loves you so much.'

He was at the foot of the cot, and if he remained there Kathleen would have to go around him. The room seemed very small all of a sudden.

'You must be tired, Kathy.'

Her father had not spoken to her in these hushed tones since she was a small girl. They would talk quietly together if she woke with a bad dream, so as not to wake Nuala. He would perch on the edge of the bed and stroke her hair, maybe humming a few bars of some song he had picked up over the years. She wanted to hear another few words before bed. It was nice to be appreciated, especially in the small hours, and she had had so little interaction with other adults these past months.

Her father did not speak again so she moved towards him and her own room. A cloud had shifted and a glow of moon highlighted the gently curved lines of his torso and his dishevelled hair. As she passed close by she caught a new scent from him that she had not known before, the horsey, muddy smell replaced by the family soap bought from Caroline's. It smelled different on him than it did on her. She wanted to ask him to come down, sit awhile by the last embers. She did not want to go down to her little, lonely room and lie awake till morning. But she knew he'd be tired from the day's work. He stood there still, a waiting shadow.

The light from the moon made a curve of the doorknob

gleam. She reached out to touch it and part of her arm became illuminated. The doorknob was cold to her touch, making Kathleen suddenly aware of how warm she was, the hairs bristling along her arms, but her father's hand where he touched her arm was hotter still. 'Don't go yet.'

She turned to face him, looking at the silhouette of his large shoulders. Softly, silently, he drew her to him. He could be so gentle sometimes, especially when it came to Paddy, and often indeed with her. She felt the weight of responsibility to Paddy then, the strain of the nights of broken sleep, the children always out with her because she had to be the voice of discipline, the only physical contact being with Paddy. She was so tired, and as the desolation of not having been held for a long time rushed over her she let herself lean on him. Through the thin cotton of her nightgown she felt the bristly hairs and the heat of his breathing chest against her. She had no bra on, of course, and could feel her breasts moulding against the shape of him, but it was all right, because here was a father giving a worn-out daughter a hug, understanding, and finally saying, 'I know how much you do, and I couldn't do it without you.' It just felt odd because it was so dark, and they had not embraced for a long while. Kathleen relaxed into her father, feeling no tension at all now, and realizing just how tense she had been. As he placed his arms around her they felt so familiar and calming and, wanting to reciprocate that feeling, she gently wrapped her arms around his neck, drawing them closer together still. Her nightdress felt awkward so she moved to the side a little, still holding on. He followed with his body, and they moved back to the centre. It was a soothing motion, and they moved together again. The light was stronger now and she raised her head from her father's shoulder to look at his face.

Her bare feet were wet with dew and a small amount of blood. She was sitting on a rock on the strand, the sound of her breathing almost drowning out the crashing of the incoming tide. The white explosions where each wave fell sent sparks of moonlit water into the cool night air. She had run all the way, through the fields of their farm and Murphy's. The chill air had dried her tears to her face and her skin felt taut and not her own. She touched her fingers to cheeks and mouth, and smelled salt and her father and herself. She cried loudly into the waves, not knowing what to do, or what had happened. She wanted to get into the water, to let it soak her through, even though she knew this would be a foolish thing to do on such a black night. The clouds had gathered around the moon again. Kathleen shivered. She stepped towards the water's edge.

At first she thought her father had followed her, but the man's voice calling was slightly higher in pitch, younger.

'Excuse me! Do you need any help, miss?'

The man was coming nearer, a shadow evolving out of the darkness. What was she thinking, coming out here alone in the night? Kathleen watched, unsure of what to do or say. She wiped at her eyes, backing away a little.

But the stranger held out his hand and said, 'It's all right . . . You ran through my field, right past me. Gave me a fright, you did.'

The man reached out to touch her shoulder. There was nowhere to go; she was not able to go back. She felt she could not go anywhere, or do anything, or know what it was that she was meant to do next. Kathleen slumped onto a rock and began to weep again, but tried to hide the sound with a cough.

'It's all right. It's all right to be upset sometimes, we all are upset sometimes.'

The man sat on the rock next to Kathleen's and looked out towards the sea. She wished he would go away. He would follow her, she knew, if she got up. And she hadn't the energy to make her body do anything other than sit and sit and sit, and forget. They sat for some time like that, each waiting for the other to speak. Kathleen thought that maybe this was not mere chance; maybe he was sent by God, so that she could confess of what she had done. She had been kissed by her father in the way she had only dreamed of doing with a nameless, mysterious boy. But what had she done? Was it something awful? It felt good at the time, comforting, necessary. It had felt as though she were communing with her confidant, her best friend, the only person who understood her and her life. And she the only one who understood him.

Kathleen shifted in her hard seat and prepared to tell the man what had happened, but he spoke again.

'I have seen you lots of times, you know, going on your errands, on your way to Mass, at your kind friend's home . . .'

Kathleen turned to look at him and recognized him as the man Dr Fitzgerald was attending to that day at Caroline's. Now she knew what he meant by 'his field'. She hadn't known she'd gone that way. She was without thought as she had fled. Despite her good intentions, she had truthfully assumed he was a tinker but she could see now, in the half-light, that, underneath his beard, he was a handsome enough fellow, with the kind of eyes that are smiling even when the mouth is not.

'It's Kathleen, isn't it?'

'Kathleen. Yes.' Her voice came out as a whisper, so she repeated it and he smiled.

'Yes. 'Tis a pretty name . . . Now, come here till I wrap this around you before you catch your death. And when you're ready, I'll walk you back up home. A nice, warm bed is a wonderful place to be when you're cold and wet, Kathleen.'

As they walked, she leaned on the stranger but felt only the form of her father beside her. It was as though she were detached from herself, as though she were sitting on the rock still, only just aware of herself walking away. She thought abstractedly of how they sat on the floor by the fire, facing one another, their outstretched legs gently resting against each other, as they chatted or just sat in the quiet. She had thought nothing of it before. But now she felt a dull, bulbous fretting beginning in the pit of her stomach. Images flickered in her mind's eye of the two of them working together on the bales and, worn out, collapsing back into the hay – his hand clasping hers for a moment – to say well done, we did it, surely . . . of him brushing her hair in the evening – a fatherly thing to do, just as he would with the girls . . . of the countless tasks of jointly caring for Paddy, for her mother – lifting her together, on her worst days; making appointments, arrangements; helping Laura at her reading and both praising her as she struggled through; holding the dog down, wrapped in a towel as she bandaged a slit paw; her rubbing cream into the sores on his feet from those wretched boots that wore holes into every sock she darned and redarned.

The man's voice wore on beside her but her mind registered no words. They sounded remote and strange, her thoughts more real than the fields before her. Exhaustion weighed down her every step and Joseph found he had almost to carry her up the last hill.

When she was a child she would often play the game of Sleeping Princesses with her twin. It always amazed them that they never seemed to wake in the same position that they fell asleep in, even if they decided between them that they would both lie on their left side, hair smoothed horizontally across the pillows, right leg straight and left foot tucked under it. They tried lying in that position while they nodded off, as well as moving around as much as possible, exhausting all possible positions and energy among much stifled laughter (their mother would be cross if she heard so much as a peep from either of them), and they tried barricading themselves into position so that they simply could not move – with cushions, blankets, winter cardigans, and each other's bodies. But no matter what they did they would have moved by morning. Nuala would make Kathleen laugh on the days she woke first by arranging her body in some comic and impossible position, then closing her eyes and pretending to be still asleep. Kathleen would wake to see her sister with her head inside her cardigan, one leg glued upright on the wall, with Yellow Ear balanced precariously on it, and arms hanging off the edge of the bed or across Kathleen's face.

Kathleen thought of this game as she began to stir from a long dream. She was aware that it was a dream, but it had been pleasant and she did not want to leave it. But the pictures behind her eyes were slipping back into her memory or her imagination, and she could sense the space left by her sister years ago in the big bed. The bed would have gone to the other children, of course, but she had been lucky. A family had moved away, the Dunnes, and they had no need for much of their furniture as their only boy had grown up and was doing well for himself in Dublin. The house they had gone to was one of the first to be electrified on the outskirts of the city, and even had its own electric cooker and washing machine. Kathleen's mother had been left the two beds, along with a mangle, a tin kettle and a good few pairs of shoes that would last them a long while.

She thought of the game as she awoke because she had fallen asleep reading her Bible and now she could feel the morning sun high on her cheek and brow, and the hard edge of the book digging into her back. There was a wind outside, which made the soft branches of the willow tree dapple the light. Kathleen could feel her eyes adjusting to the rapidly changing shadows, allowing patches of orange-red brightness to dance behind her eyelids. As she was brought further into consciousness Kathleen kept her eyes still firmly shut. The day could wait a moment longer. Nuala was with her, warm and comforting. She could not hear Paddy.

A line of warmth sat along her cheekbone. The sun was stronger than it had been any morning yet. It was strange not being roused from sleep by him. Strange to come to her senses so slowly, as she had as a child. On a Saturday their mother would often let them lie in a while and it was so blissful to just rest there, all worries hidden yet by the fog of sleep. She stretched, yawning, allowing herself the few extra minutes

Paddy was giving her – she knew she would hear him the minute he made so much as a squeak.

Kathleen lay for a long while, listening to the sounds outside the window, a thrush, a distant tractor, Jim Reilly's undoubtedly, there were only a handful for miles around. If it were not for Mr Reilly's help with the tractor her father would still be using the horse to draw the plough, urging it up the field in endless, snail-paced lines.

The memory of the other night came back to her slowly as she lay there peacefully. She scolded herself at her silly running-off in the night. It was childish and could have been dangerous – she could have tripped and fallen, or got a fever from running through the wet in bare feet, or the stranger could have been someone unpleasant. She should seek him out and thank him, but for now she just wanted to avoid him. She thought of the kiss, and she thought of the embrace, and knew she had reacted wrongly. It was merely an expression of love – such expressions are not reserved just for husband and wife. Sure, she kissed Paddy on the lips every day. And truly, their love for one another ran so deep – it transcended father and daughter, so entwined were their lives. She would show him it was nothing to be embarrassed about, or feel ashamed of, by embracing him again, or squeezing his hand. But also she wanted to do it to say thank you for being a wonderful support and, above all, a wonderful friend.

She could hear children's voices, getting louder. It was Tomás and Laura, out by the hayloft. They were arguing. Kathleen sighed and rose up onto her knees to open the window to give out to them for fighting at this time of the morning, to wait till they had at least had breakfast, so that they could do it on a full stomach.

One curtain was drawn back already, so she opened them fully, the movement of which sent an involuntary but satisfying stretch through her body. She saw Laura sitting on an upturned milk churn, muddy-eyed, with Tomás standing above her.

'If you won't listen when we explain the rules you can't play. You can't go making up your own rules, Laura!'

'I didn't get ye, how do I know there're two bases, and I can't run as fast as ye.' Laura was trying hard not to start crying again. 'It's not fair, so it isn't. You and Brendan never let me play.'

'Ah, go and play with Paddy, yeh big crybaby yeh. And there's no point going running to Mam either, she'll only ignore you like she does Paddy cos ye're both big fat crybabies!'

At this, Laura ran off behind the hayloft, wailing. Kathleen watched her go, wondering why they were up and dressed so early, and wondering whether maybe both she and Paddy had had a good lie-in for once. Her eyes fell back to Tomás, who was now kicking stones at the churn. His eyes were red. As each stone pinged off the metal an echo sounded over by the boreen. He sniffed loudly.

'Are y'all right, Tom?' Kathleen called. The boy turned his face away and wiped at it with the sleeve of his cardy. It was two inches short on each arm, and frayed to holes at the cuffs. Kathleen decided she would ask her father if she could spend some money on a new one. There was no point knitting another for he'd be out of it before it was finished, the rate he was growing. He would have the same build as his father as a man. 'You know, that wasn't very nice what you said to Laura. Go and make it up with her, will yeh?'

Tomás turned around and looked up at his older sister, his

own eyes red, and then he ran off in the opposite direction to where Laura was sulking. She would speak to his father and he would sit him down. Sure he was upset about their mother but his behaviour was unreasonable. How strange that Paddy had not woken, with the commotion of the stones and the yelling. Kathleen pulled on her shawl and hurried up to her parents' bedroom. Kathleen frowned at the sight of the room in full daylight, bed half-heartedly made, working boots and slippers gone from under it. Her heart did a little dance when her eyes fell on Paddy's empty cot. How long had she slept for? And who had Paddy? Did anyone know he was missing? Oh, Lord.

Kathleen tore downstairs to the kitchen where her mother sat in her chair.

'Hello, sleepy Kathleen,' giggled Molly, who was drawing rabbits underneath the table. The breakfast crumbs hadn't been wiped away.

'Moll, where's Pad?' Kathleen hissed, so as her mother would not hear.

'Relax, Kathleen,' said Tomás, who had just appeared at the door, shoes caked in mud, and wet shirt sleeves pushed up against the sweater. 'Da has him.'

'What do you mean your father has him? In the field? Where? Does he have his hat? Take those wretched things off your feet before you trail it all around the house. And did you say sorry to Laura?'

Tomás sighed an old man's sigh. 'I will when she comes back in . . . I was trying to rescue a rabbit from a briar near the stream, you know, in O'Brien's field. He was all tangled up.'

'But he couldn't do it and the rabbit's eyes went all big and he was kicking out, wasn't he, Tom?' said Molly. 'Wasn't he really scared?'

'He was not scared, and I could do it. He got out, didn't he? Anyway I fell in and nearly drowned . . .'

'That's a lie, you said you bet you could run faster through the water than the rabbit and then you fell on top of the rabbit, which is when he gotted out.' Molly's picture now had red crayon on the legs of all the rabbits, dripping onto some grass. 'And he didn't nearly drown, he just pretended it to make me cry and . . .'

'Tomás, where has your father gone with Paddy? I'll take over now.'

'Ah, I thought you'd got up to make our dinner, I'm starved!'

'Dinner?' Kathleen briskly gathered a knife, what was left of yesterday's bread, and some cheese. She quickly swept the table's crumbs into her hands and headed towards her room to dress herself. 'Tomás, you are old enough to make a sandwich for yourself and your sister. If there is a speck of mud on this floor when I bring Paddy back for his feed, there'll be trouble, and you'll be the one doing the mopping. And if Molly and Laura are hungry when I get back, I'll hold you responsible.'

'But, but I've never . . .'

'It's about time you had a few more jobs around the place, mister. That's why I slept in. To show you lot what needs to be done, and that I don't need to do it all. And make sure you apologize to your sister.' She turned away from their shocked faces, and felt horrible. 'And don't use all that cheese.'

As she dressed hurriedly, Kathleen felt the water in her eyes threaten to overflow. Her days were defined now by what she did for the children and when, each second. She rarely had time to think her own thoughts. The day felt strange. Paddy's morning routine was all wrong; he would be missing her, and he was sure to be hungry. She pulled her field boots on, and hurried out past the two siblings giggling away as they tried to slice the hard loaf. She would make more when she was back. She would see to Laura and set to starting another cardigan for Tomás. If it didn't fit him it would fit the girls, and if she took too long she could save it for Paddy. In fact she had not knitted him anything since her mother was pregnant with him. She had knitted everything in yellow, for a boy or a girl. Now he was here, and growing bigger by the day, he should have something nice and new of his own, not just his siblings' hand-me-downs. She would go into the store in Killnarnan and look at some wools, a lovely mossy green to match his eyes. Kathleen and Paddy were the only ones who had inherited their father's green eyes – and Nuala of course.

When he woke it was with a nasty pain in his abdomen on account of the large stone he had not noticed before he lay down to sleep, and a mouthful of mud and probably, Joseph thought dismally, various microscopic inhabitants of the mud. His drool had wetted the earth and the rising sun had begun to bake it onto his face and into his beard. He had turned around onto his back. Everything ached, like the flu. The sun shot through his sunken eyelids straight to his brain where a sharp pain trumped the general aching in his head and neck, and even his stomach. Joseph could feel that his body needed to muster a sneeze to expel bits of mud and dust from deep inside his nostrils, but it seemed to have forgotten the mechanization for this most basic of bodily functions. He was pleased at this achievement and lay there thinking about the dust and particles of earth and little creatures that he must have sucked through his nostrils while sleeping face down in the dirt. Would they be making a home in his gut now? It certainly felt like it. As long as he didn't move too much, the feverish aches and chill deep within his bones were bearable. Running after the girl Kathleen had taken its toll, confused his body. He got up stiffly to stretch his bones.

She had disturbed the pattern of things, so he had taken a walk down to the shop and bought a paper and a bottle of milk. It had felt wonderful. It was against his rules, but there was such a pleasure in using some money that he had nearly forgotten was in his bag. He went back for more. The woman behind the counter who followed him with her suspicious eyes was clearly shocked when he bought a whole pound of sweets, some bread and cheese and two apple tarts. And, as he was about to pay, he spotted some cream to go with the tarts, and then several rolls of toilet paper. He laughed inside at the thought of this intrigued lady thinking he was a tinker one day and then a man with more money than sense another. But she had treated him with polite respect, as though he were any other customer, the episode with the doctor all but forgotten.

On his walk back from the store he began to look more closely at the cottages he was passing. She obviously lived somewhere nearby, and if he knew where he could perhaps call in with one of the tarts. He regretted now not having bought some chocolate from the woman with the neat hair, but he was too far on to go back now, and the sun was getting ever higher. Chocolate would be a better treat. She probably has apple tart every day of the week, and no doubt this one wouldn't be half as good as one made by her own hand. He strained to peer casually through windows to glimpse a movement of her within, or at washing lines in gardens to see whether her yellow dress was hanging out in the morning warmth. He looked at all of the dwellings he could find, and walked up some lanes he had not trodden before. Did she live with her parents still, or with some elderly relative? He had been struck by her gentleness, the calm that immediately disguised the wild, frantic feelings that had brought her away from her bed in the middle of the night, the moment she sensed him near her. He had not told her, of course, that he had been watching her a good few minutes before he approached her. He was not sure if he should. It was dark and, to her at least, they were virtual strangers. She might have been afraid. But she seemed so distraught he could not simply do nothing.

Kathleen. Kathleen. The word whispered softly in his head. Joseph spoke the name aloud, and the sounds of it seemed familiar and comforting. He watched her often, going about her errands. He knew that she walked the road above his field, and that he might find her again on a rock by the sea in the dark of night. But it would be nice to see where she lived, where she spent her days. But what would he say to her? What had he said to her only a few hours before, when the girl must have been calling out for somebody to say something meaningful to her? He hadn't known what to do or say, so he had tried to look at the same point out at the black sea that she was staring at and had waffled on at her instead of insisting he took her home immediately. As Joseph walked he wondered why he had done this, and how unhelpful it was to the girl called Kathleen, and how sitting next to this mermaid-beauty in the dead of night had probably soothed only his own aching heart. And as he neared a turn in the lane that brought him back to the road which led to his field it all seemed to matter a little less now that he had met Kathleen. There was a chance that the hopelessness, the shame and despair of days of old, were being replaced by something new.

There was a smell under the hedgerow near his patch. A familiar smell, sweet and sickly, that drew Joseph towards it with a frown. A rabbit lay there, panting. He crawled slowly forward, placing each hand quietly, quietly. It was still alive, its small brown stomach pulsating rapidly as it struggled to breathe. Joseph drew back in horror at the sight of the bloody leg, the gloopy darkness of it making him heave, the mere fact of which ashamed him. Its eyes became wide and panicked as it spotted him there. It wanted to bolt but only its front paws jerkily moved, and its ears flattened. Joseph could not walk away and leave it in this state. He wanted to put it out of its misery, it would be the kindest thing to do.

'Shush now, little one . . .' he said.

He looked around for a rock but there was none. There was only field and mud, and leaves on spindly twigs. He looked at his boot with another man's lace on it, knowing it would be the only implement that would work.

He talked to the animal while he unlaced it slowly, but he

was not really aware of what he was saying for he had become a little detached from himself, distant from his surroundings, numb as to what he was about to do. He stood above the thing, casting a shadow over it. Its eyes were closed a little now but it still breathed rapidly. The sun was warm on his back. The boot trembled in his hand.

Joseph cried out as he flung his weapon aside. He fell onto his knees, gasping, and crept again towards the dying creature. It kicked out momentarily, flashing wild eyes at him as he began to stroke it between the ears. He shushed it again, weeping. The contrast of the soft, warm fur and the blood going cold in matted clumps was unbearable to him. The rabbit began to let him be there, and its muscles relaxed. It let its eyes close and Joseph murmured at it again as its breathing slowed.

Later, Joseph felt a deep and quiet sadness, but also a sense of peace that he had been able to be with the thing as it drew its last breath. He thought of it under its burial mound of leaves as he fell asleep, but this blood, this death did not haunt him and jump out at him in his dreams, not because it was merely an animal, but because it had gone in the right way. He had seen too many men dying alone, calling out for their wives and mothers. And in his pocket he kept still the photograph his friend held till the end. The image of a smiling wife and child, a token of hope in those bleak and frightening days.

There was a sweetness to the air that often comes when there has been no rain and a lot of heat. It was made up of moisture from the little streams dotted through the fields all the way down to the sea, combined with sticky wet rising from the neighbouring farm's silage, the not-distant-enough slurry pit and the sweat of various animals. But a breeze would sometimes lift off the scent of her mother's rose garden and strawberry patch, and be carried by the dust of some fresh golden straw and dandelion clocks and mix all the smells up, and every now and then Kathleen would breathe deeply and eternally to keep that odour of home within her. Some smells reminded her so strongly of being a child, carefree in this land. She loved this place. It was a part of her very soul, and it was where Nuala had lived and breathed. Nuala hadn't known any other place, had no desire to, and so she remained there with them.

Kathleen tried to think of where her father would be at this time of day, and headed down the boreen to the beet field. How would he be able to work and look after Paddy at the same time? It was utterly ridiculous, and she would tell him so. No doubt the poor child would be left to his own devices, without a bonnet under this scorching sun. The ground was hard under her tread, and her feet seemed to jar against it in the wellingtons, so unused was she to walking with them on ground unsoftened by rain, and so toughened by the sun.

But she could not find them in the beet field, nor in any of the other fields. The thought of going back to the house depressed her. The day felt strange. It was hot and her feet were beginning to sweat in the rubber boots, yet there was a coolness to the air and it trickled soothingly through the delicate material of her dress. There was a small brook in the bottom field, just to the left at the end of the boreen. The cattle drank from it now, but once Kathleen and Nuala had played endless games of dam-building, boat-making for fairies, and toe-dipping there. Kathleen was sure Tomás and Brendan played there from time to time, although they were forbidden to go anywhere near potential hazards, after Nuala.

Along the way Kathleen picked a few long stems of montbretia and some startlingly purple foxgloves. When she reached the gate she unstuck the boots from her heat-swollen feet and flung them over the gate, vaguely startling one or two of the nearest cows. Kathleen pulled the ribbon from her hair, which was already coming loose as she had tied it in such a hurry, and bound the handful of flowers she had picked with it. It was lilac, and had belonged to a dress of hers or her sister's long ago. Kathleen frowned at the contrast of it against the brilliant orange of the montbretia. She carefully placed the bunch in the hedge, hoisted up her dress and lifted herself over the gate. The toll of metal on metal, as the old gate clanged against its post, rang out in the still air. Not so far away a little baby sound responded.

He had not brought the pram. It was too awkward to push along anything other than a smooth road, and God knows there weren't enough of those in Ballinara. It was not an unhappy sound at all. She stood there, and it took a moment for the scene to register in her mind. There they were, the two of them, within touching distance of several cows. Some had scattered at the sound of the gate, but the more inquisitive had remained, so that her father and Paddy, held high in his father's arms, were encircled by the beasts. It was a trick he had played on all of them at some point in their childhood. Each child would be terrified at the sight of the advancing herd, the animals' intrigued, doleful eyes staring into theirs, trapping them within an ever-decreasing circle. But at the same time, each child knew the animals would do nothing to them, if only because their father was there, and he wouldn't let anything bad happen. The trick was to sit down and to let them come nearer and nearer until you would catch the spray on your face from their heavily breathing nostrils. Then you would stand up suddenly and they would all simultaneously turn and flee haphazardly across the field. Nuala and Kathleen had played this trick on the cattle time after time and the animals never learned from the day before and always galloped clumsily away from the two matching girls.

It was nice to see the two of them together, but Kathleen was less than pleased with her father. She would say nothing, though. She couldn't. It was not her place to interfere when they were having a quiet moment together. She decided to turn back quietly so as not to disturb them. Her father had not shown any sign of having noticed her and Paddy was grand, smiling and gooing at him. She was not needed here, and besides there was lots more to do at the house. Kathleen's head hurt. She had slept late, but not for long enough. She located her wellingtons, which had managed to fall quite far apart, one precariously near the stream, and headed back towards the gate.

She was surprised by two things that morning. She was surprised at the tears that came after seeing that Paddy had looked at her briefly and turned back to his father. And she was surprised at her father's voice, calling her back through the mist of those tears. So he had seen her. He called her name a few times, and she wanted to go to him to be comforted again, to feel the closeness of the night before. No one at the house would show any care. And she did not know why she could not allow herself to stay. She heard him calling her still as she ran back up the boreen.

He looked at the gate and imagined her route: up the boreen; left, along the passage by the house; left, in the door; right, check her mother. He pictured her going about the tasks she would be attending to in the kitchen, the flick of her skirt and hair as she busied herself, but he could not see the expression on her face, he did not know what was behind those eyes of hers today. Were his own as inscrutable? They were the same as hers after all, only framed by lines sketched over the years by sun and dust and grief. How comforted he had felt last night, how free! She alone knew the workings of his mind. She shared – indeed was – the other part of him. They had become melded into one, he thought, two parts of a great machine which without either one of those parts would become redundant. And so she had become his solace, his confidante. She had caught him as he fell and slowly wove her way into the daily fabric of his life and the holes never frayed any further because of her.

He smiled and settled Paddy into the cradle of his immense left arm and walked slowly towards the hedge. As he left the field he spotted the bunch of flowers that had been stuffed into the briars before she hitched her skirt up and leapt over the gate. She had on her boots and was wearing no underskirt. The flash of cream against metal and hedgerow had reminded him of the days when he and Nora would be at the céilís up at Donovan's in Carrickbrook. He would rarely dance himself, but preferred to watch his wife as she laughed and kicked and sang out with the other girls. Usually they would sneak out and find a spot in a field for a few secret moments. She was one of the most beautiful dancers in the area, and all knew it. All the boys would say it to him, and he would smile inside. Now, when he saw neighbours, the time of day might be passed, business talked of, when the farrier was coming next, when the ESB would finally erect an electricity pole for them. Now, people seemed to keep themselves to themselves. Each looked after their own, and that was the way it should be, he thought. Although there was no denying his wife's state of mind. But it was normal to him now; he often almost forgot she was there at all. For she wasn't, not really. There was no trace of the young wife he'd brought home one day many moons ago. And he did not feel lonesome, for he had all the children to come home to after a quiet day out in the field, and he had Kathleen, who had become a true friend, to talk to when the day was done.

He would put Paddy back into his cot and would let her know next time he was taking him out so she would have no need to worry. And it was so good of her to be concerned. But it came naturally, of course. The two were a picture together, the way the child adored her and relied on her, just as he did himself. He would refresh the water in the vase by his wife's table, smooth out the blankets if they were creased; she had always been particular about these things. 'We may not have the luxuries of some, but we can make what God gives us into our own little luxuries.' He could hear her giggle. It was like an echo, distant, long-ago sounding, and was gone from his mind before he really noticed it was there. Kathleen would be pleased at his thoughtfulness with the flowers. As he walked, Paddy began to nod off in his arm. He worried that this was maybe not his sleeping time, and would Kathleen be cross with him. And as he walked he thought about her, and it struck him that he had not heard his eldest child laugh for a while now, other than with the children. Not a real, honest laugh. He would catch a moment with her and say something, do something, to really make her chuckle. That would make him feel good. He would make it a daily goal, to show her how much he appreciated her, to make her a little happier every day, for who else would?

It was a lonely road, yet the air itself seemed transformed on a Sunday, with the chatter of the children on their way home, looking forward to the meal in the week that would make them feel full for once. Families walked a conscious, polite distance from each other, only a couple of the younger girls slipping in and out of the slowly moving clusters of villagers. From his hiding place in a large oak it struck him how nice a ritual it was, walking together as a family, as part of a group of people bound together for a while by the same purpose, and he regretted not having spent more time with his own family before it was too late.

Ladies in their stiff, dark dresses and clicking Sunday shoes walked past, ushering children into a more orderly fashion. The children too looked uncomfortable out of their ragged play clothes. Joseph was amused by this – who would be seeing them besides other hungry children, distracted parents and a field of cattle? Maybe they thought that God cared. But surely, if He was the God he had learned of as a child, how His congregation was dressed was surely irrelevant.

The man in the tree saw them, of course. The man in the tree who saw everything. It was quite empowering to have such a viewpoint. He could gaze at women's hairstyles or hemlines with the same freedom that a child stares innocently at a man with a large red boil on the side of his nose. He could even take in the display of varying bosoms, loosely covered with summer shawls, without the ladies even knowing, but after one or two, and especially the third, which belonged to Caroline Walsh, he felt embarrassed and schoolboy-like. So he concentrated on the ladies' faces, and it was not long before he spied her.

In fact it was her mother who he saw first. An older version of Kathleen, long grey hair flecked with yellow escaping from the headscarf that had been left on since Mass. She was slightly hunched over and had a scraggly grey shawl pulled tightly around her shoulders, held by her arms which were folded across her breasts despite the morning's warmth. He could see the family resemblance in the mouth and the lips, which, like Kathleen's, were always slightly parted. But hers were dry and thinner, and her eyes were not the same. No light reflected in them; they were misted over like a window when the fire is blazing and there is a bitter frost outside. Her feet were carrying her body forwards but she did not seem aware of herself at all. She was lucky, he thought to himself, that she had such a lovely, big family to look after her.

A few paces behind was the girl he had been looking out for. In a new dress this time. Her hands were busy holding those of two small girls with amazing heads of hair. One's was yellow, tumbling in storybook curls; the other's was thick and dark and flowing. Joseph found himself sighing a little at the thought of such a pure and bright colour fading to nothing one day, as his eyes flicked towards the older family member. Her feet were occupied with keeping up with the inharmonious skipping of the little girls, while her eyes flitted between the back of her mother's head and two more children, both boys, who were pushing a baby's pram very roughly along near the side of the road. All four children were squabbling and giggling. The boys, who looked scruffy even in their best outfits, were the noisiest of all the children walking along the road. They almost drove the pram into the furrow right beside Joseph's tree. One of them did not look related to the others, for he had a shock of red hair and so many freckles that barely any white skin peeked through. Joseph thought the dark-haired boy glanced up at him. He held his breath and closed his eyes as he could not conceal himself further without risking falling. But they passed by, and he was reassured that he remained undetected.

It was his Kathleen who scolded the pair. She took over the pushing of the pram and they did as they were told immediately. The lady who had given her daughter her wondrous lips walked on, unperturbed, as though she could not hear a thing. Kathleen was not harsh with them. Firm, but very unsisterly. Maybe the grey-haired woman was the grandmother. It had not occurred to Joseph that Kathleen might be married. But she looked too young to have so many children, and she still had that look that women have – there is a freshness, an untouchedness, about a woman who has not yet carried a child. He glanced at her again. Yes, he could see the maturity in her now, he could see the weight of responsibility on her shoulders, the tiredness in her limbs, and his heart slipped a little. She was spoken for.

Another sigh escaped him. Audible, he was sure, and he looked sharply to see whether anyone passing underneath had heard him. Of course they hadn't. But there was a man, walking on his own. There were no further churchgoers for a good stretch back. Maybe he belonged to Kathleen's family. Joseph felt a rush of unpleasantness towards this tall, well-structured man. He looked at his face. He was freshly shaven and very tanned. A farmer, for sure. Although he was still youthful looking, Joseph could see he was definitely older, or maybe Kathleen was lucky with her looks. The man was smiling contentedly to himself and absently looking ahead up the road. Joseph followed his line of vision till his own eyes came to rest on Kathleen's behind. The sun was in front of her, strong yet owning that hazy quality of a summer's morning. The material of her skirt was delicate, letting the light through, and both men could see the outline of her arse as she swished matron-like after the children. He wondered how someone so perfect could feel so downhearted as she had been that night?

As the last parishioner passed beneath him, Joseph felt listless. He did not care about returning to his spot in the field so he wandered aimlessly through the hills in the glare of the midday heat until he could go on no more; then he lay down under the burning sun. He was told by his mother many a time as a child not to look directly at it. He saw her behind his closed eyes walking alone on the way to Mass. He pictured her praying for him, as she sat still and solemn on the wooden pew, wondering when her boy would return. They had pleaded with him not to go, and had he known he would have missed her passing away, he would never have enlisted. In defiance, not of his mother, but of his body's advice, he opened his eyes and stared up at the sun till he could stare no more.

He dreamed briefly of entering a pool of cool, blue water, immersing himself completely as if in baptism. He found he could breathe and see underwater. The girl was there, all made of gold, glistening and glittering beneath the surface. He drank and drank until the whole pool was empty and when he had had his fill he stood there, naked as Adam, but no longer thirsty.

Joseph had not reckoned on how insistent his body could be, and how the instinct within to survive is far greater than any decision not to. His physical need for water was dragging his swollen feet in a desperate search for hydration, despite him thinking, This is it, this is the moment and I must switch off my mind to let nature complete its purpose.

However, nature did not believe that it was Joseph's time and so placed before him a small bubbling stream in which he soon found himself lying face forwards, giggling and slurping away like a baby. It took several moments of glee and several shouts of Kathleen's name to awaken Joseph to the reality that this was not heaven and his plan had not yet worked.

He felt as though he had slept a hundred years, like a fairy-tale character awakening to a changed world – everything was the same, yet time had moved on without him. He had lost a day at least. The hazy air had a magical quality to it. Distant, low-hanging clouds that seemed only the concern of the far-off horizon, were red and pink and dreamlike. Yet what pleased him was that no images of his dreaming remained after this sleep, and the feeling of dread upon waking was not there; that feeling of hopelessness had lessened.

He guessed it to be morning, though he couldn't be sure as he was not in his usual field. Kneeling now, through the sound of the stream hurrying over the pebbles, Joseph heard it again. Somebody was calling the girl called Kathleen. It wasn't him, surely? Maybe he had called her name aloud without being aware of doing so, a subconscious shout from somewhere beyond his slumber.

He must have looked like a madman without a cause as he stumbled here and there, and would have to get his bearings to reach his field before nightfall. But first he must see whether this was the same Kathleen, though it would surely be a bizarre coincidence if there were two in the same village who shared that name. From his knees, Joseph bent forwards, one hand either side of the little stream, and he dipped his head and lapped up the God-sent liquid. His body rejoiced and he thought of how insignificant he was in the face of water, how his body relied on the fundamental drop of it. That's what a priest would say. Water is more important than a pair of shoes without holes. Do you think Jesus worried about whether his feet would be wet, or cold, or dirty? He would say, No, Jesus would tell us to take off our shoes and feel the Lord's earth underneath our bare feet, the same earth that all of our feet walk on, that He made for us. Joseph thought that maybe he should add himself to the end of that long line of Mass-goers next Sunday. Maybe God would understand and forgive him a little. He needed someone to.

Joseph began to be able to make out his reflection in the

water. He drew back slightly so his eyes could focus on the watery image of his face. An old man looked back at him, with a downturned mouth and with watery shadows under his cheekbones. The scar on his jowl was completely hidden by an unkempt wiry beard. Joseph's first. If he were to pursue the notion that this might be the girl's home he would have to remain well hidden and come back another day a presentable man, rather than a dishevelled waif. Maybe he would take up that doctor on his offer of a few nights' board in return for running a few messages. He said it would be the only way to get Joseph better, and he could do with the bit of help. He was a kind man.

Cattle moved at the other end of the field and a rabbit sped across into the hedgerow. Joseph looked up to a strange sight. A man, tall and big-boned, but slender all the same, was doing something by the hedgerow. One hand was picking at something in the hedge, and the other hand, and most of the large arm, was taken up by holding something. From Joseph's position the parcel appeared to be a bundle of white cloths, and yet the man treated it with great care. Maybe it was an injured lamb or chicken. Or a clutch of eggs, perhaps, though why the farmer man would be using his wife's best linen for such a job baffled Joseph. As the man turned and began walking towards the gate, he could see it was the girl's husband.

He would be seen at any moment if he did not move now. But there was nowhere to go, and no time for Joseph to think of a reasonable excuse, so he closed his eyes, inhaled the scent of grass, and lay back with a gentle splash into the water.

*

She was sitting by her mother when he arrived back. The basket of wool that lived by his wife's chair was nestled in Kathleen's lap. She was knitting quickly and smoothly. He stood at the door and listened to the faint click-click of the needles and thought it strange that they sounded far off, as though Laura or Molly were tapping stones in the haggard outside. Distant, and long ago somehow, like the sound of his wife's laughter.

'If he's asleep now just put him down, but don't cover him. He'll sleep all day if you cover him. Think he's going to bed for the night.' He had been looking at the back of his wife's head and now he looked at his daughter. She had changed into more practical clothes and an apron was tied tight around her middle. The boots were off and on her feet were the knitted slippers that fastened with a button on each. There were several pairs of these slippers dotted around the house in varying sizes, and the girls were forever arguing over whose was whose and Kathleen's answer was always to knit yet another pair. He couldn't think of anything to say, and for some reason suddenly felt odd talking to her in front of Nora. Besides, he might wake Paddy. So he said nothing, nodded at her and went through to settle flowers and baby, and continue with his day.

The click-clicking stopped as he reached the door to the parlour. Seeing that his hands were full, Kathleen had put the knitting down and come to help with the handle of the door. She opened it and held it while he walked through. The door to her parents' bedroom was more difficult, and the stairs that led up to it were so small that they used to joke that pixies had lived in the house before them. She took the flowers from him so he could release the latch. The door swung against her father's arm and he turned sharply to prevent Paddy's head being knocked. Kathleen reached above his head to hold it open for him. The tricky manoeuvre of getting them both through the little door, along with the effort of having to be quiet so as not to disturb Paddy from his slumber, made them want to giggle, and the awkward atmosphere melted away. As her father regained his balance, the need to remain quiet was making the laughter bubble up dangerously. He saw the smile in her eyes and thought that maybe it wouldn't be too hard after all to make her laugh a little. She had always been so beautiful, with a sweet, happy smiling face, even as a baby. And now she was a woman, the light seemed to radiate from her. She made him want to scoop her up and embrace her again.

'Quick', he whispered, 'take him, he's starting to wake.'

Kathleen walked over to Paddy's cot, pulling back his blanket. 'Pop him in there, look ... He'll be grumpy, bless him, how long's he had?'

'Ah, ten minutes or so.'

There was more chuckling then as her father attempted to hold the offending door open with his left foot and catch it with his chin so it didn't bang.

'Ah, stop!' she said, with a tear in her eyes, coming back to prop the door open for him. 'The poor little lad ...' Paddy started to cry and as her father laid him in his cot the tears soon turned into wails.

'Ah, Kathy, you're right, he's out with me now. Come here and wave your magic wand, will yeh?'

'Whisht, would you? He'll never settle if he hears you yellin' like a tinker.'

'Sorry, miss.' It made him smile all the more, even though Paddy was now bawling as if he had been abandoned for hours on end. 'How do you normally settle him when he's like this? How does she work her magic on you, hey, laddy?'

She gathered up the cross red bundle and headed back towards the door. 'The only thing that settles him when he's like this is to lie with him.' She had to speak loudly to be heard over his tears. 'I'll close the curtains and lie in my room with him a bit.'

Immediately her father drew the curtains by the cot, and pulled back the blanket and a sheet on his own bed. 'Lie here with him, sure. The two of ye'll have more peace and quiet up here than in your room. The others'll be in and out and hollerin, about. More space too, what.'

Kathleen thought on this a moment, the awkwardness seeping back in slightly. She had not been on her parents' bed since she was a child, and that was long before her sister and her mother had gone away. She made the bed each day, changed the sheets, threshed the mattress for dust, but the prospect of lying on it suddenly made the bed seem alien, as though she had never seen it before. It felt somehow improper. But to say no would only give substance to the strange feeling, make him wonder was she uncomfortable near him after what happened. She certainly didn't want him to feel that, so she casually said, 'Thanks,' and began to hum to Paddy. Her father left them alone and she went to lie down. Paddy soon settled and his breathing calmed; Kathleen took stock of the room from this new perspective. Everything seemed slightly different. The wood-panelled ceiling had always been there, she had just never noticed it before. It was what her mother stared at night after night, thinking of Nuala. The little window to the outside world, a place that her mother was no longer part of. The sounds of their lives, echoing through the house, sounded different from up here. Noises from the farm, from the children outside playing, were muffled, dimmed. She began to feel different too. Maybe she was feeling how her mother felt.

Did she remember, Kathleen wondered, how she used to laugh and tickle the two of them when they were small, sweet children in their matching clothes? Did she remember chasing them around the hay bales dotted about the field, while their father took a mug of tea and sat upon one, watching, till they heard the bells from across the bay, and he would call them for the Angelus and the three of them would have to try to stop giggling, to be solemn. The memory of that woman was like remembering once being with an old friend, or an imagined mother, a rosy-cheeked, plump, merry sort of a mother plucked from a storybook. It was inconceivable to think that she had once been like that. The words in her parents' voices whispered at her from the past, 'The angel of the Lord declared unto Mary and she conceived by the Holy Spirit . . .'

As she lay there, enjoying the warmth of Paddy's little body, Kathleen closed her eyes and thought that she should make more of an effort to emulate what her mother used to do with her and Nuala when she was with the children. But she was so used to her own routine now, and the children used to being so free. She thought them too young to take on too many chores. There was so little time, not to mention energy, left in the day for playing boisterous games or to sit and teach Molly a bit of sewing as she had often asked. They seemed happy enough, and they were good and polite around grown-ups, and did their school work well. And they always kissed their mother goodnight before bed. They were good children. Kathleen felt a small swell of a feeling that couldn't be taken for anything other than pride and immediately quashed it with a frown and a shake of her head. It was not right to think of them as her own, no matter how strong the feeling was. She loved them as though they were hers and often had to remind herself that she was only a sister. The little shake of her head had disturbed Paddy and he sighed a deep and seemingly troubled sigh, but his breathing was slower now. She wrapped her left arm around him, and pulled the sheet over the two of them. She would lie there a little, and try to think of nothing, and try not to notice the smell of her father underneath her right cheek and in her hair on the pillow. 'Behold the handmaid of the Lord. Be it done unto me according to thy word ... And the word was made flesh and dwelt among us ...'

Her body was unused to the heat in this room. It was thicker, wetter, and heavy as a deep, deep sigh. In her sleep she dreamed of yellow corn, how it looked before it was shorn down, and how it looked after the farmers had been and done their work. She dreamed of Nuala running carefree, gliding almost, through the long ears of corn, and she saw herself running barefoot, stumbling over the brittle, harvested stubs looking for her, calling for her, not able to reach her.

When he returned to change his sweat-sodden shirt, his head inside was a tumble of large, clanging bells and monotonous aches that made him frown and his left cheek wince. He found her still there, a protective arm swallowing the baby, despite the rest of her body having instinctively moved away from this little radiator. One leg was drawn up, exposing the knee of the other, and her right arm flailed across the sea of crumpled white linen. The bed looked enormous with this slight form lying upon it gentle as a just-fallen leaf.

He plucked Paddy softly from her and laid him in his cot. The boy opened an eye and frowned at his father, but upon seeing a smile, let sleep envelop him once again. He was tired. They both were. Sitting down on the edge where there was less of her, he removed his socks. Her silken hand lay palm upward, beckoning. He turned his head away and watched for a moment his sleeping son and tried to remember how it had been when Kathleen herself was lying in the cot there, under the window. He could not. It was too long ago. And she had finished being a girl, a daughter. He was no longer a father to her. And he let out a breath that he did not know he had been holding.

Far-off sounds of his other children bickering slowly swooped in on the hot air. Inside the room was no sound. Paddy did not snuffle or stir, and behind him Kathleen was lost in her slumber. His head thudded with the dull sound of a lame bullock's hoof on dry mud. Closing his eyes, he removed the shirt that stuck to him with the farm odour that his sense of smell no longer registered. The only scent his mind acknowledged as he lay down was the sweet smell of fresh air and flowers that came from her. As he gently moved her arm upwards, away from his heavy shoulders, a puff of her own perspiration travelled through him, stirring his body into a state that should have surprised him, but didn't. What did take him aback was the harmony with which their bodies moved to accommodate each other in the bed. As if to give them privacy, the light from the small window dimmed as a long, slow-moving cloud, the first in weeks, caressed the sun.

She did not flinch when he moved further towards her, away from the edge. Her forehead was damp. She looked troubled. He stroked her hairline with a delicate finger, banishing the bad dream, whatever it was. He closed his eyes and let his hand drift down, only the very tips of his fingers touching the outline of her. His hand came to rest lightly on her hip and he found himself unable to deny the effect this had on his own body. It did not matter. They both needed comfort. And what a comfort it would be for him to feel her hand on him too. He softly guided her hand to his own hip and returned his to her own, a mirror image. She did not pull away from him as he pressed himself to her. He did not open his eyes as he breathed in her hair and, he was sure, her very soul.

Kathleen was waking slowly, like oil spilled into water, a simultaneously uncertain and directly consuming feeling beginning to ease its way throughout her being. All the worries and concerns of the day eased away. She knew that even Paddy's crying would not draw her out of this place, a place where she was free from the troublesome dreams, from the endless chores and duties, from the statue of the mother in her chair. And she let her body take over, allowing her lips to relax and her arms to welcome and envelop, to cradle this new-found comfort.

Night was coming. The house was quiet, not saying what it usually said. There were no whispers in the walls, no moans or creaks, no echoes from the past. It was the little boy who disturbed the stillness in the room first. He could not see anything when he opened his eyes, but could feel the things of his life pressing around him. The little heart God had given him tapped angrily, calling to Kathleen.

She awoke with her older heart doing the same, and sat up softly so as not to disturb her father. He slept on as she walked with the exaggerated movement in arms, elbows and knees of somebody trying to be very, very quiet. Her body felt heavy, unfamiliar to her. She was suddenly more aware of each contour of skin, each breath, and felt estranged from it. Only when she was beside her small brother did she let down her heels onto the bare wood. She bent towards him to kiss his little cheek, but as the tear fell on it and it dried too quickly, she drew back in fear. Even in the dusky evening light she could see now he was burning up.

'Pad?' The little hot form panted audibly, not asleep, but with eyes listless and staring. 'Paddy? . . . Oh, please, God.' She blessed herself, but she spoke no words of prayer. What could she say? It was a punishment for her sin.

Kathleen swept him up and thought of waking her father. She looked at him. He had turned to where she had been lying, and she saw how old and sad-looking sleep made him. But she had to reach the doctor, and waking him would take up time, and any kerfuffle might upset the other children. Kathleen glided silently through the house, so consumed by her purposefulness that she did not hear the cries from Laura that they were hungry, or notice that Molly's finger was bleeding and needed a plaster. She did not notice Tomás sitting, observing her, silent by his mother, a book, pages unturned, in his lap. As she collected blanket and bottle and water for Paddy, the colours and things of the room swirled in a confusion. The only form in focus was her mother. Sitting in her chair. At the door Kathleen paused a moment and called, 'Mother, he is poorly. Don't worry, I am taking him to Dr Fitz.'

It was Tomás who finally got up to close the door to the outside world and drew his mother's shawl around her, and the girls went to bed, wide-eyed, without saying a word. He stood behind his mother a moment or two as his hand rested on her shoulder. It was a bone under skin that had not seen enough light, and he was saddened to find that he had almost forgotten how she used to trot down the boreen with him on her back and have him clinging on around her waist, neighing like a horse. He was older now, and realized what an effort it must have been for her. He wondered whether all her bones felt as fragile as the one in her shoulder. It was as though it would turn to dust if he put pressure on it. He knew that he was too big now but wondered what would happen if he crawled onto her lap. He was afraid she would crumble. He wanted to ask Kathleen what was wrong with Paddy, but she was gone. Maybe that was why they were upstairs together for so long, because Paddy was ill.

Martin O'Brien, their closest neighbour with a car, dropped the two at Dr Fitzgerald's door and waited until the light inside swallowed them up. He wondered why her father had not taken the girl down himself. She had seemed reluctant to speak on the way up. She was flustered and slightly dishevelled, and he thought it best to let her be, so he was left to his wonderings and would ask Breda what she thought when he got back. Maybe he was in a far field or out up at Killnarnan, but it was almost dark now. He must be in the pub, although that was not like Pat Steele at all. He was one of the few farmers who did not seek solace inside a glass at the end of a long day. The men of the village used to joke that his wife Nora must give him a lot of marital attention when he got in the door, but in recent years, the jokes had died off, along with the smile on the father's face who had lost a daughter, the first child to be born into their family, followed immediately, swiftly and unexpectedly by a sister, who had seemed to grow more translucent each time she took Communion at Mass, or took a walk along the strand, whose soft voice seemed ever softer still each time she asked for a bag of flour in the shop. The men of the village often found themselves gazing at her as she went about her daily messages, a little awed by her almost lucent quality, until someone passed behind her, or spoke to her, turning her again into the solid form of their neighbours' daughter who had misplaced half of herself somewhere, and who seemed to be always on the verge of going to look for it, but was unsure where to begin. Still, he decided it would be neighbourly to let the man know and crossed over into the pub to find him.

Kathleen was surprised to be greeted by the man Joseph, who had comforted her on the strand. But she was too worried to be embarrassed about their strange moonlit meeting. She began to explain Paddy's symptoms but he promptly dashed up the stairs calling the doctor by his first name. It was afterwards that Kathleen realized he must have read the seriousness of her call not by a quick visual examination of the child, for he had not taken a look at him, but by looking at her own face.

After the doctor had handed Paddy back to Kathleen, and explained his instructions, the little boy began to grumble and complain, which Joseph commented, pointlessly, was a good sign. So far, throughout the examination, he had hung back, ready to hand the doctor whatever he needed, or to offer a reassuring word or sound to the girl Kathleen. Now both girl and doctor looked at him, as if noticing his presence in the room for the first time.

He moved his weight away from his right hip and scratched at his chin. His scar would be visible, but at least he was smooth. And clean. But he could do with a shave again, to be extra soft. He thought of her stroking his face gently, and imagined what her skin would feel like under those overalls of hers. The skin under his fine stubble grew warmer and, he knew, redder. What would she think of him having inappropriate thoughts in such circumstances? He stiltedly offered his services in any way he could be of help and the girl thanked him, and gathered the child and the doctor's comfort in her arms as she walked backwards towards the door. She smiled as she went but Joseph could see she was still worried.

Outside, the man of the house waited. He had with him a blue trap that had seen better days. Kathleen got in without a word, the little bundle squirming and crying with the heat, the sickness, and the confusion of being out and about at this time of day, everything unfamiliar in the dusky light. Joseph sat down in the whiteness of Dr Fitzgerald's consultation room and waited till the rest of the world had gone quiet. He thought of the baby and knew that he would be settled now, and that meant Kathleen herself was settled too, maybe not in her own bed, but near to him, on a few cushions and a blanket. Would her father check on her to make sure she was not coming down with it as well? He had discovered it was not her husband, learned of the condition of her mother, and many more things about the villagers and the history of the place – there was more than one benefit to staying with the doctor, Joseph had found.

Joseph came to check on her and Paddy over the next few days and in time it became a little routine. He usually arrived at about two o'clock, when the doctor was off on his rounds, Kathleen's mother was having a rest in bed, and her younger children were distant shouts and ripples of laughter in the heat of the farmland. He made gentle conversation, while Kathleen continued with her chores or tended to the sick boy. She did not sit with him while he drank the milky tea she made, but folded sheets and tidied the cupboard, or swept the hearth.

Visitors normally sat in one of the good chairs by the fireplace, but Joseph sat at the table. He would talk of nature mostly, and she found it soothing to listen to. He spoke of the sea and the land as if he had never seen them before, of the wildlife that was around her always but which she took little notice of. In the week or so since Dr Fitzgerald had taken him in, he seemed to have opened up, become more confident with the villagers. They had been pleased to see him at Mass, she was sure. She thought that he must think her shy, but she enjoyed the stream of talk. It masked the silence that hung there each day like a presence, distracted her from her own thoughts, blotted out the image of that night. He had a soft way of speaking, yet it had a slight huskiness to it. She wondered daily, as she grew to know him, what had driven this man to such desperation, and she longed for him to talk of that above all else. But she did not want to ask him, that would not be appropriate at all. So she let him sit and talk to her of the things he chose to speak of.

He talked because he needed to. He and the doctor spoke in their own, sparse language already. It was the language of carpenter and apprentice, farmer and son, of priest and altar boy – the unspoken instructions whose responses were pre-empted anyway by the intuitive understanding of what was needed. It had been a long time since he had had a real conversation, and Kathleen opened up a new train of thought each time he saw her. He waffled on, he knew it, but she seemed to enjoy his company, and so he continued until one of the children came running in, patting dry mud over the floor that had just been swept. There was a look she gave to those children that Joseph could remember his own mother giving him – it was the look of, If I didn't love you so much, I'd kill ye. And Joseph would take his mug into the little galley and rinse it, much to her polite protestations, and he would reluctantly leave her, jealous of the dirty beds and uncooked food and unwashed potatoes that commanded so much of the girl's attention.

As he left one day he resolved to ask Dr Fitzgerald for a little money for a new shirt, or maybe to borrow one of his, although the doctor was really a much larger man than Joseph, having had the good fortune of many nights' dining at the villagers' homes. Each woman cooked the largest dinner she could, with her best linen on the table – partly to impress the doctor, but partly, of course, in silent competition with the other women. Joseph thought that the doctor could have a good meal out most nights of the week if he so chose, stopping at the monastery on the way to Carrickbrook on a Sunday to boot.

He was aware that the girl had noticed his scruffy attire, despite his clean skin and trimmed hair. In fact the scrub-up only served to draw attention to how worn his clothes were. Though they had been washed, they harboured old stains and had the odd hole here and there from his adventure in the field. Yes, it was best to refer to it as an adventure. That might stave off the doctor's daily questions on Joseph's mental state. 'And how are we feeling today, young Joseph?' or 'Let me know if you are feeling a little low now, won't you?' or 'You've not been off wandering, have you?'

They came to see more and more of one another. It was the only way Kathleen could put a distance between herself and her father, to avoid having to be alone with him. Joseph was the one person not connected to their lives, the one person who had not known Nuala. He didn't seem to mind her mother's condition, and in fact seemed to relish any chance he had to help.

When he was gone each time, Kathleen was not saddened by his absence, even though she saw him more and more and became used to his company. She did not feel what he felt, the worry and the excitement between each meeting. They would sit close to each other on the hill sometimes and he would look into her eyes, searching for a way into her innocent soul, but she did not let him in. She would look away after excruciating moments as his eyes bore into hers; she would let him sense the power between their fingers as they held one another's hands.

Kathleen felt his skin, warm and comforting, but there was nothing on or in the skin of this man that made her want to squeeze his hand and smile. No matter how hard she tried, she could not make the feelings she knew were within her arise for this good, kind man who had come to love her.

In the stillness of the early morning, among a whip of grass thick with the last daisies of summer, Kathleen waited. She knew he would come. Even if she had not seen him, she sensed him there always. He watched her. He loved her. She thought of this, but she did not think of him, just of his love, and it made a furrow in her brow. The daisies had not yet woken for their day of worshipping the sun, following it around in a slow, devoted arc. They were still closed in on themselves in their private, petalled chambers, flecked with pink here and there – the girl ones, Nuala always said. The plain white ones were the boys. Her shoulders, bottom, legs, heels were damp with dew, and she knew that if she raised her head there would be a thick stripe of hair at the back where the moist grass had worked tight curls around and around. She thought that he liked her hair a lot. He looked at it more than her face. He would look around it, at her feet, her hands, her shoulders, and commented on her hair often, reached out to touch it – and she let him, for she wanted to feel for him what she knew he felt for her. He was not a shy man, that was not it, but slightly distant from the world. Removed, as if his mind were always somewhere else. He was a deep thinker and took small matters to heart, which was endearing.

Kathleen lay as still as the air around her, eyes closed, breathing slowly. Only the outermost strands of leaves on the weeping willow swayed sleepily, as if to tempt the others to join in their gentle morning dance. Her world at this moment was as calm and smooth as Paddy's forehead at the deepest destination of the journey of sleep. She often watched in fright, hand held to her own heart, while she waited to see a breath. With the other hand she would cup his rib, willing fingers to feel the moment of his breathing. It would always come, of course. And she could then let her own breath out and smile. His fever had lasted a week and she had barely slept for watching over him. The little interaction between herself and her father focused on Paddy's illness, and soon enough time had passed that both knew neither was going to bring up what had happened.

At first Kathleen thought that a cloud had moved in front of the sun, but then she knew that it was him. He had come. 'Kathleen,' he said. He spoke her name softly always, as though it were something delicate, something precious to him, and he lay down beside her. She turned her head to him, eyes still closed.

How wonderful, he thought, to be lying with her in this field that had been his home, his world, that had once represented his despair. It had been, for weeks, a limbo between this life and the next, between his recent horrific past and the calm nothingness that he could see so vividly when he had gazed into the sky for hours on end. But it was not futility and dejection that engulfed him here now. It was hope, and love. Now his purgatory was his new sanctuary.

His eyes saw a new sky now, with this woman beside him. A girl or a woman, he could not decide. Neither could she, he thought sometimes. He knew so much of her – the way she moved, her routine, how different she looked when she was free of the children, her hair, her skin, her smell which travelled now across the few blades of grass separating them. Each time she breathed out, he could smell her sweetness as it disturbed the static air into something more magical. He looked at the blueness of the sky in between the new, pure white clouds dotted here and there, and found it beautiful. Joseph breathed in time with the girl next to him, and marvelled at the irony of having travelled here to die, only to be injected with such a feeling of life and wanting to live.

'How is it going at Dr Fitzgerald's?'

He turned his head to look at her, and raised it onto his arm, held high by his elbow, underneath which the parched earth pressed. When she spoke to him, he had to look at her. Her voice was an angel's. He heard it in dreams and he would wake subsequently with that immense and deep peace one feels after finally recovering from a terrible bout of flu. He would wake suddenly, clear-headed and with happiness flowing through him, feeling as though a cloud had passed and he could do anything. Her lips moved in such a tantalizing way when she spoke that he was compelled each time just to watch them forming the shapes of her words, although often this left him unsure of what she had said.

'Dr Fitzgerald . . . oh, it's fine. Good. He's a good man, very generous, as you know.'

'He is, he is . . . and did he say how long you can stay with him?'

'Oh, he said he would speak to someone in the city, to make my position official, you know, but it should all be fine.'

'Great, Joseph, that's really great.' Sometimes she caught him looking at her in a way that she knew meant he hoped one day soon for more than friendship. It had always been at the back of her mind that she was unlikely to meet many prospective suitors in this part of the world, and considering the little free time she had. While other girls her age would go further afield to attend céilís, Kathleen would be needed at home. But now that there was a spare man in the village, she could not find the desire within her to embrace him, to welcome his advances. She could not imagine feeling with this man what she had felt that day in the little attic room, that wonderful, awful feeling.

They met each day, when they could. A few minutes here, half an hour there. Joseph had a more structured day and larger chunks of time to himself, so often he would just sit and wait somewhere for her. He, of course, knew all the paths she trod, and generally what she would be doing and when. At first Kathleen found this a little odd and was unsure if she was pleased at his little surprises – popping out from behind a bush, or waiting by the wall at the village pump – but she supposed it was endearing.

He spoke to her of the things that he witnessed with those clear, grey eyes of his, and what lay behind them. He told her of dreams he had had – of her running toward him in the sunshine, followed by a flock of beautiful wild geese, and of terrible things that alarmed him and made him wake in the night, shaking. She said it was to be expected, that it would take time to forget.

He told her of friends he had had, comrades who were like brothers to him – he would see them as clear as day in his sleep but then on waking would recall that most were gone now. Kathleen thought that if only certain people like Brigid Callaghan were to hear him speak of the horrors he had seen and the quietness they had instilled into his heart, perhaps they would judge him less harshly.

She spoke sometimes of her childhood, and very occasionally of her sister, whom she obviously missed dearly, and Joseph listened enraptured by those pure lips and the knowledge of his being her only confidant in this relentless life of hers. He would help her escape it one day. That was what he was working towards. He was studying the books on the doctor's shelves in every spare moment when he wasn't either helping the man or seeing Kathleen or dreaming of her. He would one day have enough money to rent the two of them a small place near to the farm, as he knew she would want to visit her siblings. Maybe she would bring the little one, Paddy, as the two were so attached to each other, and the child's mother the way she was. At first he thought the bond strange, and rather unhealthy, but the more Joseph observed the family, the more he saw how much the eldest and the youngest depended on each other. She was like a mother to him. A wonderful one.

Kathleen spoke of the villagers, as she knew Joseph would never feel part of the community as long as he did not know about Father Nolan's corns, Jimmy Neely's strange manner, and the many grievances of Brigid Callaghan, but mostly it was he who talked and she who did not. She listened, and let the sounds of his words fill the quietness left in the wake of the children gone outside playing. But she longed to tell him now of something else. As they lay side by side, she longed to tell this man who loved her of the thing that was worrying her more than whether the children would be hungry by Friday. She longed to tell him of the ache in her back and the dizziness at around midday if she had not eaten something. She wanted to tell him about the sickness and the heavy feeling in her breasts each morning and each night. But it was surely nothing. She longed to tell him that for the past few weeks she had been pretending – no, trying to love him back. But she knew that if she mentioned any of these things he would walk off into the mist of his nature and lie down in a field. And that was a fate worse than all of those that circled her sleepless mind.

Kathleen turned to look into the eyes of the man who appeared more youthful and alive with every sultry day, and searched for herself within them. He was a different man from the one who had arrived in Ballinara, and now he grew in strength and happiness by the day. To her surprise she found her lips relaxing into a smile. Her fears were only fears after all and her mother had always said she was a worrier. A pure white butterfly dazzled past her head as he smiled back, melting, and pressed his own lips gently to hers. She knew what she must do. Joseph's lungs filled with the scent of honeysuckle and dry hay, the scent of the woman before him.

TWO

It was soon to be Paddy's christening. Each of the older Steele children had been baptized within a few weeks of entering the world, but with this little life they had all waited, the village holding its collective breath for the day when his mother would return from her reverie, so that she could enjoy the day. But days and weeks trickled by and the baptism of the last Steele child was forgotten by all, except, of course, Father Nolan. Each Sunday after Mass he would say, 'Patrick, are we ready yet?' And the child's father would reply each time with a regretful smile and pat his wife's hand in answer as he led her on up the road.

But this day when the priest advanced towards Paddy's father, Pat Steele spoke first, saying, 'I think the little lad's about ready now. Sure he'll be able to help you pour the water over his head in a month's time.'

And Father Nolan had smiled and said, 'That or he'll be fighting me off. We'll do any Saturday now, you just let me know when is best for Nora and yourself.'

Nora. He had not heard his wife's name spoken for such a long time, it seemed. No one asked after her any more in the street or, if they did, they referred to her as 'She' or 'Her' – everyone knew who that referred to. They would ask after the children of course and coo over Paddy if one of them were out with the pram. He spoke to her himself less and less. It pained him so to see the nothingness in her eyes no matter how he implored her to speak, to smile, just to look at him. In fact, now he would walk around to the back of the house to come in through that door, so as to avoid her vacant stare out of the window, through him, the motionlessness of the woman who seemed to be fading into a shade of cobweb grey. Visitors to the house had become more and more infrequent. Friends of Nora or Kathleen grew visibly uncomfortable and stuck for what to say. It was by slow, silent, mutual agreement that they put an end to these stiff and strained cups of tea, with all the children sitting straight-backed on their chairs, itching to get away from the atmosphere, and Kathleen responding politely to any questions asked. And all the while the figure of Nora sat motionless and, as with some gross disfigurement on a stranger, visitors would not know where to look.

Nora. The children had never spoken her name. He wasn't even sure if the little girls knew their parents' names. He would ask them. Or not. They seemed afraid of him sometimes, he thought. They never asked to play with him, were always eager to please, looking up at him from their small height. But they seemed happy enough in each other's company. Thinking about it now he realized he had put much more time into doing things with Nuala and Kathleen when they were small, such was his joy and his wonderment. But now it seemed an impossible task to play with his young daughters. He just wanted to sit a while in the quiet with Kathleen after the day was done. But he should. He would tell them a story, one of his father's about Finn McCool.

But Paddy now was a different matter. His little Paddy who looked so like him, and such a good baby. There would be no more children now, and he wanted to savour these short days, when he could bury his nose deep into the warm life of a baby and breathe the scent of innocence. If he were to attempt to give Tomás a kiss he'd get a kick in the leg, while Molly would run off wiping the offending area and hollering, 'Yukyukyucky!'

Kathleen took it as a bad sign that the christening was going ahead, and so too did Tomás. It made the unspoken more tangible all of a sudden. It was as if their father had said, Children, your mother is not coming back to us. Ever. She will remain in that chair for the rest of her life and Paddy will never know what it is to hear his mother's sweet, sweet voice singing 'The Rare Oul' Times' and the little sisters will forget her. They will forget the sound of her laugh, her voice, which will be easier than remembering her and missing her, but not at all as awful as never knowing her, like your baby brother.

Of course, she was pleased that Paddy would finally be baptized and welcomed into God's family, but she knew what it meant and that changed everything for her.

And there was a feeling within her that she had not truly understood before now. As she walked she thought back, very hard, until she realized just how long it had been since she had washed out her rags. Too much time had passed for it to be ignored any longer, and the fear at the back of her mind was confirmed, and hurled to the forefront. In a small moment that day, Kathleen's lungs took an involuntary, reverse breath, and the pattern of her breathing was changed then, the course of her being altered from what it had been since the moment she was born, to what it was now, and would forever be.

Kathleen broke apart from the procession of good villagers, of husbands and wives and children and grandmothers and feet clad with shoes that shone for Sunday only, before being scuffed and muddied by real life. She slipped between the families and, when no one was looking, removed her own shoes, tying the laces hurriedly and placing the length around the back of her neck, and began to run. She ran and ran and her freshly shined boots slapped angrily against her chest, sending darting pains from her nipples to deep within her. But she could not make her body stop its feverish crusade and when she reached the furthest cattle field she knew that none of the churchgoers would be able to hear the sob that suffocated her throat so. She released the weight of her body then, and her bottom and right side hit the ground with a ferocity that made her suddenly concerned for the little life that she now knew was inside her.

The sound that was released from somewhere within her made her recoil in horror. It was the sound the remaining children had heard the moment their mother had learned of their sister's death. It was a deep and sickening sound that caused each child simultaneously to retreat into his or her self and reach out to another sibling, any other being, for some kind of comprehension, some morsel of comfort. Kathleen was not aware that her body could make such a noise; it was her mother's voice. She was a woman now. How did it happen? She had not noticed herself changing. Which day was it when her voice took on the smooth, deep tone of her mother's and grandmother's? When she first took over the housewife role? Or when she lay with her father?

It was almost as though that day had never happened – it had not been discussed. A fear, stronger than she had ever known, rose up inside, bewildering her. Her hands trembled, sweating. She was in shock. She could not move or think properly.

But wasn't she still only a child herself? Just because she looked after the children and ran the home – it did not qualify her for this, she did not want it. She wanted to run to her father and tell him and hear his words of comfort, but what could he say? What could anyone say? God was to punish her for her sin, and rightly so. She was ashamed, sickened. What would Nuala have thought of her? It would have been the ruin of them, of their special relationship. They were becoming separated by time and by Kathleen's actions. God was not content to keep them apart through taking her for Himself. Now He wanted to estrange them from one another by causing one to remain a pure, sweet angel, while one grew fallible and old.

She wept for a long time, till her stomach ached and her face was taut. She felt helpless, at the mercy of a God who was showing the side of Himself that Kathleen had seen when Nuala died, the one that made her want to turn away from Him. But she knew there was no one to blame but herself, and she had nowhere to turn, except to Joseph. Maybe he was a second chance, a saviour of sorts, that God had sent to her. She would go to him when she was calm, when she had had time to think carefully of what to say.

Tomás imagined his big sister in heaven. What was it like there? He did not imagine heaven as most children did. He did not envisage colossal white clouds and serious angels garbed in shimmering white. All he could see was a hole in the ground, peaceful, quiet and cold. And as his own mother faded in colour and palpability she would become clearer to Nuala, they to each other. He knew that was where she was going. Soon now, he thought. One day he would check on her and fleetingly touch her cheek with his lips in the way of young boys' kisses and she would be icy cold. And she would be gone.

He knew it because he had felt the skin of Brendan's dead pig a good few winters ago. It had been the runt, a scrawny little thing with eyes that looked too big for its face. And it had struggled on for a good few months till Brendan got sick himself with flu and could not tend it. When Brendan had recovered enough to check on his pet it was not there. It had crawled out towards the cottage to look for its friend but did not know where to go. As night fell and the piglet lost the scent of its mother and the warm straw of its shed, it lost its bearings and settled into the rhubarb patch, underneath one of the giant leaves, and slept awhile. It was still sleeping when Brendan finally found it. He ran to tell Tomás that his little pig would not wake. Could he bring some of the poitín that his father kept, maybe that would help? It was said by some of the older folk that it could cure all manner of ills, the magic glass. Tomás had not been sure at all but he emptied the remainder of the milk from the jug and filled it with a little poitín and lots of water. Brendan would not know that it was not pure poitín. He did not want his father noticing.

The drink did not work. The pig's mouth was stiff and taut and cold. The placebic liquid spilled out of its mouth and over its nose. The coldness of the animal was what stayed with Tomás, because he knew what that must mean, without having to be told. But his friend did not know. So he told him, and Brendan had run away inside to his mother saying, 'Tomás says the pig is dead, the pig is dead,' and had heard his friend crying. Tomás would not tell the other boys at school that Brendan had cried over a cold, dead pig and, when they played together next, Brendan knew that his friend had not said a word, and at that moment a life-long bond was formed and the two would be like brothers for ever, even when one of them left on a ship to a faraway land. There was a hole dug by Brendan's father and the pig had been unceremoniously thrown into it. In secret the two boys made a cross and drew a picture for the poor animal. *RIP Willie*. Tomás hadn't known Brendan had had a name for it. He had noticed that there were things about everyone that other people never knew, and perhaps were not meant to know.

It was the harvest time following that when his sister died. And all the family and the aunties and the uncles and the neighbours and the priest and the doctor and the well-wishers, and those curious to see what a beautiful young maiden looks like when she is dead, gathered around. But Tomás did not. Tomás did not want to look at the skin of the arms that had held him but two days before, arms that had been warm and soft and had freckles and had the blood of life blobbing through them. He did not want to be tempted to touch this skin that he knew would be tight and cold.

Now, in the day, when he was not with Brendan Reilly, Tomás had work to do. He did whatever his father needed him to do on the farm, obeyed Kathleen as she gave out her motherly instructions and tried not to argue with his younger sisters. And all the while he observed things, without anyone knowing. He observed the comings and goings of the villagers and held his breath as he peered at his mother for a sign of her returning. He observed the man who had come to Ballinara. He followed him sometimes, for he did not understand this strange newcomer, and the only way to learn, thought Tomás, was to watch and be patient.

Joseph had been crying. Weeping. His tears were returning to him. He had not played his spying game today, except for early that morning as he watched Kathleen usher two of the children outside to feed the dog and bring in some eggs. He had wanted to get going early as he had the thought that he might go to their Mass again. He stood at the back, concealed by his lateness and by the large form of Mr O'Brien. He had found the emotion and the atmosphere of the service overwhelming – the poetry of the words in the messages being sent from God via the priest and the intensity of the belief of all those people, the way they chorused in one droning voice, expressing something from deep within them. He looked in wonder at the conviction on the sea of faces before him, a conviction that he had discovered could not be rocked in some no matter what they might be subjected to. He had yet to discover how, when a man has seen only sorrow, he has faith enough to appeal to a God when drawing his last breath.

He liked his position at the back, and would leave before or after the rest of them, for confined spaces full of bodies made him feel nauseous. If, when he visited the store, there were a few customers there, he would walk up the road a way and then back, so that they would not be pressed in on one another in the little room.

After Communion he fled and retreated to the comfort of his field, where he sat in contemplation. The priest seemed, at times, to be speaking directly to him, understanding him, but the man could not have known Joseph would come along and therefore could not prepare for it. Perhaps it was the divine intervention of an understanding God, but also one who was telling Joseph that there is more to life than the unhappy things that happen to us, and that there were many worse off than he, that he should be grateful for having survived when so many had not, that living with the horror of memory was a relatively small cross to bear.

And as he walked back to his field he tried to remember the words the priest had spoken, words that had seemed to be specifically for him: 'For my days pass away like smoke, and my bones burn like a furnace. My heart is smitten like grass, and withered; I forget to eat my bread ...' He had felt guilt then again, and sorrow, as the man continued to speak of Joseph's isolation: 'I lie awake, I am like a lonely bird on the housetop ... My days are like an evening shadow; I wither away like grass.'

He had gone on to say that, although we may all feel like this from time to time in our lives, He is always there, ready to comfort, that there is always hope around the next corner if only we are to look for it. He did not know what he thought of God, or of the orderly, mechanical way in which they worshipped Him, but he did like the way the words had touched his heart. He liked that, somehow, those words had shown him that he had turned a corner and had found things again worth living for.

He was kneeling down, with his head in his hands, against the ground. He could smell the earth and the parched grass and tried to remember the smell of freshly cut grass through the ever-pervasive smell of manure. And then he heard a sound that touched his heart like a silken ribbon, that wound its way around the organ, making it beat a little harder, a little faster, and as the sound drew nearer the ribbon gave a tug, causing him to lose his balance and frown at the recognition that the sound was Kathleen's voice.

She was weeping also, again. She was feeling something akin to what he had been feeling, and she had stumbled into his field. His father had once spoken to him of Fate, and at this moment, after being in that holy place, Joseph understood what this strange word meant. Real Fate. Two people lost within their own troubled thoughts, thrown together in a space where time and possessions and money did not matter. They both needed somebody at that moment, and here they were to happen upon each other. She was drawn to him without realizing it. She would see it, too, feel it, and be glad of him and his open arms.

But Kathleen did not see Joseph as she ran. She hurried on,

but she was making little headway, weaving clumsily through the long grass of the middle of the meadow. Maybe the farmer was superstitious about this field as it had not been used for crops for many a year, he could tell, and no animals were brought to graze on it. Or maybe this was another element of Fate. A space in time, a space on this earth that had been reserved for Joseph Foley to be reborn, to find his one true love.

Joseph rolled back to sit on his feet, to await her with his arms open. His joints ached, and he tried to hide the wince that this induced. He had thought of mentioning these aches and pains to Dr Fitz as he had not had them before his time in the field and now they were there to some extent throughout each day. But what did a little pain matter now? She did not slow as he rubbed at his eyes with the rough cuff of the doctor's jacket. He stood up, smiling, feeling the aches melting away as she neared. She ran on, and so he called her, but she ran on still. She had seen him; he saw her eyes pass over him as she glided stumblingly on through the grass. Standing up and frowning, he swayed slightly and looked skywards as the first grey cloud in weeks began to cover the sun. It was a pale grey, advancing slowly, and there was a faint crispness to the air as he raised his head to the sky and imagined he could smell rain from this one lone cloud. He thought briefly of how it would have been in the field with endless rain instead of endless sun. Surely he would not be standing there now.

Joseph watched her and found himself running too, without having thought through the mechanisms of the movement, and he stumbled stupidly across the small hillocks of the unused field, her name echoing in the vast space as he called out to her. His voice had a hoarseness still, at this volume, with this effort. She ran faster, stumbling herself. He was nearing her and could hear the frantic, worn-out breathing through the choking tears. As he ran on after her, calling for her to wait, he searched his mind for what or who could have upset her, and he wanted to reach her and embrace her, and breathe deeply from the scent of her. He would bury his face within the mass of hair that would smell half of her and half of the air that had been tossed through it with her running. He would gently but firmly caress her back as he held her close so that she would be reassured, that her tears might stop. She would see that there was no need to feel ashamed, only relieved and comforted. She would look up at him and smile, and neither would need to say a word, for that is the language of love. If he reached out his arm now, he would be able to touch her shoulder.

'Joseph, no!' She turned and stopped abruptly, causing him to collide with her breasts. He regained his balance, and stood before her, offering still the warmth of his arms to her. Her eyes were red all around and her pale cheeks had pinkish blotches on them. 'Joseph ... leave me be! Can you not see I want to keep going, I want to be on my own.'

He looked to her like a lost lamb then, his eyes questioning, not understanding. There was a wildness in her own eyes, an urgent pleading in her voice.

'Kathleen, whatever's the matter? Let me help you. Let me comfort you.'

She was shaking her head, frowning. 'Please ... I'll be all right if you just leave me be for now. I must ... just give me a while.'

'All right so, Kathleen, but you must know that it grieves me to see you like this. I will come to you tonight, when all the children are in bed and you need think of nothing, and we can walk together . . . we do not have to talk even. Just let me do that, make sure you're all right . . . I'll be outside after nine.' He did not wait for a reply, but walked back the way he had come.

He stole through the darkness, and tried to quieten his breathing lest someone should hear him as he passed by. He removed his shoes and left them at the top of the boreen. On the grass the doctor's socks dampened with the night's moisture. His energy was still not what it should be and he found himself having to slow his pace. He would soon see the lights of the farmhouse, if there were any still lit. He concentrated on his breathing and thought of what he would do when he got there. Maybe nothing. Maybe she would not come. Maybe he would just catch a glimpse of her, see that there was a smile to her eyes and then he could walk leisurely home.

He softly crunched around the corner of the boreen and padded across the haggard. A single window was leaking yellow onto the path that ran all the way around the house. Joseph stumbled on a makeshift wagon cleverly constructed with the skeleton of an old pram. A white cat appeared, shining brilliantly in front of him. It was ready to depart but made time to look this intruder in the eyes for a moment or two before slinking off into the night.

She did not come at the sound, and he waited, plotting stars and bristling with excitement at the thought of seeing her in the dark of night. Where was she? She had not been keeping a lookout for him. He could not knock at the door, of course, as the hour was so late, so he silently scratched in his mentor's socks along the length of the house. As he neared the window he realized that if somebody were to look out, they would be face to face and, no doubt, he would be chased off the land with a shotgun by the father, a much stronger and bigger man than he. A raised bed of rose bushes was planted a few feet from the house. As he crept around behind them their strong, sweet smell filled his head and made him feel more brazen. He would romantically throw a pebble up to her window, and maybe hum a bar or two in a serenade.

He hopped up, soft as a cat, onto the low wall of the flower bed, just out of the light. And there she was, perfectly framed by the window, candlelight glinting off her skin as she washed herself. A large bowl sat before a mirror, on which a couple of pieces of paper were pinned. He could just make out a scrawl of crayon on one of them. The thought that they were draw-ings done by her dead sister filled him with a deep sadness and made him feel a little afraid of the night.

The steam had clung to her hair and worked curls into it and it glowed again in that mysterious way. Why did she insist on tying it back so tight like that? But still, she was beau-tiful and innocent and, most importantly for Joseph, there was nobody else around to court her. And she was calm now. That comforted him. She did not look red-eyed and desperate as she had in the field. She must have forgotten he'd said he would come. He would leave her. He did not want to be bothering her; she should want to come to him.

*

When he found her the next day she was sitting, very still, looking out to the island on the horizon. On a hazy day like today, the island seemed to float on a strip of mist sewn atop the sea. There was no breeze. The grass did not sway, no butterfly flitted as he crept over the last patch of field. He was the only moving thing. No puff of air teased at her wisps of hair that strayed free, her skirt did not give the slightest hint of lifting. He was on edge. How would she be? Would she be crying again?

He had reached the fence, knotted here and there with yellowed sheep's wool stiffened by salt. If he cleared his throat she would be startled out of her stillness. But he watched her a while, upon the rock with her legs drawn under her. It was almost as though she was leaning, ever so gently, against something. He imagined her sister there, her grown twin the mirror image of her; he could almost see the girl. Maybe Kathleen was thinking of her. Maybe that was why she was sad. He felt again the guilt that he had felt after Mass, that he did not deserve to feel such despair, having only witnessed loss. Maybe she could not get the image of her sister out of her mind, just as he could not rid his own mind of images in his first days here.

If he stole up behind her and loosened those pins, her hair would fall tumbling down her back. A fisherman passing on the far-out tide might look through the haze at the mermaid sitting there. He would not question his eyes, despite not believing in the stuff of fairy tales, and the other fishermen in the pub that night would share furtive, concerned glances as they heard their friend tell the story of his mermaid, how he will never set eyes on such a beautiful creature again. And each of the fishermen friends would experience the fear that every solitary sailor has from time to time – the knowledge of what too much time alone at sea, with only God and his own thoughts to keep him company, can do to a man – and their wives would wonder why they received an embrace so large that night.

Only the bottle-green water moved. It was as though the ocean and his breathing were in tune with each other, almost as if he were controlling it. The sea performed her relentless, cajoling assault on the edge of the land. And Joseph too, always an onlooker, felt that he was encroaching on the world around him – at first the field and its little ecosystems, then Dr Fitzgerald's, and now Kathleen's farm and her family.

He was so deep in contemplation and concentrating on trying to stay still that it was he who got the fright in the end. She had not stood up abruptly, or begun to move towards him; she had not even turned to look at him. But she had spoken. She had sensed him there behind her.

'Sorry I didn't meet you last night . . .'

Climbing through the largest gap in the thick wire fence, he went to her. She turned to look at him. She seemed to have stopped crying a while ago. Her eyes were not red, but the marks, like beautiful snail trails, were there yet. He looked upon her face where the colours of the sky were reflected. Many a man would give up on such a sad soul, but not Joseph. He saw a kindred spirit, someone he could love and bring back from the sadness. He had come back, and so could she. He would help her.

He hoped, as he stepped down the rocks, hand held out to her, that the tears would eventually rid her of whatever this pain was, and he hoped that he might be given the opportunity to make her forget the source of the pain as well. For he could see that the worry behind her eyes was not a childish or insignificant matter, and it was not the look of concern tinged with fear he saw in her the night the little boy Paddy was taken ill.

And upon the touch of this man's hand a layer of her seemed to melt away. She needed the comfort of touch. She stood before him on the deserted strand that she had known as a part of her since her mother had first brought her, snuggled up in a blanket, as a baby. She stood there now stripped of something, exposed to the sand, the sea, and to him, and she was able to step forwards and let the tears be absorbed by the smooth fabric of his shoulder, the connection between her and her mother a distant, ghostly whisper in the sea's swish. Underneath the shirt and the faint smell of disinfectant she could feel his collarbone against her cheek as he gently rocked her. His whispering was loud in her ear as he spoke the words, ''Tis all right, it'll be all right,' and she thought of Paddy listening to her whispered words in the darkness as she held him close in the night in the upstairs room. But she did not feel safe, nor as comforted as she had with her father. And she did not feel the sudden pulse, the shock of electricity that switched something on deep inside.

Kathleen knew that the frown that had come to the smooth puddle of her forehead would never leave her. She knew that some women would recognize the frown within, even when she smiled and said, 'Beautiful day again, isn't it?' That they would see that finally she too had something so unfathomable inside, an unspoken thing that even God would hardly comprehend.

But of course God knows everything about us. And that was what she said to him that day. That was all. 'He knows everything about us,' she said, 'because He made us, and whatever we do with the life He has given us is between Him and us. I am not going to tell you what is grieving me because it is fine now. I have thought a long time on it and I needn't think on it any more. And I won't cry any more. You are very good to me, Joseph . . . I do not deserve a man like you. But I would like to spend time with you . . . be with you,' and she tried to feel a small comfort in the uneven way the bones of his fingers grasped her hand. And she smiled at him and led him away from the rock.

Many rocks along the mile or so of that strand held a significance to her and she would seek them out as she walked, to extract the memory that each particular one held: the tall one with a bump that used to be her horsey, her parents either side, minding she didn't fall; or the wide, flat one where she and Nuala would play nurses. One of them, usually Kathleen, would lie on it trying not to giggle, trying to look ill. Her sister would choose from the neatly organized array of shells and stones for ointment and medicines, and seaweed for the bandages, to perform her operations. As they walked along the strand, back up to the road, Kathleen stole a glance back at the rock where Joseph had unknowingly offered her a chance in her life, for her baby's life.

It was the young brother Tomás who learned of the romance first. His sister appeared to be what they call In Love. The man who had arrived in their village had chosen Kathleen as his. Tomás watched from up in the hayloft where he looked out for pirate ships on the distant horizon, as his sister lay down with this man among the heather in the next field. And Tomás that day learned that people may show their love for one another before Father Nolan pronounced them man and wife.

Tomás had only ever seen his parents' sleeping bodies lying next to each other, with perhaps only their shoulders touching, or a hand lain gently upon a hip. He had seen Brendan's boar and sow, heard the foxes, and watched as the bull, brought into a field of his father's cows, sought out its first victim. As a child these acts of nature had frightened, even repulsed him, but in the last year or so they had become less vulgar and more intriguing.

They might see him if he climbed down now and he would die if they thought he was spying on them. So he climbed higher and lay on his stomach so that he would be almost completely concealed. He would keep an eye on him. After all, had he not joined the other boys in speculating as to whether he was a tinker, a prison escapee, or even a pirate? He had overheard the women in the shop one day talking about him having been a soldier and being unhinged because of it. Maybe he would have to climb down and rescue his sister. He whimsically wished to be in possession of a bow and arrow. But the man looked different now, the gossip had lessened, and the mothers of the village seemed to think of him as a harmless and rather kind man, now that he worked at Dr Fitz's.

But what if she had not gone with him willingly? He was after all holding her by the hand. But, no, it was she who had been in front, as though leading him.

The boy stole another look down. The breeze was at last beginning to re-emerge. He could hear the waves coming in on the wind from behind him and below him. And leaves swished over and about the image in front of him. The rhythmic movement of green before his eyes disguised at first the movement of the stranger above his sister that he tried not to watch in the gaps.

The man had removed his top, but not his boots, or trousers, which were thrown about his ankles. His sister's dress had been pulled up about her, but the buttons from her neck to her waist had been undone so that her white flesh was bright against the dark purple and green of the heather. They must have chosen this spot for the length of the grasses. The small white blob of his arse pumped up and down urgently. Tomás could not see Kathleen's face. He wondered if it hurt her. There was no difference, in Tomás's mind, between man and bull – it was disgusting, and even more disgusting still that it stirred him in the same way a dream in the haze of the early morning sometimes did.

The house was still. A quiet hung in the air like a watchful presence. Patrick Steele checked once more that the baby was settled and sound asleep for his daytime nap, then he moved through the heavy milk of this quiet; soundlessly, like a lumbering ghost, an intruder. He was a well-proportioned man, whose hands and feet betrayed him as a farmer; big, strong, rough appendages so used to the farm work that they were awkward anywhere else. But the past few days his hands had been cleaner. There had been an unspoken agreement that Kathleen would no longer see to all of Paddy's needs: before his nap-time, their father would take him off into the field with him.

At first, Kathleen had pottered about the house anxiously,

or needlessly tended the roses in the garden, waiting for them to return. She would hear them coming up the boreen from the fields. Paddy was never crying. He was wide-eyed, and eagerly listening to the soft, deep murmur of his daddy's voice, talking of flowers, butterflies, footballs, the snow that would one day come. Paddy listened to Kathleen's words attentively too, as though he yearned for more, cooing sweetly in the gaps of that giving stream of baby talk. But never was he more enraptured than when he was with his father.

How strange it was to see him developing a true bond with someone other than herself. She had spent whole days trying to cajole their mother to talk to him, to smile, to look at him as he was placed to her breast. He would suckle noisily, dripping milk down his chin, as she stared blankly ahead. Little fingers would explore the contours of his mother's skin, or tug at her hair. But Kathleen did not have the strength or the time between nappy changes and washing and wakeful noise-filled nights to continue this mission, and it was she whom he had begun to feed off in all other senses. And it was true too that she fed off him.

She had begun to go for walks so that she would not have to see him inevitably growing away from her. When she awoke each morning and went to fetch him, she told herself she must not have such feelings for this baby who was only going to grow into a Tomás and tut at her as she told him to drink up his milk, or to take the potato peelings out to Waggy's bucket.

She was in the chair facing the window again. Sometimes she slept there all the night now that the evening chats between father and daughter had stopped. One of the children would place a cushion on a milk crate upon which they laid her slippered feet. The slippers had been a gift a few Christmases ago. He had heard of a man over from London and had taken the trap out over to Duncarrig to examine his wares. He gave the slippers to Laura and Molly to wrap in old newspaper on which they had potato-printed angels and stars. Nora had been delighted more at the wrapping than the present, and the girls were enthralled that their mother was so pleased with something they had given her. There was still a scrap of it saved somewhere, he was sure.

He had chosen a yellow dress with a lace trim for Kathleen, sweets and marbles for Tomás, and ribbons and matching red shoes for the little girls. That Christmas was special, and had eaten considerably into the savings. Nora had surprised all by having a good week, as she did from time to time back then; she had even joked about her unstable state of mind. But St Stephen's day was a melancholy affair, he remembered, with the sticky smell of turkey bones that sat mutedly rattling away in the pot on the range hanging in the air all day. His wife had not resurfaced since. He did not expect her to. Each doctor had said it was likely to be for ever and, looking at her now, he could see that for ever might not be so very long. She was fading away. There was no hint of the woman he had married.

He thought that he should tell her, even though he knew she wouldn't hear it. But Kathleen seemed grand and Nora was oblivious, so it wasn't a sin really. It wasn't that bad. And he thought that maybe, in fact, it was a good thing that it had happened; inevitable, like. No one regarded Kathleen as his daughter any more, surely. They had a new family set-up, the two had naturally become closer in the circumstances, and what other man would not have done what he did in his situation? And although he would make sure it did not happen again, he was able to put it out of his mind, for now.

But Patrick Steele had begun to see a restlessness in Kathleen in the past week or so that he was sure had not been there before. He surveyed her from atop his mug of milky tea as she went about her chores, sweeping the floor, rubbing the cutlery shiny in her apron, straightening Laura and Molly's mess of dolls and colouring, and finally setting to the dough to make the day's bread. This was a task that he enjoyed watching. It seemed always to coincide with his cup-of-tea time. He suspected that she would not take such care if it were her own house; she and Nuala were never mindful of tidiness when they were children. 'You'd think I had two boys with these two, Da, traipsing the mud here, there and everywhere.' But their mother would never be cross, so enormous was her love for her two beautiful girls. They could do no wrong for her, and she was so proud to take them out into town in their ribbons and shined shoes for to be admired by old ladies. No one called him 'Da' any more: the girls tended to say 'Daddy', Tomás only 'Dad' or 'Father', and Kathleen . . . what did she call him now? To the children, 'Your father', 'Him'; she did not address him by name. It occurred to him that she no longer really had a name for him. He watched a puff of flour envelop her as she dropped the turned-over dough onto the surface. Most of it settled down upon her hands, the dough, the surface, a cup, but some rose up still, like a cloud of white fairies, that's what little Laura would say. And she would see it in slow motion as children can, as he did now. No Tomás to burst in the door and tell the earth that fairies are not real, to send his sister off crying. No distraction at all. Just this moment in which the world was still and in which for a moment he could imagine that Kathleen was still his daughter and his wife was still his wife, and that Nuala still lived.

The flour landed so softly and secretly that Kathleen did not notice, and she continued to work away at the dough, kneading and massaging. He wanted to take a cloth dampened with a little spittle to dab it from her face. But she would know then that he had been watching her. He wanted to be able to share his younger children's beliefs – that fairies and Santy are real and that the worries of the grown-up world are silly, boring, irrelevant. He wanted that profound belief that children seem to have that everything will be all right, their innate trust that the grown-ups around them will always make everything better. But he was the grown-up now, and he did not know how to make it better.

She was not talking again. Now he thought on it, she had been distant, quiet, the last couple of weeks. They rarely spoke now. The silence pressed in on them, and on the room. It emanated from the two women now. He could not bear it. He had never concentrated on the sounds of her labour before – the soft slap and pat of dough against oft-used wood; the smooth sound of her floured hands dusting each other; the rub of apron against the edge of the counter as she moved in rhythm with the kneading. Usually there was her humming, or even quiet singing, or the occasional sentence or two – about the hens, the weather, one of the children, the neighbours. Today there was only the sound of the bread being made, and the sound of him drinking his tea; the liquid inside his mouth, travelling down his throat, the soft thud of his mug on the table, quieted by the cloth lain out over it. His was the only mug in the house. Even male visitors were offered tea in a cup, on a saucer. He felt himself ridiculous when he had to join Father Nolan or the doctor in drinking out of these feminine, flimsy receptacles. Yet they seemed to carry it off without seeming oafish and clumsy.

He could not hear the children outside playing. No dog barked nor hen squawked. His wife was not asleep so there was not even the faint rhythm of breathing and creaking coming from her and her chair. She was awake but staring and silent. Kathleen too was staring, into the wall ahead of her. But she was as much awake to the world inside the room as his wife. She looked out at whatever she was seeing past the flour, past the peeling yellowing wallpaper, through the stone of the wall and further, beyond even the air and trees and sky. She was thinking of it, he knew. It had not seemed to bother her so much before. He thought they had an unspoken understanding of what happened, both knowing it would never happen again. They had had a few evenings together by the fire and she seemed her normal, happy self. But lately she had been out walking at night, wanting to be alone.

The two women were lost in the depths of their minds then, lost to him. Again he felt an intruder, ashamed to be occupying the space between them. Maybe she was waiting for him to say something. To apologize. What if she thought he had taken advantage of her? That could explain her mood. But surely she would have said something, made it clear to him that she was unhappy. The image of them together came to him in sudden graphic detail. He saw her naked skin, saw his body against her. He saw her as a child running up to him, arms outstretched. He saw her reading to the children, then himself reading to her and Nuala. The images became mixed together.

He wanted to spit out the tea in his mouth. He wanted Laura to come tearing in crying, arms up, needing some comfort for a bleeding knee, a bruised elbow, though he could not recall the last time she had come to him for such a comfort and thought briefly, horrified, that maybe he shouldn't embrace his small daughters at all. How could a father deserve such a thing now? He willed something to happen, for some movement in the room, other than the kneading and shaping of dough. He emptied the last dregs of his mug and had to swallow twice to get it down him. A surge of sickness emanated from his stomach to all parts of his body.

He could bear it in the room no longer. He stood to leave, and the door swung loudly against the wall, startling Kathleen and her mother. Kathleen turned, wiping her hands upon her mother's apron wrapped about her waist. Unnoticed, Nora Steele blinked and turned her head slightly. But the little girls were in from their playing just in time to see their father on his knees in the hall behind a puddle of vomit, and their sister over him, a hand in his hair and one on his shoulder, just as she did with them. They were afraid. Their father, the big, gently fearsome man whom they had seen in only a handful of poses – straight-backed, sitting at the head of the dinner table with huge hands working away at his food; a distant stooped figure in the fields; or a kneeling, solemn man, with bowed head along the line of them at Mass; or towering in front, even as he knelt, receiving Communion. They had each other now, and they were growing older, and he had Paddy to dwarf in those hands of his. But the large proportions of him seemed diminished in front of the two now as they stood hand in hand, bathed in the mid-morning light of the porch windows. As he knelt there gasping and groaning, he was smaller to them, and feebler.

'Will . . . will I get you a cloth, Daddy?'

At the sound of Molly's soft voice, still high-pitched in its innocence, Patrick Steele hung his head lower still. He gave no answer but concentrated on regulating his breathing. The two looked to Kathleen. Her hands were not on him now, but at her hair and face where she had noticed the flour at last when she caught herself in the mirror as she crouched down to comfort him. The light had not reached the two adults so the specks of white were not illuminated on her skin. To the small girls in this moment it was just a bit of flour on their big sister's face. There were no fairies.

'Girls, ye're very good, but we'll be fine.' She rubbed at the flour on her cheekbone with the back of her hand and she said, 'Your da'll be fine, he's just a bit sick. Came on all of a sudden it did. You go off out again and play.'

'But we want to help him feel better.' Laura's eyes twinkled threateningly. The edges of Molly's mouth were sucked in, but she would not let herself cry. She looked at her father, who had slumped back against the wall under the mirror. He made strange coughing sounds.

'All right so. I'd say a nice cool drink of water would do

him just fine. Go to the boreen and fill a cup each. Ye're always thirsty after too, aren't ye?'

'Yeah, and it helps get rid of the nasty taste, doesn't it, Moll?' Delighted to be of use, the two sprang to life, jumping over the puddle and through to the kitchen.

That night there was a feeling in the Steele house. Each member of the family noticed it without knowing that it was shared by the others, so they felt strange and lonely as the darkness blotted out trees and cattle and outhouses one by one. Each lay awake a while longer than usual, sensing that something important had changed in a way that was scarcely noticeable.

Seeing her father squatting there on the floor had made Laura afraid. She had lost a sister, but she was still only a baby really at the time. In a sense she had lost her mother, but for her father to have become fallible too left a frown upon her forehead as she lay against her sister, back to back. She wanted someone to cuddle her but Kathleen, who was like her mammy, was so busy with Paddy all the time. She knew that Nuala and Kathleen had slept in their womb position most nights, even towards the end when they were both quite big, much bigger than she and Molly were now. Maybe they would even now if Nuala was still there. As Laura finally nodded off, she wished Molly would turn around and sling an arm over her, but it had never been their way.

That Sunday afternoon Joseph Foley waited. He had become used to waiting for things, had felt his body gradually adjust to the slowness of his new life. Time was something almost palpable in this place, in this new chapter of his being; the moments that made up a day were far apart from each other, and stretched out like long expanses of sea, broken only by his two short shifts helping the doctor. He sat and waited for the cloud to move that had been hiding the sun all the morning. He watched as it crept past the ball of light now low in the sky. He waited for his stomach to still itself. Willed it to, as he waited for Kathleen.

They had not arranged to meet, but he knew she would be passing this way at some point soon, returning from whatever her message in the village had been. And she knew that he would be waiting for her, just as she knew he had noted her on her walk down into town. He would be by the pump, or on a low branch of the tree by O'Brien's. Or somewhere on the farm itself, hidden in the shadows so that only she would find him.

She wanted to tell her friends in whispers after Mass; she wanted to hear them say how romantic it was, to be excited. But she was not excited, and in any case she had no friends, not really. Only the few who had been close to her mother, and they were much older than her. And Niamh, who had always been more Nuala's friend than hers, and who she saw infrequently after she moved down to Kerry with her fisherman husband. And when Niamh came back to visit her mother and father, a silent sadness hung above the two old friends. Gossip and amusing stories seemed inappropriate as they each gazed upon features that startled the mind with the memories they held. They could not reminisce without conjuring up Nuala's ghost. Niamh spoke of her husband. Kathleen spoke of the children, and enquired as to whether Niamh would be having any children of her own, now that she was married. Niamh would look out in the direction of the sea in response to this and ask if the weather had been as treacherous here.

Kathleen thought of her friend Niamh as she walked up the long hill by Callaghan's. She wondered what Niamh would say when she saw her next. She would be showing by then. Maybe it would bring them a little closer. Maybe they would become real friends, talking in whispers and giggles like children again. Babies can do amazing things to a pair of people, no matter how they are connected. Maybe talking to Niamh would make it seem more real, and she would tell her that everything would be all right, just as Kathleen had said these past few years for the children. Maybe Kathleen could tell her how afraid she was – she had witnessed her own mother giving birth enough times to know the harsh reality of it, and she knew that things could go wrong, with the baby or for the mother. She was scared. If something were to happen to her, who would look after Paddy? He would be at a loss without her.

There was Caroline, of course, although Caroline was more of a surrogate mother to her than a friend, and the shame Kathleen would feel in telling her would be unbearable. And she could not tell her friend of those deeper, darker feelings. The dread that lay beneath that someone, some day, would find out the truth of it. The lies and deceit that would now underpin her every day. She could not confide that, although he was a dear, dear man, she did not love her Joseph, that she was deceiving him and all who knew them. Her friend could not help but judge her.

But Joseph Foley was oblivious. And besotted. The girl he had first seen in the distance from his lonely spot in his field had seen something in him, given him a second chance in his life, shown him what it was for. And it had taken him so long to gently gain her friendship and trust, and now she was willing and they were beginning to spend more and more time together. He was filled with a schoolboy excitement each time she came into view. And she was so wonderful and perfect and sweet, she suffered with no grand ambitions, and the place where she came from was so simple and good. There were no other young fellers knocking on her door, and she was too busy and shy and disinterested to bother going to the céilís. He was content that she would be his, and that he would one day be welcomed by her family, and that was his only ambition.

Standing in his trailer, fixing the string on his last bale of the day, Kathleen's father could see the figure of a man partly concealed by a wild cherry tree at the edge of his own cattle field. Its blossom had long since bloomed and dropped, but still, from afar, the twigs and branches merged into a natural awning so that it was hard to see beyond it. He watched the man a while to see if he moved from his horizontal position, but he did not. He knew the man was not injured, and probably not asleep, for he was sure it was the same man he had caught glimpses of over the past few weeks. Patrick Steele left his work and put his shirt back on. Sweat seeped random patches onto the white material. He needed water anyway. Again. Kathleen had said he should take it easy for a day or two to get over the illness, that he should rest in the house, but he knew that to be away in the fields was the only remedy. They both knew he did not have a bug. The sickness was in him, was him, maybe. Neighbours would surely talk if they saw him working away on a Sunday, and goodness knows he would be spoken to by Father. But he had to escape from her and from the house and apply his mind to something else.

As he watched from the pump, refreshed, he thought of how to approach the man he had seen, as a ghost, on his land and his neighbour's, here, there, disappearing at a blink. Nothing had been stolen, not even an egg.

'Are yeh all right there?' he called from a good bit away. 'Mister . . .'

The man did not seem to hear so he stole closer, placing each heavy boot as gently as he could. If the man was dangerous, he did not want to startle him at close range. His eyes were closed, his face young in his apparent slumber, though he was surely only ten years or so younger than himself. The man breathed slowly, hands resting on his slender stomach. The world had moved without the man noticing and the shade no longer covered his bare feet. Droplets of light lay delicately on his toe hair. His soles were hard, showing dry intricate lines of black and brown.

Pat Steele moved closer. He was the doctor's man. The waif, Foley, whom Fitzgerald had taken in and fed, even dressed, had been creeping about them like a bandit. And, yes, the man's clothes were slightly too big, and did not match the boots which were tossed to the side of him. It was plain to see that the boots were his own, and not a doctor's shoes. They were brown, sturdy and scrubbed old through cleaning. Patrick had heard that he had been off fighting. A brave man. Braver still for coming to a place like Ballinara after that. Patrick wondered for a time what to do with him, and decided that the best course of action was to return to the top field and his baling. His head throbbed and he needed more water already. He would leave him and have a word with Fitzgerald, and maybe the doctor would understand more clearly the kind of talk there had been in the village. It was very charitable, of course, everyone agreed that, but ''tis a bit strange, 'tis all', the women would say.

As he was about to turn away from the sleeping stranger, Patrick Steele detected the faintest sound of humming. It was a melody of his ancestors, old and mysterious, and reassuring in its familiarity. The female hummer was moving nearer, on the road beyond the strip of furze. What a beautiful thing it was to him in the stillness of the warm day, being in the presence of a man who didn't know he was there, in part of his own land where he had never had reason to linger before. The singer's place was hers alone, moving with her, carrying her along the road. He took a few steps back. Surely the mist of notes in the air would wake the man as she passed by.

He looked at him, and noticed the stillness of his eyes and the downturned lips on an upside-down face. This stranger was not sleeping – he was smiling. He was breathing in the presence of this hidden woman also. They were like two foxes, lying in wait, stealing satisfaction from an unwitting vixen.

A sun-dappled foot twitched. The man smiled on slightly, as if he had heard this music before, while Pat Steele frowned, uncomfortable, as though intruding on something quite private. He backed away and climbed up on the trailer in the field where he had begun that morning. It was quieter now, the air, the world; the quiet that only a farmer or a sailor might know. And the only moving thing that his eyes could see was the figure of a woman in Kathleen's distinctive blue overall drifting serenely towards the house, and the only movement in the immobile air was the resonance of the earlier quavers and minims of a haunting tune that a father once sang to his child.

When he looked down again towards the lower field it was empty. His eyes searched and searched but the man was gone and, when he looked back to his house where the boreen started, so was his daughter. The world around him was still, the cattle in the next field were muted. But inside, the little tune burned him as he rocked Kathleen to sleep in his arms, somewhere far away in his memory.

There was no one to see the silhouette of a farmer standing astride a bale of hay up on his trailer, sky all around, above and behind him. There was no one to offer him water for his parched lips. No one to explain why the tears began to roll again down his weather-worn face, as wrinkled and cracked as the stranger's foot, and no one to warn him of the effect of his crying on the young boy as he hid behind a nearby furze bush.

It had been a long while since Tomás had seen his father cry. The tears that had rolled down his cheeks at Nuala's funeral had frightened Tomás and he had been afraid that his father would never stop. But now he was bigger it simply seemed odd to him. He felt no fear, no desire to comfort, no need to make it stop.

Tomás observed his father as he stood up there watching Kathleen and Joseph walking away down the road together.

They would be passing by the field where he had spied Laura playing earlier. He did not understand why this would be upsetting and thought that maybe he was going mad. Why did grown-ups get affected by things so? Couldn't they just get on with life like the children are expected to do? Maybe he was sad because he thought Joseph was going to take Kathleen away and he'd be left to look after their mother.

He took one last glance at his father and headed off to take Laura back to the house. He did not want her to have to see or hear Kathleen and Joseph. She was too small to understand these things, and he did not want to be the one to have to explain them.

Dr Fitzgerald's visits remained frequent, despite the lack of change in Nora Steele's condition. She neither deteriorated nor improved; the doctors at the hospital had anticipated as much and had been happy for her to be at home with her family, provided there was adequate care for her. It was not his duty so much as his kind nature, and his liking for Kathleen's homemade scones, that brought the doctor up the hill every other Wednesday afternoon, after surgery hours. Over the months, less time was spent talking about Mrs Steele and more was spent taking the tea that Kathleen made him and those scones, buttered thick, just how he liked it. He found her such a delight, and admired her so; a silent mother and a virtually silent father among an ever-enthusiastic clutch of noisy children. But they were never dirty, never aggressive to one another, and always minded their manners. She was doing a grand job.

The doctor felt it unnecessary to have his new assistant

accompany him on his visits to Steele's farm, so while he was there Joseph delivered prescriptions to the villagers, determined whether their complaints warranted a trip to the doctor, and collected deliveries from the chemist up the road in Killnarnan. Dr Fitzgerald would lend Joseph his bicycle and this arrangement suited him, too, as the longer walk justified a longer rest, which meant an additional cup of tea. Besides, Joseph had begun to seem to the doctor more youthful by the day, and surprisingly handsome, given the state he was in when they found him.

He had taken it upon himself to take Joseph in. He was the only medic for miles around, and one of the very few with no mouth to feed but his own. For the first week or so he had nursed him with water and regular morsels of food. And when Joseph had begun to regain some strength he had encouraged him to talk of his feelings, for he had done as much as he could for the man's physical well-being. When he looked preoccupied the doctor said to him, just as he had once said to Nora Steele, what his own mother used to say to him when he was a boy: 'A merry heart doeth good like a medicine; but a broken spirit drieth the bones.' And gradually he had noticed that as the young man began to talk about what he had seen and what he had done, he started to sleep better and have a more positive outlook.

The doctor's evenings were a little less lonely now, and the long, quiet walk up the stairs from surgery to living room less daunting. Often he had sat in his armchair, drink in hand, with only the ticking of his carriage clock for company, waiting till he was tired enough to go to bed. But now he had the task of helping Joseph work through his emotions, which in time became less of a chore and more of a friendly conversation. Joseph was a good man, and the doctor enjoyed having him around. He had begun training him informally and Joseph was a good student, eager to learn. He had even remembered his old chess set that had been abandoned in the back of a cupboard, and although he wasn't sure that the man was very fond of the game, he played along as best he could.

Laura lay on her stomach, sheltered from view – and from the sun – by one of her father's hay bales. Even through the cushion of thick woollen cardigan and knitted rabbit she had lain out, the stubs of corn stabbed at her, poking rudely into her daydream. She was observing a butterfly just in front of her nose atop a lone stalk that had somehow been spared the reaper's lethal swipe. If she squished her cheeks upwards so that her long black eyelashes (her father's eyelashes, she was always told) made a lattice in front of her eyes, the blueness of the butterfly merged with the blue of the sky and she could hardly see it. It didn't know she was there, and it let its sky-blue wings be fanned gently by the breeze that had finally, blissfully, come in the last week or so. The wind had been picking up, and there had been the hint of a winter draught in her room that made her cuddle up more closely to Molly. She wondered what the butterfly was thinking, a thought which made her sad. How small it was in this big field, the world. And how small she was. When she stared at the map of the whole wide world that Miss Ahern had pinned to the wall, Laura found it so hard to imagine the smallness of Ireland, of her house, a tiny dot among all the pink, green and yellow shapes of the other huge countries that dwarfed her own.

The breeze shifted, disturbing the butterfly's meditation, and the white-gold softness of the hair on her arms bristled momentarily. Again, Laura thought of the draught from the window at night. She would not ask Kathleen to fix it, nor her father – they were both too busy with the house, the farm, the baby, their mother. She would use some plasticine, or even a sock. She would not ask Molly to swap to be on the side under the window, next to the cold outside wall. She did not want to annoy her any more than she seemed to at the moment, although she could not think what it was that she had done in the past weeks that could have annoyed her. She looked on as Molly played out more and more with Marie Sullivan, who usually played with the boys, and Laura was left playing their fairy game with just herself and the pretend Molly whom she imagined beside her still. She wondered at the back of her mind whether Kathleen spoke to Nuala still. She was sure she used to, but Kathleen was a grown-up now, and grown-ups didn't do things like that.

And at home sometimes, Molly would run off with Tomás, no longer wanting to play the games the two girls had always played. Gone were their private, sisterly giggles. Molly would fall asleep straight away at night now, and not play the shadow game or the lists game that had been part of their nightly routine for so long. While Laura lay awake reading and re-reading Kathleen and Nuala's old books, Molly would wriggle and squirm, and Laura would move closer to the wall so that her sister would not fall out; Molly would turn onto her stomach, further away, blankets following her, clinging to her simple, straight back, and Laura would look upon her sister and think that maybe it was because they were not the same. They did not have the special connection that Nuala and Kathleen had had, being twins.

Laura had a faint memory that she used to go into her big sisters' bed for cuddles sometimes. And they would be fitted together, as a conker fits just perfectly inside its spiky shell, or like two wooden jigsaw pieces; but they would always part, remould and make room for her between them. Molly and Laura had never had a sleeping position, not like their older sisters. Their mother had said it was because Nuala and Kathleen had clung on to each other in her tummy, been side by side before they were even born. They didn't do it on purpose. They didn't know any other way.

She had been so small then, when it happened. If it wasn't for Kathleen, maybe she would forget all about her other sister. Sometimes it seemed as though Nuala had never been there, that the family had always been as it was now. And their mammy didn't smile any more. That was where Nuala was now, in the space where that smile was gone to.

Laura often cried on those nights because she knew that she should not have such feelings when Kathleen was, of course, in more pain than any of them could know, even Molly and herself. Even now. At least she still had Molly, and she told herself not to be envious of whatever her older sisters had shared, and to be thankful that she had her Molly, a little bit bigger, almost a twin, to play with. But those thoughts made her think of dying and of heaven and of their mam, and she could not help the corners of her mouth turning down and a bubble of hot tears forming in her eyes. She tossed her hand crossly at the corn stalk, sending the butterfly fluttering away in sudden, jerky movements.

'Tell me,' said Joseph. 'Tell me about how it was.'

'About how what was?' They were beneath a tree watching the blue and white sky above them through the leaves. One or two leaves had begun to succumb; their edges had become a gentle pear-yellow and one had a red-tinged caterpillar hole. But they were only a couple. The rest remained happily swaying to and fro in the gentle, just-warm-enough breeze, still green.

'Your home, you. Your family.' He turned onto his side, head propped on curled-over pale fingers, smiling a smile that he hoped would say, I will understand. I love you. Tell me, because you love me.

Kathleen sighed quietly to herself, and continued to look upwards, at the leaves and through them. She did not want to do this, but she knew she must play the part. She did not want him to ask her the unanswerable questions. She internally willed, begged him not to ask again. She only wished to carry on enjoying this brief time of togetherness in which she was trying to create something meaningful, lasting, between them. It seemed to take all of her energy when she was with him not to think about the ever-growing circle of baby within her.

Things that there were once words for had become private and internalized. Nuala had changed into something unreal and unspoken, she was ingrained within the memories and objects in their home, a lingering presence, beautiful but uncomfortable. The effect of their mother's sickness, also an undiscussed entity, had rippled outwards among their little community and into the treatment by neighbours; even to the significance of times in the year – Kathleen's birthday, Nuala's anniversary, Lughnasa – even certain passages in Gospels at Mass. It was what her state of mind represented: a gruesome and continual reminder of Nuala's death, not allowing a one of them to properly move on and set the grief aside. Words in the Steele household had been replaced one day by glances, avoidances and fleeting, sometimes imagined, shadows from the next room. Excitement and smiles and children's spontaneous outbursts had overnight been stifled. But Kathleen had noticed early on that Joseph had an open nature and inquisitive mind; he wanted to look for the meaning in everything, even when there wasn't one. And often when there was a meaning, it was better left unspoken. And so, he ascribed each of her sad episodes to Nuala's death.

But slowly, and with time, some peace came back into their home. All of them, she supposed, were kept slightly removed from the rest of the world by Nuala's passing. Initially there was a restraining of childish emotions and, once they began to forget, after a few months, the rawness of their loss, they had emerged different, subdued. The little ones had begun to forget much of what made her Nuala, the details that made her a distinct half of The Twins. Kathleen was sure they had all forgotten how infectious her laugh was – she would involuntarily snort at the end of a phrase of laughter, which would set them all off again. She was a clown, a daredevil, whereas Kathleen was more reserved. But the differences were slight, and no outsider would be able to tell the pair apart. 'I'm Nuala,' 'And I'm Kathleen,' they would chant when asked by an elderly relative, or the priest after Mass. For the rest of the family, Kathleen had quickly realized, the good memories were almost more painful than recalling the awful day itself. And so everything was unsaid. It was easier to lock it away from everyday thought. But Kathleen kept Nuala alive within her. It was easy. She was lucky. But she did not know how to begin to say any of this to another person.

'What was your sister like? Was she very like you, as Fitzgerald says?'

'She is, yes . . . was. We were exactly the same, down to our little toes.' Kathleen smiled at her mother's words. Their voices sounded similar now. Suddenly, Kathleen felt an acute anger towards her mother for not being able to support her now, at the time in her life when she needed a mother's love and advice. Her mother, whom she used to love so dearly.

Joseph moved his head and rested it gently on her chest. His chestnut-brown hair was soft and warm under her chin; like a cat, Kathleen thought. He was waiting, she knew, for her to continue. He wanted to listen, to know. He wanted her to pour her heart, her love, out for him. And as she began to form the words that had gone unspoken for so long, he heard in her voice something that seemed new to him, but which was really very old – an animation, a passion almost, that was once a part of her, of them both. He knew that, were he to raise his head and look at her, her beauty would be even more radiant, her skin aglow, her eyes aflame. But he did not want to disturb her. She needed to speak as much as he needed to hear her.

But Kathleen sat up and scrabbled into a sitting position as the flow of memories came tumbling out of her mouth. She told him of how they would go on the pony and trap down to the strand at Kerry when it had just been the four of them, when Nuala and Kathleen were the only Steele children. She told him of how close she and her twin were, of their secret language that not even their parents knew about, of their grandmother who would make a tart with the blackberries the two picked, and the smell of the apples as they cooked whilst they picked splinters out of each other's legs from climbing the apple trees.

He learned of when the parlour used to be full, with the priest, the doctor, the neighbours – the Sullivans, O'Briens, Walshes and Crowleys – and sometimes the cousins from down over Killgorney way; and how it was their mother who was invariably asked to start the singing. Her husband would always stand at the door, leaning on the frame, surveying his wife and the room and topping up mugs and glasses. Kathleen stopped momentarily and let out a long, soft breath. She went on, and he listened as she conjured up the two little twins who would sit either side of the fire, or snuggled up together on a big chair, legs and arms entwined, listening to the stories, dozing, or when they were a bit bigger, offering their own invented songs, or ancient songs of Ireland, in harmonies handed down throughout the generations, in other parlours in other places, in bygone times. And Joseph could see the oldest of the gathering closing his or her eyes in contentment and regret as the melody told its tale.

He could not imagine the room being used for any such gatherings now. He could only see in his mind's eye the stillness and the treading quietly around the stationary woman. It was the mixture of sadness for Kathleen and latent anger at Mrs Steele's selfishness that sent Joseph's hand tightly around hers. He did love this girl, all would be fine, and he looked into her face to see if she too felt the immense emotion of the moment. But Kathleen had barely noticed his hand and kept on as though afraid that these words, these memories, would disappear if they were not all spoken about, remembered aloud, turned into something real again, if only for a few moments.

These were the images that kept her company and sometimes, conversely, were cruelly lonesome. It was as though a knot of stiffness in her mind and her chest were being loosened, as kneaded dough, as Laura or Molly's matted hair when she poured water over them. She talked, and Joseph listened. He gazed at her, at the dappled light on her hair, and had to keep looking at her mouth to maintain a concentration on what she was saying. He had not thought of his previous life for days now. At moments like this they were the only two in the world. When everyone knew, when it was no longer a secret, things would still be well for them. People would forget that he was once a desperate, smelly stranger, and would see only the happiness he brought to her.

They had discussed it and thought it best if Joseph, in the presence of one or other family member, asked to meet Kathleen at Reilly's forthcoming do for a son who was emigrating, and they could then begin courting. Joseph would no longer have to think of pretexts to run errands along the Farm Road, and Kathleen would surely be excused some duties of an evening for the sake of their new romance.

'It is nice,' said Kathleen as they walked, 'so nice, to have someone to share a walk like this with.' She was smiling. There was no frown, no faraway look that Joseph so often noticed, and which he thought made her look all the more beautiful. And it was such a simple beauty, nothing too accentuated or unusual – her lips were not wide and full and her eyes were not the brightest, but altogether each little feature, down to the tiny freckles on the palest, most translucent skin, fitted together to make an image of perfection. She was calmer now, and he felt privileged to be the one to have heard her memories. She did not aspire to wealth or wish to know about the lives of the ladies in the city. She was pure and happy walking along the hedgerow with him, counting petals, laughing as he inelegantly tried to catch butterflies. He believed it was the simplicities, the joys that could be found in nature, that pleased his Kathleen.

She grasped his hand, the immense relief of speaking about Nuala, and of feeling she had been given a second chance by him, making her giddy – and he could see her breathing in the air of her world, her tiny patch of Ireland. He knew that, even if there were another potato famine in their time, if all their crops failed, if everyone they knew moved away, she would not leave this land in search of a better one, like the young Reilly lad, and like so many others, for to Kathleen there was no better land. This was where she knew. It was Home. She could never leave it because it was where Nuala would always be. This ghost, thought Joseph, would either keep each member of the Steele family members close to the farm for ever, or send them far away.

'Do you think Tomás will get the notion to leave when we go to Reilly's on Saturday?'

Kathleen stopped and looked at Joseph, half frowning, half smiling, as if to say, Don't be so ridiculous, and she said, 'He's only just thirteen. What a notion, Joseph Foley.'

'All right . . . what I meant was, you know, with all the talk of leaving away on the boat, the adventures to be had, the wide open sea – and what lies beyond it. It's bound to make him excited, and for him to wonder.'

'I wouldn't worry', Kathleen said. 'He's the oldest boy. He has the farm to take on.'

'But what if he doesn't want to take it on? Not all sons do, you know. When I was small, my daddy used to tell me such wonderful stories of the sea – pirates and treasure, ships with sails as big as a house—'

'You never talk about your da, your family,' Kathleen interrupted. 'Is he as fanciful as you?' she said, playfully knocking her hip against his, setting him off balance for a moment.

'He is a good man, Kathleen. I'd like to be a bit more like him. I hope you meet them one day . . . But you never talk about your own da. Of all the Steeles, he's the one I know the least.'

Kathleen's face lost its smile. She could feel it happen and tried to put the smile back on, tried to conjure back the carefree happiness she had been feeling a moment ago.

But it had not gone unnoticed by Joseph and his face mirrored hers. He stopped walking and said, 'What is it, Kathleen?' She did not turn around to face him, but stopped also, her heart galloping suddenly. He was sure to see it. He would be able to read her eyes. She could not tell him, but what if he guessed? He couldn't, surely. She must think.

'You think he will not approve of me.' Joseph kicked at a pebble that lay near his boot and sat down heavily on the stile. 'He will not want his daughter being with that boy from the field, or Scarecrow Man they call me, isn't it?'

Kathleen stopped him, and put her arms around his shoulders, stroked his neck in the way that she had come to like doing. It was soft there, and as smooth as Paddy's skin. She was relieved that she did not have to think up a lie to explain her expression. And she was sorry that he had these feelings hidden within him, that he would doubt himself before ever thinking she could do wrong. Such a good man. Too good for her.

'No,' she said with a smile. 'No, no, don't be a silly. No one says anything of you. Not now, now that we all know you. And children can say such cruel things without really knowing what they mean.'

'True.' Joseph breathed in the scent rising from the top of Kathleen's head. It was sweet from the soap she used, and sour, too, from the vinegar rinsed through to make it shiny. Such things about her were becoming familiar to him.

'And children – they don't know that adults have feelings. They do not know that grown-ups are as uncertain of what lies ahead as they are . . . so ignore whatever people say and live the life that God gave you.'

And to that, Joseph murmured into her hair, without knowing he had spoken the words aloud, that he would like nothing more than to spend the life that God had given him with the life He had given her. It was a notion that needed no contemplation or deliberation by Kathleen, as she had been waiting and hoping for it. She let her hands drop down from his neck and into his, and said simply, 'Yes.'

When Kathleen arrived back her father was in the kitchen, with Molly on his lap. She looked as though she had been crying.

'How come you're in?' she asked of him. 'Are you all right, Moll?'

There was a long moment of quiet and dust in the air till he said, 'Where were you, Kathleen?'

'I went to pick some flowers for Mam.' Molly hopped off his knee and ran outside to find her brother.

'All this time, gone. To pick flowers.' He looked at the bunch she was holding. 'Those late poppies only grow down in Murphy's field. Why on earth were you there?' She stayed silent, though she began to feel an anger towards him for speaking to her like a child again. But she said nothing.

'We needed you, Kathleen. The children needed you.'

'They seem fine.' They could both see four children out the window playing happily with a ball and two dogs, Brendan Reilly's having followed him.

'Well, they weren't fine. You should've been here.'

Kathleen breathed deeply, the anger bubbling up inside her. 'How can you talk to me like this, like I'm a silly little girl? Moll was upset because she can't decide whether she is seven or seventeen. You leave them to me, and I'll leave you to your grass.'

Her father slammed his water glass down hard on the table and stood up. 'Oh, my grass. My grass, she says!' He laughed briefly, falsely. 'That's right, because I have it so much easier than you, because all I do is go out in the field and cut the grass a bit, while you have all the children to play with—'

'Play? Do you think I have time to play? In between the washing and the cooking, and running around after them, after your children? Do you think I can even remember what it was like to play? Do you think that I am not working till I am so tired that I cannot stand, so that they may have some sort of a childhood?' She stopped and swallowed back a sickly feeling. 'Because I certainly didn't.'

She stopped again, breathing fast, knowing her cheeks were flushed and that the children could have heard her voice from outside. Tears prickled threateningly. She did not want to be arguing with him like this. They never had harsh words and she had never raised her voice to him before, but now she needed to. She looked him in the eye till he hung his head. He dragged a chair out from under the kitchen table and sat down heavily. Neither spoke for a moment or two. They listened to the sounds from the children outside, the carefree cries echoing over the land, and to the thoughts and feelings rushing around in their own heads. Finally he spoke, with so clear a tone of regret that Kathleen immediately softened and felt terrible for speaking to him so.

'. . . If it is in any way because of me . . . If it is true, if I have taken away your childhood, then I am truly sorry, Kathleen.' He was crying. She could hear it in his voice, though his head was in his hands now. 'I thought . . . you did . . . I thought you wanted it too.' He gulped back the emotion but tears were steadily dripping onto his lap. 'I would never have . . .! I don't understand why we did . . . if you didn't want to . . . I know it was wrong, I just . . . I thought it was both of us, Kathy . . . It hasn't left my mind since, and I feel so sick when . . . Oh, what have I done?'

Kathleen went to the door and turned the key so that the children would not come in. It would be too much for them, especially Laura and Molly, after seeing him in that state before.

Then she got a cloth from the scullery and dampened it and went to kneel on the floor in front of him. She wiped at his lap and his feet where tears had fallen. She patted at his hands, prising them away from his face. As she wiped his eyes, cheeks, lips, she spoke to him, softly now: 'I didn't mean it, any of it. I don't really know what I said now, I'm not myself at the moment. But it was not you who stole my childhood. No one did. The child in me died along with Nuala, God rest her soul. I couldn't go on being carefree and giggling, with her dead in the ground. And that is the fault of no one. It's just the way things are.'

Kathleen paused to frown away her own tears and her shame at what Nuala would think. But this too needed to be spoken about. 'It was a mistake and we will put it behind us now, for it will not happen again.'

'I know, I know, I know. May God forgive us, Kathleen.'

'May God forgive us.'

They stayed like that for some time, unable to say any more, or to think any thoughts. And as they held hands nothing passed between them. That confusion in their life was over. It was a chapter they felt had passed. Like Nuala dying, like Kathleen's childhood. They were father and daughter once more, and that was all. But the reality of the life inside her had not gone.

She stood up and went to unlock the door, her body casting a shadow over the stone figure of her mother as she did so. She hesitated, but then came back to him and said, 'Stand up.' He obeyed. His eyes had red veins in them and looked swollen. She waited till he looked into her face. She needed to be sure that he understood, for it was not something that she could bring herself to say.

She took her father's hand, turned it slightly and stepped closer towards him. Then she gently laid it against the hardened wall of her stomach. In the moment or two that it took for him to realize, she hurriedly said, 'It's all right. I have found a man who will marry me. He doesn't know. We'll go far away if we have to, but ...' And then she fled, running through the door, chased by the sound of his wailing, a sound that was more terrible than any of them had made at Nuala's funeral, more haunting than anything Kathleen had ever heard in her dreams. She knew the children would hear it, she knew they would be scared and would want her, and she knew that she should be there, but she needed with all her soul to get away.

Tomás didn't go down to the strand very often. If Kathleen was taking the little ones he would usually stay behind on the farm or go up to Reilly's. The jolly colour of the sand and the children playing, sandcastles being constructed – it was a contrast too far for him, disrespectful. But occasionally on a quiet day, when he knew not a soul would be there, he would take the rusty blue bicycle along the roadway. He would let it pick up speed and tear down the hill, racing Waggy to the bottom, the wind drying the whites of his eyes, hoping that no tractor was turning in Murphy's boreen along the way. He would dump the bicycle by the rocks and run as fast as he could all the way to Mermaid's Point and back again. Then he would find a collection of stones and throw them as hard at the sea as he could.

The running felt good. It helped clear his mind. He wished that he could get his mother down there and make her run along beside him. But she had not been down for a long time.

Kathleen and their father had given up on that. It was such a rigmarole bringing blanket and slippers and yoking up the horse to the cart – for she couldn't manage the walk up the hill – and Kathleen and her father would quietly bicker with the effort of trying to mind the children and their mother, and keeping Paddy happy.

Mass was the only thing for which they now presented themselves as a family, and he was beginning to think that it was only he who listened to the words. They didn't eat together any more. Their mother was usually in her chair while the others sat at the table, and sometimes Kathleen would feed just the three of them, and she and their father would eat leftovers later, after they were gone to bed. He would lie awake listening to their murmuring through the wall.

He did not look out for neighbours as he pedalled furiously down the hill. He did not think to see whether Joseph was in any of his hiding places, waiting. He did not check whether O'Brien was out baling or in the hedgerow smoking a Woodbine. He did not want to observe life any more, to know the people around him and what they did in a day. He would just concentrate on himself and his mother and one day he would be a man. That is what reassured Tomás – that everything would one day be all right because one day he would be a grown-up and when you are a grown-up you can fix anything.

He had nothing to be upset about. He had misunderstood. He had seen through a window, after all. It wasn't as though he was in the same room as them. But still, while his father's tears in the field had not bothered him, that awful sound he had made in the kitchen terrified him, and he had seen Kathleen putting his hand on her stomach, had seen the look on her face. Why could he not be even a year younger? Then he would not understand.

And as he ran, images of his father and his sister flashed through his mind. He was confused and sickened. He thought of all the evenings they spent together by the fire, talking in hushed tones. If Kathleen's gesture had been her way of telling their father that she was going to have a baby because of Joseph, he would not have reacted like that. He would have been furious, maybe even have hit her. But he would not have collapsed into that agonized wailing, and Tomás would not have been chased away by the sound of his father retching in the hallway again.

'Kathleen?' She had been trying to ignore the little voice at the door. 'Kathleen? . . . I need you.' It was Laura. That was all right. Any of the others she would have sent away, despite loving them all equally. Laura was such a sweet girl, had such a soft nature. 'Come on in, love,' she called in a loud whisper from her bed where she lay wrapped around Paddy's sleeping body. It was a new thing, this needing to be held until he was in a deep sleep – a sign that he was more aware of himself and his preferences. Whenever she so much as moved a hand, his face would crumple and redden and she would have to place it back in position immediately lest he should wake fully. Until recently she would put him down in the cot and carry on with her chores or, as was happening more and more frequently, steal away to see Joseph. He was always eager to see her and, despite often feeling so overcome with tiredness, or fuzzy with the sickness, she knew she must keep him in love with her.

Before, as she fed Paddy his milk, or rocked him back to sleep, she would think of what needed to be done in the house, or of her mother, the way she was before, the lives of all of them before Nuala. Memories of Nuala would play continuously behind her eyes with such clarity and frequency that, when she blinked, she was often surprised to see a blank wall in front of her, and not her sister on Christmas morning, or splashing water on her face, or tying a ribbon at the end of her long braid for Sunday Mass. In these quiet moments of the day, Kathleen's mind had always looked back, never forwards, for she had had no reason to think upon what she might do in her future, because it was already laid out before her. She had accepted her role caring for the children without ever wondering what would happen if her mother got better. It never crossed her mind that Paddy, like the rest of them, would one day grow up and move on. Even if he stayed on the farm he would become a man, non-dependent, and the need for affection and closeness that would surely remain for ever with Kathleen would be gone from him, extinguished by maturity.

But she did not think of this. Until now, until she was given a different path to walk down. It was a path she felt unprepared for. She did not own the shoes for walking it – how would she do it? She saw herself standing at the crossroads by Callaghan's at the edge of the village, bewildered. She would have to leave the farm, her home. She would have to try and love this baby inside her. But how could she love any baby as much as she loved Paddy? She would have to leave him – but they would be lost without each other. Who would settle his tears? The thought of him crying for her in the night and her not coming, not able to, was unbearable. It would be that choking, hiccoughing cry that babies make when they are so bewildered as to why they cannot get what they want, what they need.

Laura had come in and shut the door gently behind her. She had stepped softly because she had seen the small mound of Paddy's bottom rising up under a blanket behind her sister's leg. She had wanted to ask Kathleen if it was all right to borrow some beads of their mother's to wear up at Brendan's. But she stopped as she saw that Kathleen's eyelashes were shiny. Laura thought at first she should go out again and leave Kathleen and Paddy alone, but then she thought that now might be a good time to try being a little bit grown up.

'Do you miss Nuala?' she said softly. It did not cross her mind that there would be anything else upsetting her sister, and it felt nice to speak of something so rarely mentioned.

'I do, yes, love.' Kathleen looked at her small sister, proud at the brave question. 'Do you?'

'I do, sometimes.' And she snuggled down on the bed with her big sister and her little brother. 'Sometimes I . . . I think that if you and her weren't exactly the same I'd forget her.'

'Little Laura, don't say that. You'll never forget her, she's always with us, she watches over us. You know . . . any time you feel sad about her, or anything, you can tell me . . . even if I'm far away.'

The two sisters lay with the baby, thinking their own thoughts. The younger one had forgotten all about wanting a sparkly necklace and instead began to think about the thought her sister had put in her mind – that one day she would leave them too. One by one everyone would go away, Laura thought, till it was just her and Paddy left. She tried to imagine herself as a grown-up, looking after her baby brother, but it seemed a hundred years away, and she was sad that things in life had to change. She wanted everything to stay the same, just for a little while, without anything bad happening.

As the days passed and the hard curve of womb within her began to swell, though still perceptible only to her, the change that this little life would cause to all the lives around it was dawning on Kathleen. She knew that, although your first child takes longer to show than those that follow, it really isn't all that long. The need to make their engagement public worried her. Her breasts were already fuller and the insides of her thighs had begun to rub when she walked. Perhaps the most noticeable change was the appearance of greyish crescents that hung permanently now under her eyes. Her legs, arms, head, mind were so tired. It was a tiredness the like of which she had never known, and she could see already why her mother and Caroline would say, 'No more now, love,' to their husbands after each one. 'That's the last one now . . .' But still they carried on, as all mothers do, and so must she.

Kathleen thought about this for a while as she examined her face in the bedroom mirror. For years it had been such a comfort to her, to look upon her own reflection. But now a puffiness had arrived on her cheeks and about her chin, along with the age that exhaustion can bring about the eyes. She had to search a little to find her sister there.

But was she as strong as all those other women? Her circumstances were so different. She wasn't ready. How could she carry on, like other mothers? A mother. She would be called 'Mammy'. It did not sound novel to her. Each of the older children had called her that name by mistake at some point in time. But maybe she did not deserve this little gift from God, for that is what it was, not a punishment. No, God's punishments did not come in such wondrous forms.

Her father had begun to change too. He began to look old to her. Old, worn out and baggy. Kathleen felt guilt, along with her shame. He could not look at her, talk to her. If she entered a room, he left it. There was no communication any more. But the children hadn't seemed to notice. She tried to catch him in the evenings but he would retreat to his shed, or to Pat McCarthy's where he had found a new solace at the end of the bar. She would be left alone in the evenings that were now growing cold, and she would sit on a chair by her mother and sew what needed mending. She supposed she should start on some baby clothes, but could not somehow. When the children were asleep, she could not help but weep. She could not speak of it to Joseph, and her father was bewildered by it. She would look at her mother dozing by the fire and long to tell her, to say she was sorry, to ask for her help.

It was Saturday. Clouds had been forming in the west and were creeping in. 'A day the Good Lord Himself would want to be ashamed of,' as Caroline had said when Kathleen had stopped by mid-morning. The little girls had unearthed a pair of dresses that had belonged to her and Nuala. Two pale green chiffon Christmas dresses that had been made by their grandmother when she was still the bright, cheery granny that only the twins had known, the granny who, by her death, had been spared the pain of losing a granddaughter. Kathleen had been so surprised that they both wanted to wear the same thing for once that she had clapped her hands and squealed with childlike delight when they ran in with them in their arms, Laura asking was it all right. Kathleen's joyful reaction prompted the two sisters' excited laughter, and an atmosphere of fun began to seep through the house that morning, despite the bleak day beyond their windows. It was liberating to have a reason to be excited for a while.

Kathleen watched the girls united in their giddy anticipation. It was so nice to see them getting along the way they used to. Laura was glowing with contentment, eager to do anything Molly suggested.

'Why don't we try them on now and see do they fit?'

'Oh, they'll fit all right,' said Kathleen. 'Your one might be a bit big, Laura, but it doesn't matter. Go on, pop them on. I can't wait to see you. You'll look like a pair of princesses.'

'No, no, fairies!' exclaimed Laura. 'They're greeny-blue, just like a flower fairy!'

'Yes, definitely more fairy than princess,' said Molly, 'but fairies don't exist so—'

'Well, I know that, of course.' The sweetness in Laura's young face made Kathleen smile. They would be fine, the pair of them. Molly just couldn't wait to grow up, and was waiting for Laura to get on with it, while it hadn't yet occurred to Laura to be anything but a child.

They were holding the dresses up to themselves, gently pushing against each other to see themselves in the mirror. Strands of Laura's strawberry-blonde hair, as unruly as Kathleen's, were getting entangled with Molly's thick, straight black hair. Hers was the hair of the boys in the family. Their father, Tomás and Molly. They had yet to see what Paddy's would be like, of course. Kathleen thought of how her mother's hair had seemed to change with each pregnancy, sometimes dramatically – she had heard from Caroline's mother how she had lost her curls when she had Nuala and herself: 'Gave them all to you two curly-tops!' After Tomás it went smoother; after the two little girls more curls again, but loose, soft ones; and after Paddy it became all fuzzy and wiry. What little physical contact had existed between their parents was not what it used to be. Gone were the days when his fingers worked through the coarse tufts and greying waves. Kathleen thought of her own hair and she thought of him and, blinking quickly, returned her mind to the children before her.

'Ah, Molly, you have Nuala's one, look.'

'How can you tell?' The two stood facing each other, studying the gowns.

'Yours has a little hole, see?' said Kathleen, kneeling down between them, touching the waistband where the hole was. The feel of the fabric transported her back to a Christmas scene, so strong and clear that her stomach heaved.

'Well, I don't want the one with the hole in it!' Molly said hotly.

'I want Nuala's one,' Laura responded quietly. 'I mean, I don't mind having the one with the hole.'

As the two girls swapped dresses and the green fabric passed before her like a beautiful, swishing wave, Kathleen felt as close as ever to the memory of her dead sister. She smiled with relief, knowing that the changes in her body would not make her grow away from Nuala. She turned to Laura and said, 'Well, that's all right then, because Mammy used to just tie a green ribbon around her tummy, and no one ever knew it was there.'

'Do you still have the ribbon?' Laura's eyes twinkled.

'Sure, I don't have time to look all the morning for a ribbon that's probably all moth-eaten, but I'll go down to Caroline's when I take Paddy for a walk and I'll see does she have an oddment or two. If not, I'll stitch it, love.'

Kathleen could see that Molly now wished she had the dress with the hole so that she could have a ribbon tied in a big bow on her back, but she knew better than to complain, after rejecting something that had once belonged to Nuala.

'Will you help us try them on now, Kathleen?'

'Why don't you and Laura help each other? You can do each other's buttons up at the backs . . . I have to change Paddy before I head off.'

She left them in her room, a picture of two sisters, helping each other. She hadn't told them that the ribbon's original purpose was to allow people, including their parents, to tell Nuala and her apart.

Kathleen fetched Paddy's bonnet and a blanket from the press. It had been a few days since she had taken him out walking; his father tended to take him out into the fields now after his sleep.

'Don't forget, girls,' she called, knocking on the window from outside. 'If I'm going off to get ribbon, you'll have to do a couple of jobs for me.'

'We'll bring in the washing,' called Laura's smiling face through the pane.

'And you can put his nappies in to soak for me when you've swept the parlour.'

'Nappies! . . . Ewwgh!' Molly made a face and Laura copied. They both giggled and squashed their noses at her against the glass. Tucking her little purse under the blanket, she set off up the boreen. Pushing the pram uphill to the road seemed harder than usual. She was out of breath and sweating before she was halfway up. But once she was up on the road and Paddy was nodding off with the gentle motion of the pram, Kathleen was free to think. There was relative harmony in the house, and a sense of anticipation. The tight ball just under her ribs began to relax, remedied by a little moment or two of carefree happiness. She tried to keep her thoughts away from her recent troubles and concentrated instead on humming one of her and Nuala's favourite nursery rhymes, mainly to herself, as Paddy was now fast asleep. She let her mind wander back to the day when that hole in the dress was made. It had been at Lughnasa, on the last occasion that the village had celebrated the festival together. And now that she thought on it, it must have been out of respect to Nuala that they stopped, with her dying only a week before the following year's festival. That year the festivities were cancelled. Someone must have had to send messages to those in the surrounding villages who usually came. She wondered who it would have been.

She could see them as clearly and plainly as she could see the child in the pram before her. They had been down at their fairy dell at the curve in the boreen in their good dresses, the two of them bedecked with daisy-chain crowns and bracelets and dandelion earrings. They had called them earrings, but by the time they had wrapped the stalk around the top of their ears and fastened it with a slit in the stem, they looked more like huge dandelion ears. And both knew they looked silly because they needed only to look at each other for a mirror. They would spend hours some sunny days making daisy and dandelion jewellery, and they would arrange them all for their shop. And then one would be the shopkeeper and the other a variety of customers. The shop lady always had a very posh voice and a very grand bonnet fashioned from meadowsweet that made their pillows smell of it at night. Their father had called for them when it was time to join the other villagers and Nuala had jumped down from Kathleen's back, from where she had been reaching for the uppermost blackberries. As she did so the dress had caught on a briar, and they had presented themselves to their mother blackberry-stained and with a good dress ripped. She had given out to them something fierce that day but her cross mood had not lasted long. The harvest festival put a smile on all the faces in Ballinara.

With all her reminiscing, Kathleen had not noticed the sky quietly darkening and it was just as she reached the corner before the shop that the first few drops bounced off the warmth of the road. She hurriedly pulled up the hood of the pram and quickened her step, the memories snatched cruelly away. She scolded herself for not bringing a shawl. By the time she had reached the door to the little store with its welcoming tinkle of bell and promise of shelter, the heavens had truly opened. Brigid Callaghan, who was just about to leave with her basket of shopping, was peering out at the weather, asking Caroline whether she would mind putting the kettle on now that she was stuck here and no more customers would likely be arriving.

'I will so, Bríd,' Caroline said with a little wink to Kathleen as she removed Paddy's blanket and flapped off a small shower of droplets resting on the outermost filaments of the wool. Brigid would find anything a reason to stop and request a cup, and any 'news' she gleaned from Caroline, or by eavesdropping on customers as she supped in the back room, would be elaborately retold to the two waiting at home. Seeing Brigid Callaghan in her black wellington boots and black shawl, Kathleen recalled giving Tomás a clip round the ear one day for saying the Callaghan sisters, all of whom were spinsters, resembled the three witches he had learned about in school. She hid her smile and scolded herself for her own impertinence.

'How are Aggie and Moira?' Kathleen enquired.

'Oh, my sisters are grand. Not a bother on them.' Brigid had slinked over to coo at Paddy in the slightly misjudged and exaggerated way of a woman who has never really been around children. 'Cute as a button, isn't he? Looks like his da, wouldn't you say, Kathleen Steele?'

'He is. He's a good boy, aren't you, Paddy?' she replied. Paddy looked up at Kathleen dreamily.

'Patrick. A good strong Irish name.'

'Yes. That's right. We all take our names from Father's side of the family.'

'Ah, but names are given, Kathleen Steele, not taken. And a very important job it is, naming a child. Now my name, of course, reminds me that I am expected to be as holy and charitable as I can be, even though I may not have a lot myself, just like the good St Brigid.'

Caroline's head emerged from the door of the back room, which framed the perfect picture of a small parlour. Kathleen loved to sit in there and sup tea with her. It was one of the few places where she could easily put her worries aside. It was neat and orderly and always filled with light, even on a day such as this. There was nothing grand about it, but anyone who peeked in could see it was a happy home. 'One sugar or two now, Bríd? Sure, you think I'd remember after all these years.'

'One now, thank you. Only the one. The Lord does not advocate self-indulgence, Caroline Walsh.'

'You'll have a cup, won't you, Kathleen?' Caroline saw how wet her friend was. 'Jesus, you're soaked through! Let me get you a towel.'

'Ah, no. I'll be heading. I just came to see do you have any ribbon for the girls – to spruce an old dress up, like.'

'Have a look on my side, under the counter there. In the drawer with the wobbly knob . . . I must get Jim to look at that . . . I'd nearly forgotten what rain was. Oh, yeh can't go back out in this.'

'I thought maybe you might have an oddment, you know, a leftover in your sewing box? Only—'

'Kathleen, take as much as you need, love, put it on the slate if you must.'

Paddy was stirring and called at the ceiling like a little bird. She felt uncomfortable, squeezing by Brigid Callaghan, whose only favour would be the tea on offer in the back. But she wanted to get home before the rain worsened. It could be bad all afternoon, and the chores wouldn't do themselves.

'Thank you, Caroline. You're very good.'

'No, no, but you must come and bring that beautiful baby brother of yours in the back till I see how he's growing.'

'Really, Caroline, I must be going. A lot to do before tonight. Are you away up to Reilly's do?'

'I am, but . . .', and Caroline nodded and raised her eyebrows as if to say, Best not to mention it in front of present company in case the Callaghans aren't invited.

'Don't worry, we'll be there to see him off. Sure haven't I known Finbar since he was in nappies,' called Brigid from where she was now sitting in the largest and most comfortable chair that was usually reserved for Jim Walsh.

Kathleen went to choose the ribbon. There was no green, only blue or white or yellow. She wound a length of the yellow around two of her fingers and tucked in the end. Then she went in to say goodbye to Brigid.

'Kathleen, you and Paddy can't go out in that awful rain.'

''Tis grand, he'll like it. His first experience of it really.'

Caroline sighed and went to fetch a spare cot sheet which she then fashioned into a protective covering for the pram. Paddy squirmed and gave a few grumpy squawks. They fastened it on together with several wooden pegs. And, as Kathleen couldn't very well hold an umbrella, Caroline lent her a raincoat with a hood.

'But you bring that back to me tonight at Reilly's or I'll end up looking like you . . . a bit of vinegar through it, love, and you'll be stunning again.'

Kathleen looked down at herself and then at her reflection in the window and touched a hand to the frizz of hair haloing her. Her dress had gone see-through with the wet, and her cardigan clung to her every contour. She hoped that her friend could not tell, the way a mother often can.

'A sight for sore eyes you are, miss. Let's hope you don't meet a handsome rover on your way home.' They both giggled and embraced briefly, while Caroline whispered into her ear, 'Thanks for leaving me with oul' Boring Brigid!'

'It'll be your turn soon,' Brigid said with a nod towards Paddy.

Kathleen could feel her cheeks flush alarmingly. 'With God's blessing it will. Goodbye now.'

'You'll need a man first!'

'Don't be crude, Caroline,' Brigid tutted, and at that moment the door in the other room jangled and Joseph's voice called through. 'I'm just dropping in an order here from Dr Fitz . . .'

Caroline and Brigid guffawed at the timing and Kathleen tried to smile and hide her cheeks from them.

'Sent from the Lord in a shower of rain, what? He's not half bad, you know . . .' Caroline whispered to Kathleen as she passed by through to the shop. Kathleen followed her, conscious of the swell of her bust under the wet cotton.

Joseph grinned at Kathleen and gave her a less than surreptitious wink. 'How're you, Kathleen? Looking forward to seeing yeh up at Reilly's.'

'Joseph. How are you? Well, I hope . . . I must be running, lots to do, you know.' She joggled the pram around him and had a foot out the door. The coat Caroline had given her was acting as a second waterproof cover for Paddy.

'You can't possibly go out in this, it's lashing . . . at least put that plastic on, Kathleen!'

She had to get out.

'Sorry, Joseph. Yes, see ye all later.'

It was folly, of course, not to mention irresponsible, to think she could make it back up the two long hills without the two of them getting soaked through, but she could not remain in the shop any longer. She could not face the tedious inquisitions of Brigid Callaghan, in between her disapproving looks towards Joseph, and the mere fact of keeping something so huge a secret from Caroline, especially in Joseph's presence, made her guilt so strong that she had found it hard to breathe.

Sheltering in the porch of St Francis's, she unpegged a corner of Paddy's cover and peeked into his cocoon to find him sleeping and oblivious. Kathleen sat down and tried to imagine the face of her baby, of any baby other than Paddy, but she couldn't. He was so like his father, and Kathleen was so like their mother, and it dawned on her that her baby might be a boy, might resemble his father as Paddy did, and how women like Brigid would try to see Joseph's face in him. She could hear them now: 'Not a bit like his da, is he? . . . More like his grand-dad . . . Oh, but he has his grandfather's eyes . . .'

The gasp that preceded her tears echoed around the damp porch. The chill from the stone underneath her seeped into her body and she sat shivering there. She couldn't go back to Caroline's, and she couldn't go home. Closing her eyes, she thought maybe she should go inside and speak to Him, ask for His help, but surely He had forsaken her. And rightly so, she said to herself. She would sit here a while and try to empty her mind. She gently teased the raincoat from the pram and laid it about her knees.

'Is that you, Kathleen?' She could hear the voice of Father Nolan calling her out of her uncomfortable half-slumber, calling her to hear him. 'Kathleen? . . . Kathleen . . . come on now, child. 'Tisn't the weather for . . . for this. You'll be frozen now in those wet clothes. I'll see to this little man and I'll be back in a moment.' He took the handle of the pram and pushed it with difficulty up the stone steps and in through the door of his church.

How very odd it made him feel, to be momentarily assuming a role he was never destined for. And what a strange sight, a priest in his cassock, pushing a baby's pram. The child rhythmically jolted as the priest rolled the pram over the ancient slabs and then soundlessly, smoothly up the aisle, away from the draught of the door. Father Nolan installed him beneath the statue of the Virgin Mary cradling baby Jesus, who smiled eternally, despite His crown of thorns. He had never liked the statue. It wasn't till He was a condemned man that the crown of thorns was part of His story. But maybe He already knew, as a mere innocent infant, the course His life would take.

Father Nolan looked down upon the Steele baby who was still resting, his dreaming breaths audible in the echoing cavity of the church. Gazing at him, he had a fleeting feeling – he would have to pray for forgiveness later – of purposelessness; having no family, his spirit and ideas would go on living only among a handful of his diminutive congregation. He would tell that to Kathleen now, remind her of the good fortune of her home and family. Yes, he was glad he had a moment to formulate some sensible-sounding advice.

But when he opened the heavy door, he found the porch empty. There was a pile of wooden pegs strewn about, but no Kathleen. Seizing an umbrella, he quickly checked around the back but was met only by the disorderly rows of fallen-in gravestones. A mild panic rose in him – what would he do with the baby? What if it cried? He had tomorrow's sermon to finish, and his shirt to iron if he was going to make it up to Reilly's.

He closed the door and went back inside. His congregation never saw the church as it was at this moment, dark and cool without the candles. Nor did much light filter through the windows, so thick and dark were the clouds today. He had become used, over the summer, to the comforting rainbow of pattern that performed its slow dance across the interior on sunny days. He let out a long sigh.

'I'm in here, Father.' Kathleen's muffled voice spoke beside him. She was in the confession box.

Father Nolan instinctively stooped to light the candle in the bulbous red holder, checked that he had refastened his collar after dinner, and stepped inside. There was a pale light from his side, a blue-green, where the weak rays filtered through the bottom of the Mother Mary's dress. He waited for Kathleen to say the words, but she remained quiet. They listened to the silence together for a while. It was broken momentarily by an echoing gurgle from the baby.

'What is it, child?' There was no reply, but through the gloom and the grille he could see her shifting on the wooden stool. He could tell that she wanted desperately to speak. He needed to get on. This was not, after all, an allocated confession time, and he knew it could not be anything serious.

'Pull the curtain there if you like, and we can talk. You can tell me anything, child. God the Father will listen and He is always forgiving.'

'No!' Like a rubber ball, the syllable careered about them in the box and out among the rafters.

He waited. Outside, the rain thrummed on the plastic sheet underneath which his bicycle sheltered from the elements. It reminded him that the chain needed fixing – he would ask that new feller down at Diarmuid's to do that for him, and he would take the opportunity to let him know the times of confession. He had noticed him at Mass every now and again, standing awkwardly at the back, but he never seemed to catch him before or after. The priest let a small sigh escape unbidden. He hoped Kathleen had not noticed. She was such a sweet girl, and so good to her poor mother.

'Forgive me, Father, for I have sinned.'

'I am listening, my child.'

There was a deep pain there – the tone of an older woman behind her words. He would let her talk and would speak only when she had finished.

'I have committed a truly awful sin and I am truly, truly sorry ... I don't know what to do, Father, and I am asking you to help me. But I don't know how you can help me, and I know that the Good Lord cannot and indeed must not ... He could not forgive it, but I do not want Him to turn away from me ...'

'Calm down, child ...' If it were not for the metal grille separating them he would have reached out to her, overcome as he himself was by her emotion. He was not used to this level of sobbing. This needed a woman's touch.

The sudden noise of the door opening startled them both. Her sobbing softened slightly as she stifled it.

'Ah, that must be one of the Callaghans,' he whispered. 'She said one of them would come by to pick up my robe – I keep tearing them on my bicycle pedal – although I did not expect her to come in this weather, I must say. You'll be all right in here for a moment while I see to . . . errm . . . I always forget her name, 'tis terrible, isn't it? They're all the same person to me . . .' He laughed momentarily in a whisper and stood up. He took her silence as consent and, rather awkwardly, he got to his feet.

But it was not Brigid, nor either of her sisters. It was Kathleen's father. He had gone out looking for her when she had not returned to fix the children their snack. He had called in at the store only to be told by Caroline and Brigid that she had come and gone a good hour before. He had called at all the homes she could reasonably be visiting, which was not many as they did not tend to visit anyone these days.

So there was nowhere else they could be sheltering. At first he had been mystified but then it struck him. With a wild panic rising in him, he had turned the horse at Callaghan's Cross and clattered the cart back up to the church.

It was not the unattended Paddy by the statue that perturbed Pat Steele, nor the eerie light that hung fog-like before his eyes – it was the little red glow across the pews. She was there, confessing.

And it was without thought, or intake of breath, that he scrabbled noisily across and over the pews, calling to her, sending 'Kathleen's echoing about him. He had flung open both doors, with a force that caused a swirl of air to extinguish the candle, and stood between them, catching his breath and dripping dark patches onto the stone floor. After a silent moment, when he had gleaned from their faces that nothing of significance had yet been said, he staggered back a few steps, back along the path of muddy footprints that led from the door of the church to his daughter.

He sat down heavily on the long, cold, wooden bench and hid his face in his hands. This, he reflected, was the second occasion when he had spoken Kathleen's name aloud in a silent, listening church. She had been crying the first time, too, when he and Nora first gave the girls their names before God. Kathleen Theresa and Nuala Margaret. The memory and the cruel juxtaposition of the two events were so alarming to him that he barely noticed the priest saying softly that he would pop into the vestry and make a pot of tea. He touched them both briefly on the shoulder before he departed and, as if freed from a spell, the two looked at each other and stood up.

They did not speak, so much as correspond with nods and facial expressions of understanding and regret. They clasped hands and, as they walked around the back pew and up the aisle where they both knelt down in front of the altar to pray, Patrick Steele thought how small and soft and childlike Kathleen's hand felt in his. And she noticed how rough and clammy his was, and how glad she was that he had arrived at that moment. Asking for forgiveness through Father Nolan was not the way to do it – he was a human being, after all. Only the man Himself offered any chance of redemption.

The priest reappeared with a tray of tea just in time to see the little family heading out into the rain. It was darkening now, the villagers would all be donning their best garments for the evening's excitement. He set the tray down on the step where Kathleen and Patrick Steele had just been kneeling together and took his cup of black tea in his hands. He never took tea in any other room than his own or, very rarely, the vestry. It felt rather decadent. He walked over to peek through a clear section of the stained-glass window. They had safely set the pram into the cart and the child, who was now whimpering, was swaddled close to Kathleen, a large blue blanket wrapped about the two. Her eyes were pink and sore-looking, but she was smiling. Pat Steele seemed all right now, too. He could see them talking but he could not make out what they were saying. Maybe they would explain it to him later, at Reilly's.

Then he watched as Pat Steele jumped from the cart and approached the church again while his daughter and baby waited in the rain. The door opened, amplifying the rain, and Kathleen's father called through it, 'I'll return it later, Father. We need it . . . Sorry.' The priest jumped, teacup tinkling against saucer in his startled hand, and hoped he had not been seen to be spying on them. He watched from the doorway now, gave a little wave, and saw Kathleen and the child huddled under the clear plastic sheeting that had been covering his bicycle. He watched till they had gone from view – the image of the girl under the plastic, all blurred and patchwork-like, resembled a stained-glass window to him, a light-blue cloud passing through the thrashing grey of the land. He hoped that the poor girl was all right. She seemed to be, now that she was with her father. When he could see no more of them he fetched his bicycle in under the porch from the rain and undertook to say a quick prayer for them before a morsel of bread and cheese to keep him going. Then he would get ready for the evening ahead and wait to see if any villager with a covered cart would appear to offer him a lift up to Reilly's.

The atmosphere of anticipation had pervaded the doctor's house too. Gatherings were few and far between in their little slice of the world. Christmas tended to be a private, family affair, and an unattached doctor could feel very out of place at christenings or at Easter. People did not want to bother him with their physical complaints, but felt compelled to anyway, and then found they had nothing else to say to him. But Joseph's childlike excitement infected him with good spirits. He had come to enjoy his presence. How long ago it seemed when he was slightly wary of the wretched, hungry man he had taken in for a meal.

That evening, as they got ready, they might have looked like father and son if viewed from the street. Through the window, a passer-by might see the younger one fixing the collar of the older one as he sat shining his shoes, newspaper on his lap to keep his trousers neat. It was a job performed only by the doctor and the priest of Ballinara. The farmers' Sunday boots, if they were fortunate enough to have a second pair, were simply cleaned of mud. Or, at the bedroom window, one might see the older, more rotund one holding aloft a selection of shirts, neatly ironed by Moira Callaghan, and the slighter man choosing one based not on its whiteness or newness, or indeed its tailoring, but its size. Dr Fitzgerald had kept the clothes that he had worn as a younger man, in the conviction that he himself would one day take the advice he gave out to those patients who were partial to a drink or two and to Breda O'Brien's apple tart with cream.

Beyond the window, Joseph was preoccupied. He was determined to use the occasion to show them his true nature. He would be clean-shaven, he would be polite, even endearing – but not too talkative or opinionated. It was important to him to become part of this community, for it was where his heart now lay. It was his new life, his future. His old life seemed so long ago. Dr Fitz had told him when he first came to live with him that your family had to have lived here for at least two generations before you were considered a 'local' and that they, as well as Father Nolan, were just visitors, travellers passing through. Although they might play important roles, might influence, even change, the village, they would always be outsiders. Joseph, he said, was like him and like the priest in that way.

But Joseph had done a little more than the priest or the doctor to belong – he had found the most beautiful girl in the county and had claimed her for his own. And he had claimed a secret bit of their land, too: that space where he had vowed to sap himself of life, that had become his saving.

The contrast of the fresh, salty air outside and the sudden fuzz of warmth as they stepped inside brought an unsteady, sickly feeling to her. But it passed, and she smiled her hellos to those who caught her eye. Kathleen and her father were greeted by Mr Reilly, who took their coats and helped her father manoeuvre their mother in through the narrow doorway. They put her by the fire, near where Joseph sat engrossed in conversation with Finbar Reilly.

Reilly's kitchen was full of people. As well as the neighbours, Kathleen recognized many from nearby farms and those from Killnarnan who attended Father Nolan's Mass. The few unfamiliar faces looked so like Síle Reilly that she took them to be cousins from further afield, come to send Finbar off. She could hear one of them telling of the fine ceremony marking the erection of an electricity pole connecting up the outlying farms around the town of Killgorney.

'And yeh don't have to cart your batteries all the way into town to be charged any more, you just plug the radio in and away yeh go.'

'That's marvellous, Mickey, isn't it? Have they forgotten us altogether?'

Kathleen ushered the children through the kitchen and into the parlour where the other children were playing. Caroline Walsh was there, bent down, scolding the middle of her three boys for being too rough with his brother. 'Hiya, Caroline ... how're ye, boys? Don't ye all look smart?'

'Hmph, and long may it last.' Caroline stood up and, with a last threatening look at her boy Colm, she greeted her friend. 'Are you all right? You look awful flushed.'

'Oh, we were racing to get here – I'd not realized how long it would take to get everyone organized at this hour of the day.

And then, of course, Paddy needed changing at the last minute.'

'Typical!' Caroline said, laughing. ''Tis awful warm in here. But we should welcome it after the weather today.'

'Yes . . .' Kathleen replied, attempting to arrange her face in a neutral way, still embarrassed about the episode in the shop. 'I have your plastic here for you.'

'Thanks, love. Well, he'll be ready for his bedtime soon, won't he? Síle's a cot in the room there, but he'll be having to share it with Anne, of course. Oh, she's teething something terrible at the moment.' She then turned to the children, saying louder, 'So, you hear, ye little rascals, little Annie and Paddy'll be letting us know if there's any silly carryings-on going on in here, won't they? . . . and keep the noise down.'

Laura had appeared at Kathleen's side and was patting her, gently imploring, on the leg.

'What is it, love?'

'Do we have to stay in here, Kathleen?' She looked from Kathleen to Molly, who was already sitting on the floor under the sill with two boys from the playground. They were chatting with disdainful expressions as they gazed about at the smaller children at their games.

'You'll be grand, little Laura, won't you? You don't want to be in with us boring oul' things,' Caroline said as she moved a pair of candlesticks onto a shelf, out of arm's reach.

'But Miss Ahern hasn't seen my ribbon dress yet.'

''Tis all right, lovey, you can come in with us. You look just like an angel in that dress,' Kathleen said.

'She does too, and so do you, Kathleen. You're looking very

well tonight – better than earlier ... and drier! ... Oh, look, and Molly has some ribbon in her hair, I see. That's nice ...'

'No, not an angel, a flower fairy!' Laura gave a little twirl as if to demonstrate the difference. Nuala was almost close enough to touch for a moment, and then she vanished.

Kathleen smiled, 'Come on then, Flower Fairy. Let's go get you a drink.' She glanced at Molly – she looked slightly crestfallen and Kathleen saw that, actually, she would quite like to come in with the grown-ups and Laura and show off their matching dresses, but in front of the boys she felt stuck. Kathleen gave her a big smile over her shoulder and said, 'Don't forget I need you to help me with Mam in a few minutes.' Molly smiled a grown-up girl's smile and looked so very like her father that Kathleen's briefly lifted spirit sank again.

It kept happening. She would try to forget, to put it out of her mind by busying herself, or by conjuring Nuala, or by trying to imagine her life as Kathleen Foley. But this was worse than dwelling constantly on it: each time it hit her it was like the shock of plunging into the icy sea, or of a blind man who walks unexpectedly into something on a path he has always known to be clear. Yet she had felt a little absolved after praying with her father. The two of them had felt some of the weight of their secret lifted. She thought she had found a little peace within herself and with God, but she knew she was naive to hope this feeling would last.

Tomás and Brendan were enlisted in helping Finbar take a couple of horses into the stable. The doctor and Mr Reilly covered over Steele's cart as best they could and joined the other men in sharing a pipe while they discussed the crop news, the next market day and, of course, the effect of the day's long-awaited rain. Kathleen could hear one old feller telling the others loudly about a hole in the roof of his chicken coop: '. . . 'Twas only this evening I realized it. Sopping they were, wet feathers all over the feckin' place.'

'I'll come and help you fix it tomorrow, Nicky.'

'Not too early though, eh, Pat?'

The men laughed at this, at the promise of the good night that was ahead of them. 'Now, how about a little poitín, Neddy?' This was followed by several cheers and more merriment from the men, and numerous pairs of rolling eyes from the women gathered at the table, setting out the sandwiches, pies and tarts, cream and sugar. Kathleen and Caroline joined them and, watching Joseph trying to involve himself in conversation, she could sense his discomfort, his feeling of exclusion. Her heart warmed to him. He did not have a farming background, he did not know the history of the place, the age-old connections between families. When he caught her eye, she smiled and, excusing herself from the ladies, went along the hall to the little room used as the family's formal sitting room. They would assume she was going to the bathroom, which she would happily take the opportunity to do while she was here – it was a highlight for the children when they came to the Reillys', the indoor bathroom with bath and shower. It was by far the largest house in the area and the Reilleys seemed to add to it all the time – she had overheard stories between her parents in the past about a wealthy and aged aunt up in Dublin and about how, on market day, James Reilly spent more time chatting than haggling.

Kathleen opened the door to the sitting room. The parlour

had become, over the years, a room for the Reilly children to play in rather than a room for visitors – the armchairs were worn and there were chips in the wood panelling, which her own father had laid and occasionally came to replace and repaint. But in this room the armchairs were pristine and the cushions upon them were bought rather than home-made. She must have gone to Roche's in the city, or maybe they were a gift from the aunt. In the fireplace gleamed a beautiful set of fire irons, clearly not made locally.

The door opened and she dropped the cushion she was holding. He had given her a fright, even though she had fully expected him to follow her. She giggled, glancing about her with raised eyebrows, as if to say, 'Wow.'

'Kathleen ... I can't give you this. I could never afford such luxuries ... but I—'

She stopped him by embracing him and saying, 'I do not want anything but you. I need you, Joseph Foley. You don't know just how much I need you.'

He sighed a long, contented sigh and took her by the hand and led her to the window. Darkness was almost upon the land, but Kathleen could just make out their farm down the hill. How different the view was from just a little further up the hill, how much more she could see from here. The familiar view felt unfamiliar, as though she had been displaced. She could make out each square of their own land, the dairy and the hayloft. She could see her and Nuala's favourite climbing trees, spooky and alive-looking in the dull light. And what would her new home with Joseph be like? Where would it be? She dared not hope to stay near here – to be his wife was such a great mercy to her, she knew she dare not ask or wish for anything more. She caught him watching her reflection in the glass and she relaxed her brow, placing a smile at the corners of her eyes.

'What are your thoughts behind those beautiful eyes of yours, Kathleen Steele?'

'My thoughts?' She tried to brighten her face a little more, turning to look at him. 'No thoughts, Joe, except the one about how wonderful it will be to be Kathleen Foley.'

'Kathleen Foley,' he echoed, beaming. 'Yes, it does sound lovely, doesn't it?'

'Kathleen Foley.' They stood there awhile till she said, 'And what about what's behind your eyes? You do look so very sad sometimes . . . are you wishing you had not asked me, because I would understand—'

'No, no.' She had not seen him so handsome. 'You sweet, sweet girl. What a silly thing to say, my love. You know . . . I miss some of the fellers sometimes. It was . . . it's hard to forget, you know . . .' He trailed off. 'Besides, I thought it was you who was having doubts, and of course that would be understandable.'

'Joe . . . no, I am yours, and only yours, not just from our wedding day, but from this day, from the day you asked me. I'm sorry I may have seemed . . . a bit faraway, like . . . Have I? It's my mother, and Paddy, you know, I'm very tired sometimes . . . But why would you think that, Joseph?'

'I thought that was why you were gone to see Father Nolan. He told the Doc, you know. Please don't be mad at him, he was so concerned. I couldn't help but overhear them. Oh, my love, why were you so aggrieved? I thought it must be because you realized I had little to offer you, and . . . and, you know, how I was when I arrived here . . . and that you did not have the heart to end our engagement, being the sweet girl that you are. Maybe you didn't mean to say yes.'

There was a little bubble of fear that had been somewhere within her, near the baby in her stomach, that she now identified as the fear of someone knowing. It hadn't occurred to her consciously until this moment. But Father Nolan and now Joseph and Dr Fitz were aware of her unexplained outburst of emotion. Rumours spread like the measles here.

'Ah, Joseph, you're the sweet one. You will never know how much you offer me.' She leaned back, resting on Síle's polished sideboard. 'Really it was nothing. I was feeling a bit emotional is all and St Francis's seemed a good place to go; there's never a minute's quiet at home.'

'But Father Nolan said you were distraught. You'd tell me, my love, wouldn't you – you can tell me any of your troubles from now until we die. It makes me so sad to hear you have been hurting . . . I just want for you to be happy.'

'I am, Joseph Foley.'

'That you want to be with me makes me more happy than I can say.' Joseph wrapped his arm around her and swung her briefly in a waltzing movement. What would it be like to dance with him? She had not danced with any man, but surely that is what should come first. How did he not think her brazen to have lain with him before they had shared any other intimacy? His low chuckle in her ear and his features made quite handsome in the soft light gave Kathleen a sudden confidence and she chose to start the lie for him then.

'How lucky I am to have found you here in Ballinara.'

''Twas you that brought me here, but I didn't know it then. Only He did.'

'What? . . . Oh, Him up there? He's a good friend of yours now, is He?'

'Don't tease me, you. To think how I was before . . . You have a way of showing a man the right path in life.'

'Well, I don't know about that . . . But you know, Joe, you mustn't worry about my silly behaviour at St Francis's.' She found she had to moisten her throat by swallowing a couple of times before she said, 'You know, Caroline says that women can get all teary when certain changes start to happen to them, to their bodies, like . . .'

Kathleen waited till she was sure he knew what she was referring to and, despite the heat in her cheeks which she knew was visible, she carried on. 'And she says with all her little ones she'd be crying all the time for no reason at all.' Kathleen let out an awkward laugh but Joseph did not seem uncomfortable at all.

'Do you mean . . . when she was expecting?' Kathleen nodded. 'Yes, I've heard women can get very—' And he stopped abruptly. She saw his dawning comprehension and closed her eyes to shield herself from it. But a laugh crackled loudly about her and Joseph squeezed her tightly, scooping her up and swinging her round. 'Oh, Kathleen, do you think? . . . I mean to say, well . . . that's wonderful!'

'Well, no, it's just possible that I might be.'

Joseph's face was alight with glee and pride and all the other feelings Kathleen had seen before on men's faces when good news was broken. She again noted his beauty, but it was a strange and still unfamiliar beauty. One day, though, his image would be as familiar to her as her own, but the thought did not comfort her. He was talking quickly now and pacing the room, leaving on the rug boot-shaped imprints that faded almost as soon as they appeared.

'. . . not the ideal time, or situation, of course, but don't you worry about that. And I do not care . . . no, Kathleen, I am not ashamed that things haven't been done in the proper order, so we shall ignore any comments from Brigid and Fitz, and the older ones, but of course they do not need to know, we'll just bring the wedding forward, tell them of our love sooner . . . but you must rest more and not run around after the little ones so much . . . Ah, but anyone can see what a wonderful mother you already are, Kathleen . . . and for me to be a father! Well, I had never contemplated it, such a prospect!'

Kathleen had to sit. Relief overwhelmed her. He was not angry. He was elated. It was a dream. She felt at peace for the first time in three months, but she had thought of every scenario and so expressed to him clearly, as she had rehearsed, how she thought they should proceed.

'Now, Joe, love . . . it is only a possibility, but it would explain why I have been a little off-colour of late. But I think, so as not to upset my family – they've been through so much – that we should announce our engagement first. We'll say we've been seeing each other secretly, romantic like, and keep this to ourselves for the time being. 'Tis still very early days, after all. That is, if it's all right with you.'

'Of course, my dear. Of course. Anything you like. Oh, little Kathy . . .' And he pulled her to her feet again, knelt down and lifted the layers of her dress like a child unwrapping a delicious sweet. She watched his hands working through the material until he found a spot on her stomach where he deemed it appropriate to send a little warm kiss in through to his baby. The touch of his lips made the skin of her stomach quiver, transporting her back to the fateful day – she could see his huge, delicate hands caressing her, she could feel him against her again, and she quaked inside both with the memory of a new-found pleasure and with a profound disgust.

Joseph caught her as she wobbled slightly, going pale. 'Sorry, Joe, I don't feel well.'

'All right, girl, hold on . . . are y'all right? . . .' Joseph sat her down and fussed over her. 'There now, 'tis to be expected, what? Don't you worry, I'll be looking after you all the way.' The sensation passed and Kathleen felt the colour returning to her face and she painted a smile there for him.

They stayed in the room longer, they knew, than was appropriate – their absence would undoubtedly be noticed, but it would make their announcement an unspoken one, which was easier. The thrum of rain and the hum of voices were mesmeric. Time seemed stilled for a while. And then, slowly breaking the spell, these rhythms were interrupted by the notes of an accordion striking up. The volume of the voices dimmed and a bodhrán began its mellow rhythm as if in mockery of the rain, as though trying to out-beat it.

The two returned to the gathering and the music flooded their ears. It was a space of candlelight, warmth, whiskey breath upon smiling men's faces, and music that made all forget their labours and sorrows.

'You play the bodhrán too, don't you, Joseph?' The doctor had come away from his station at the table of food, still with a mouthful.

'Oh, poorly, Diarmuid, poorly,' Joseph replied. Kathleen looked at him and raised her eyebrows as if to say, 'You dark horse . . . I didn't know,' but also thinking to herself, How little I know of him.

'You'll give us a go, though.'

Joseph smiled.

'Go on, Joe, I think you should,' said Kathleen. 'I'm sure some of the older folk still feel they do not know you quite as well as they wish.'

'That's settled, then,' beamed the doctor with almost fatherly pride. And, as the reel came to a climactic end, Dr Fitzgerald ordered that they make a little room for their newest neighbour, Joseph Foley. 'Hand over your bodhrán there, Pádraig . . . that's it . . . there now.'

And Joseph was installed between Finbar on the box and Pádraig, who was now in possession of a tin whistle. Any initial shyness on Joseph's part disappeared as the men discussed something and laughed uproariously before beginning a lively jig that Kathleen had not heard before. The doctor had weaved his way back to Kathleen.

'He looks the part, doesn't he?'

'Oh, yes, just like one of us.'

'He admires you very much, I think, Kathleen. As do I . . .'

But Kathleen did not hear the last part as she had simultaneously excused herself. 'The girls brought their whistles too. I must call them in . . .'

As she stood in the doorway to the parlour she felt as though she were standing on a very thin line between two worlds – one which she had once been part of and one to which she must now belong. The children were playing, oblivious of and uninterested in the grown-ups next door. That had been her once. Her and Nuala. And it never mattered if they felt left out of a game at these get-togethers; they always had each other.

But the warmth and sense of inclusion she could derive from the world in the next room – the freedom of adulthood, the partnership offered by Joseph – was welcoming also. She must check on Paddy, and call in the girls. The bodhrán began to beat a new rhythm. He played well. The music had become louder, faster, and the warmth of the fire and all the people in the kitchen had followed her. She swayed, unsure suddenly why she was standing here watching the children, why she had left the kitchen.

There was dancing now – she could hear whoops and feet stamping out a set on the slate floor. Chairs were being scraped back to allow for more room. Kathleen thought how hot they must be, dancing in there. It was unbearable even here. The sound of the bodhrán, faster still, was hurting her ears. There were more whoops, this time from the children as a crack of lightning emblazoned the land outside. They all ran to the window to await the next one and listen out for thunder. The blurred image of the girls flashed before her eyes and she thought she saw Nuala for a moment in among them.

Slowly, Kathleen took a few steps backwards and turned towards the kitchen. Her feet and legs felt as though they no longer belonged to her. They felt light as air, but at the same time so heavy that it seemed near impossible to make them move. She thought vaguely that she ought to eat a bit of bread and cheese as there had been little time for food in her strange day. Maybe that would settle her.

The door to the kitchen was open and she could see the back of the doctor and Father Nolan tapping his feet and clapping in time to the music. The volume was unbearable to Kathleen now, and she just wanted to sit down. There was a loud rushing noise in her head, louder even than the music. Behind her the children shrieked again and the bodhrán continued to beat its urgent pulse. As she reached out to hold the door frame she could see sparks flying from the stone floor as a couple of the old men with their hobnail boots had taken centre stage. Her hands tingled, sweating. Everyone in the circle around them was clapping eagerly. Joseph's face blurred with her father's and they swirled before her. She felt her legs wobble and give way. She could hear her name being called in her father's voice, as if from very far away.

Patrick Steele had seen what had happened and had pushed past an indignant Callaghan sister to reach his daughter. He must have called her name aloud for the cheers and clapping transformed into a flurry of concerned gabble and gasps and cries of 'Oh, Lord! and 'Fetch some water!' from the ladies. And Joseph had lain down his borrowed instrument as gently as a man in a mild panic could.

'Pat, if you just move aside there, I can see to her.' Dr Fitzgerald spoke softly but firmly to Kathleen's father, who obeyed. He bent down to look at her. Her eyes were closed, her lips dry. 'She needs a bit of air and some . . . ah, water, well done, young Joseph.'

'Mrs Reilly says to use her room . . .'

Kathleen's father looked up at the man whose worried face loomed above them, the man she was going to marry, who would be a father to the child.

'No, I'll do it,' he said as Joseph bent down to lift her.

'I really . . . Please, sir, I'd like to—'

'I said, I'll carry her,' and he clutched his daughter and carried her out of the kitchen and through the parlour to a side bedroom. She looked at him briefly, like a child. She had left her hair out for the evening, save for two small braids in a band around her head, and it trickled soft and long and wild down the side of his arm. She was coming to as he laid her on the bed. He sat beside her and pulled away some strands of hair that had become stuck to her face.

Kathleen's eyes opened, blinking slowly. 'I'm sorry, I . . .'

Her father put a finger to his lips and looked into her fuzzy vision. 'Hush now, love. The doctor and your friend Joseph are here.'

There was a faint buzz of chatter from the kitchen and much loud whispering coming from the parlour, but there was no music, of course, and Kathleen knew there would be no more merriment until she had returned.

'Yes, take your time now, Kathleen, and just rest awhile there.' She turned her head to look at Dr Fitzgerald, who was holding her wrist between chubby thumb and fingers, looking into the air with a slight frown. Joseph was standing behind him.

'Hello,' she said to him, and then looked at her father. He looked away at an imagined something on the floor.

'You had a funny turn, Kathy', Joseph said. 'Are you feeling better now?' Pat Steele raised his eyebrows at the abbreviation of her name, which only he had ever used.

'Yes, I think I am.' She sat up a little, and admired yet another room in Síle Reilly's home. She lay upon a beautiful quilt, and beside the doctor was a dressing table with silver brush, mirror and powder set neatly laid out. Her father reached for a richly embroidered cushion from a chair and popped it behind her back.

'There now.'

'Thank you. I really do feel fine now, I don't know what came over me. How embarrassing.'

'Maybe 'tis the prospect of the handsome Fin Reilly leaving town,' Dr Fitzgerald joked.

Kathleen managed a small laugh. 'I really think it must be because I forgot to eat anything much today.' She could feel her father stiffen and glance at her.

'That may be so, Kathleen. But that should not affect a healthy young girl like you so.' The doctor looked slightly uncomfortable as he continued. 'Joseph said you got caught in that awful rain today ... that you got quite wet through.'

'Oh. Yes ...' Kathleen fidgeted and looked to her father for support. But he was again looking intently at the floor.

'Hmm ... But you do not have the signs of a chill.'

'Really, Dr Fitzgerald, I'm grand now, honestly. I'll rest here a moment or two longer – ye all go back in and I'll join you in a minute.'

'There were just a couple of other things I wanted to . . . to ask you, Kathleen.'

'All right so.'

'Maybe you'd like a private consultation?' he asked, looking at her father and Joseph.

'Oh, no, they're grand. Go on. As I say, I'm perfectly fine now,' and as if to illustrate the point she sat up further on the bed and set to fixing her hair.

'All right so . . . I hope you do not mind . . . I don't want to be presumptuous.' The doctor looked as though he were working through a complex problem in his mind, so intense were his features. 'I have to ask, young Kathleen, I'm sorry . . . as your doctor . . . is there any possibility that you might be . . . with child?'

Kathleen and her father both looked up at him sharply.

'Of course not. Don't be so ridiculous, man.' Her father stood up, a strong pink risen in his cheeks.

'As I said, I do apologize, Pat, but I have to ask certain things, especially considering the evidence.'

'Evidence? What on earth are you getting at, man?'

'Calm down, Da . . .'

'I mean, it is very common for women in the earlier stages to suffer from fainting episodes, especially if she does not know she is expecting, and is not keeping an eye to her food and her rest . . . And there are the emotional imbalances – I hope you won't mind Father Nolan confiding in me, Kathleen dear – and the more physical signs, of course . . .'

'Physical signs?'

'Yes. Does she not look a little pallid to you, heavier around the eyes perhaps, a little heavier in general, and – I hope you do not mind me saying so, dear – more . . . well, womanly . . .'

'Good God, man. I don't know . . . I don't . . . I don't look at my children in such a way!'

'What? Calm down, man . . .'

'Da! Really . . . what are you saying? I think I will allow Dr Fitzgerald to examine me alone now. And it will be known before long anyway, won't it, Joe? I know things haven't been done in the proper way . . . but Joe and I . . . people need not know.' She smiled and Joseph stepped around his mentor as she held her hand to him. He took it, sitting beside her, touching her hair briefly.

'Mr Steele, please do not be angry with me. It would not be such a terrible way to begin our lifelong acquaintance. You see, I intended to marry your beautiful daughter before this happy event occurred. And now that it seems certain, I will do all in my power to provide a home, and love, for Kathleen and for all the children we may have.'

Kathleen thought there was going to be another outburst from her father but he merely nodded, saying gruffly, 'You have my blessing.' Then he rose and tramped out of the room.

The doctor had politely busied himself by taking various implements out of his bag.

'Well, what a surprise, Kathleen. And Joseph. But you speak as if you already know for sure?'

'I've had my suspicions, Doctor.'

'Is everything all right, Diarmuid?'

'I'm sure it's all grand, Joseph. Why don't you go get a bit of something for Kathleen.'

Joseph leaned in to kiss her forehead. 'I'll fix you a plate of something nice – if Caroline hasn't done it already.' And then he left Kathleen and Dr Fitzgerald alone for the examination.

'Just pull up that quilt there, Kathleen, over your legs, that's it. I'll need to . . . need you to lift your dress up there to have a listen, but I doubt very much we'll hear a thing yet.'

Kathleen did as she was told and watched as he placed the little trumpet-shaped stethoscope on her stomach. She noticed that his hair was thinning as he breathed heavily on her skin and wondered how old he was and why it was that he had not found himself a wife. She had listened to Laura and Molly's heartbeats through the wall of her mother's stomach and remembered how loud and fast they were. She felt at ease for the first time since she had found out, and a little excited. She was finally getting some proper advice. And things with Joseph were coming together. She tried not to think of it as deceit, and although she knew it was, he was as happy as could be, and surely would prefer not to know the truth.

The doctor raised his head and Kathleen's heart sank as she saw his frown.

'What's wrong?'

'No, no, nothing's wrong. It's just . . .' He bent his ear down again for a few moments. 'I can hear a heartbeat and it's very strong, is all.'

'Well, it is a Steele baby after all,' she said, grimacing inwardly.

'Yes, you were all big babies . . .'

He moved the stethoscope around on her stomach. Kathleen

could hear some music starting up again – they must have persuaded them that she was fine.

'Hmm ...'

'What is it?'

He listened for a while longer and then popped the stethoscope back inside his bag. With a tentative smile he told her, 'Let's hope they'll be little angels, like you and your dear sister Nuala were, God bless her soul.'

It took Kathleen a moment to understand what he was saying to her. And when she realized, her eyes filled with a gasp and she did not know whether the immense sensation that washed over her was joy or fear.

'I ... two heartbeats?'

'Two heartbeats, Kathleen. I'm almost certain of it. It runs in the family, but ...'

'Two heartbeats. Twins ... thank the Lord I'm sitting down or I think I'd have fainted again.'

Dr Fitzgerald did not share her wonder. He said simply, 'Now, Kathleen, I'll want you to come and see me on Tuesday, and make sure you eat lots and drink lots ... you might not feel like it ... although ...'

'Oh, it's all right, I'm ...'

'... past that point, I know. I would say you're about three months on, although we'll know better on Tuesday after a proper consultation. Have you been sick at all?'

'Yes, Doctor. But ... as you said, that has passed now.'

'Well, you may feel unwell again, so keep your fluids up ... not tea so much now, but water. Plenty of water, and milk of course.'

Kathleen began to feel perplexed again. He paused a moment and gazed at her with a troubled frown. But she stood up, preparing herself to rejoin the celebrations.

'. . . Dr Fitzgerald? . . . I would appreciate it if you were not to mention it to anyone . . . and I'd like to tell Joseph about the heartbeats and . . . the date and . . . you know how people talk. I wouldn't want to upset . . . well, it is delicate, not the ideal timing, like.'

'I do, Kathleen, I do. Whatever we discuss is in my strictest confidence.'

'Thank you, Doctor.'

'And Kathleen,' he said as he reached for the doorknob, 'I know you'll make a wonderful, wonderful mother.'

Kathleen thought she saw a slight regret or sadness in his face before he turned around and left her alone. But her thoughts soon returned to herself, standing now in front of Síle's ornate mirror. She smoothed her dress and borrowed a comb from the dresser to settle her hair.

She examined herself. The angles on her face were softer, and her hips and her arms were more rounded. The freckles sprinkled on her nose and cheekbones were effervescent with the rosiness in her cheeks. How silly she felt, but she would not let that be known. She would compose herself and then go and sit with Joseph and chat a little and observe, and let the women make a fuss of her – to attempt to stop them from doing so would be taken as an insult. She would hold his hand and return his smiles as a sweetheart does. And everyone would know they were to be engaged soon – they would be the talk of the village.

But she would not let them think she was ashamed. It was a relief that the story was as she wanted it to be.

She took one last look at her ever-changing self and saw that two of the four buttons on her neckline were still undone after Dr Fitzgerald's examination. Rather than buttoning them up and making haste, Kathleen unbuttoned the last two, relieving her chest of a tightness she had not noticed before when wearing the dress.

She sighed, looking at what little remained of her sister in her face, touching her fingertips to the mirror, having caught a glimpse there in her smile. The door creaked open and Kathleen's hands flew to her chest.

'Jesus, Mary and Joseph – Joseph!' Kathleen's shock startled him, and they laughed in unison. 'Sorry, Joe. Terrible language. Forgive me . . . You just gave me such a fright . . . I was in my own little world there . . .'

He stepped towards her and helped her fasten the dress. 'You'll say, and do, whatever you desire when you are my wife . . . looks like we'll be needing some new clothes for you, 'tis a bit tight. Isn't that uncomfortable for you?'

'No, no, I think I'll just borrow this shawl to cover up a little. I feel a bit exposed now.'

'Do, do . . . but are you all right to come now? The Father has his eye on your plate of food.' Joseph daubed softly at a couple of leftover beads of glistening sweat on her brow. 'You know, I've had a thought on a name already . . .'

'Whoa there, mister. Let's just get used to the idea of it first.'

'Well,' Joseph swept his arm towards the window, and, as

though he and God Himself had planned the timing, a low rumble of thunder sounded. 'Mug Ruith.'

'Mug Ruith?'

Joseph could see her furrowed face trawling through memories of legends she'd learned at school or through stories from old men around fires.

'You know . . . the ancient god of storms – after tonight, what do you think?' He chuckled, turning her mouth upwards gently at the corners with warm fingers. 'Only messing with you, Kathleen.'

'Oh, I remember . . . didn't he have a daughter – a witch, wasn't it?'

'No, no, not a witch. A sorceress.'

'Well, we might be needing her name, too.' She took his arms and placed one on either side of her stomach.

'Of course . . . it could be a girl. I had just imagined a boy. And what a beauty she would be – like her mother.'

'I mean . . . we might be needing both names.'

Kathleen was a contented observer as she sat by a window looking on at the dancing, enjoying food that was all the more delicious for having been made by somebody else. She had insisted on staying, despite Joseph's protestations. She felt fine and did not want to cause any more disruption to the celebrations. While the other guests sat down to rest their legs and quench their thirst, Finbar Reilly's father began quietly in a corner to sing in Irish, a song so sweet in its melancholy that even the children in the adjoining room hushed to hear it: '. . . ag dul thar sáile, agus deora a mháthair ag tuitin ar an dtalamh.' In a strange, converse Last Supper she had the Callaghans on her left eating cake with Caroline and Síle beside them, and to her right Joseph and the doctor, Brendan, Tomás and her mother, Finbar and his little brother, all sitting with half-empty plates, heads bowed to them as if in prayer. He sang of the hope that lies across the ocean, of the space in the family that is left when a young man moves on, '. . . onto a ship, across the sea, his mother's tears falling on the ground, waving him for ever goodbye . . .' He had sung his song all the while with eyes shut and, as he opened them to find the eyes of his grown son, there was a quiet in the room.

'Ah, Da, you know I'll always come and visit ye. All of ye.' Mrs Reilly stood and busied herself with slicing yet another tart at the table, even though everyone was full. Her tears dripped little circles onto the dusting of sugar. She knew of no man who had left for America and had ever returned.

'How about you, Joseph Foley, do you have a song for us?' someone called to him. 'Do you sing as well as you play the bodhrán?'

'Oh, now, now . . . I wouldn't want to upset your ears, lads.'

The men laughed, and Caroline's husband urged, 'Ah, go on, you will.'

'Well, I don't have a song, but I do have a story. An old, old story fit only for a night such as this.' He glanced over to Kathleen.

There was a shuffling and a couple of giggles coming from the doorway. Molly spoke for the children, 'Can we listen too?'

'Ye can, o' course,' said Síle. 'Brendan, throw over a couple of cushions there for the little ones, will yeh?'

'Well now,' Joseph began when the children were all gathered in a half-circle around the fire or on relatives' laps. Laura yawned and laid her head against her father's leg. 'As I said, this is a very old story. From a time long before that of your grandparents, or their grandparents.'

Kathleen sat up, caught by his change of tone. 'And longer back than even Ned's grandparents,' he said with a wink towards the oldest man in the room. The children gasped.

'Ah, Jaysis, Neddy ... it must be one from the Bible so!' someone called out and everyone roared. The old feller Ned smiled a toothless, shut-eyed smile and raised his glass of poitín in acknowledgement of the joke.

''Tis a story about a god – not like our God now, not like *the* God – but a magical, blind god, called Mug Ruith, who could grow as big as St Francis's church, who was stronger than a herd of bulls all charging at once, and more powerful than anything you could imagine.' Kathleen noted the disapproving looks that invariably emanated from the Callaghan sisters at any story other than a Bible story, and settled back in her chair, closing her eyes. The warmth of Molly leaning against her was comforting. Hearing the gentleness and the animation in Joseph's voice, she imagined him telling the story to their own children.

'Well now, he was not an angry god but, at his choosing, he could summon up all the power of the skies and cause the most great and fearsome thunderstorms you could ever imagine. If you were scared by the lightning tonight, well, imagine Mug Ruith's lightning – it would be like tonight but tenfold, all over Cork and Kerry, with thunder crashing as loud as a wave is to a little tiny sand creature, or like a cannon going off right by your ear.

'Now, of course, the people of Cork and Kerry were getting fed up with all the rain and the thunder and lightning, especially as they never had any warning of when Mug Ruith would strike again. Sure, their homes were damaged – not as sturdy as ours are today, you see – their cattle were killed, and other animals – horses, cats, chickens – all frightened to death. And Mug Ruith began to realize that there must be other places to go and annoy people who really deserved the fury of his storms – might teach some naughty people a lesson, see?

'Well now, he had an idea ... and it was a very good idea. He ordered his servants to construct the most wonderful and marvellous thing that would transport him from one place to another so he could play with the power of his storm-making and – best of all – practise turning the baddies into stone!'

'How'd he do that?' asked one of the enthralled children. 'Did he get a tractor?'

'No, no ... something much more amazing than a tractor – a flying machine. It was the most beautiful chariot, made of silver and gold and studded with jewels and pulled by magical oxen and it could fly ten times around the earth before you could say "Ballinara" ... And Mug Ruith rode about in the skies for a year with his beautiful daughter, who was herself a powerful sorceress, because he couldn't bear to be without her ... And some say it is Mug Ruith's fury still on a really stormy night like this.'

'Wow, that was great, Mr Foley!'

'Yeah, does he still exist – do yeh think that was him tonight?'

Brendan tickled Molly to try and scare her, and Caroline's little one whimpered.

'But how could he do all that stuff if he was blind?' asked little Johnny O'Brien.

'You don't need your eyes to see what's happening around you, silly,' Tomás said to the little boy. Kathleen looked and saw that he was looking straight at their father. A momentary horror rushed through her. She sat up and studied her brother's face. But it was only fear causing her imagination to run away with itself. Sure, he was too young to understand anyway.

'Ah, now, children. 'Tis only a story,' proffered the priest with a raised eyebrow, looking at Joseph.

'Course it is. Just a silly oul' fable . . .' Joseph looked uncomfortable, as though he had given the wrong answer in school. Kathleen stood up and reached for Laura and Molly's tin whistles. 'Maybe you girls would like to give us a go.' She knew that Laura loathed performing. She would go red and breathless with the nerves, but they were so sweet when they were playing a little jig or air together.

'All right so,' said Molly. 'But only if Tomás does one too.'

'Ah, now, Moll,' began their father.

'No, it's all right, Father. I'm sure Mammy would like to hear us all play, wouldn't you, Mam?'

Their father opened his mouth and drew in a breath to speak, but the ripple of furtive looks about the room halted him. Instead he said, 'Go on, son. That would be nice. Bren, pass over your bodhrán there.'

'She can hear, you know,' Tomás said quietly, looking intently at his father. Dr Fitz took the last long sip of his whiskey and

Joseph thought he saw his mentor shaking his head slightly. There was a sadness to his features that made Joseph see that his care for Kathleen's family went beyond merely a doctor's concern. Such was the way of this place. And Joseph thought himself fortunate to be part of this family, this community, to be putting down roots for his children, who last week were not even in his thoughts. He had grown into the man he knew he wanted to be; he had a purpose, finally.

He turned to the fire and watched the flames dance in time with the air being played, and tried to imagine two childlike Kathleens performing such a tune in their matching party frocks in years gone by. He thought of how wretched he had once felt and how surprising and healing life itself can be if one just lives it. And he knew that the only thing that would make him feel wretched like that again would be if something happened that caused Kathleen or their children to be taken from him. He would write to his father, inviting him to the wedding and telling him the good news. Then he sought Kathleen out and they shared a secret smile.

The old man Ned called for Kathleen's father to sing his song, 'Nora'. He would always be asked to sing it – to make her blush when she was well, and since then as a kind of lament. There was a pure and soft resonance to his voice that instantly hushed a room, and immediately there was a ripple of 'Yes, do,' 'Ah, go on, you will . . .' He looked at his daughter and Joseph noticed that she shook her head, ever so slightly.

'Ah, now, listen . . . I've not sung that one in a while now.'

'Ah, do, Pat.'

Tomás stood up suddenly and said, 'Well, if you won't, I will – she wants her song to be sung, don't you, Mam?'

'Tomás!' Kathleen was shocked, and a little embarrassed, at this outburst, and besides, Tomás had never sung at a get-together at all. Discomfort rippled around the room.

'No, no, Kathy. Let him sing it. I don't have it in me any more.'

'Go on, Tom,' Caroline interjected. 'We'd all love to hear you sing.'

It was in her dreams that night, goading, haunting her: '. . . our hopes they never have come true, our dreams were never to be, since I first said I loved only you, Nora, and you said you loved only me . . .'

THREE

The days grew shorter and the evening air cooler, and the routines of farmer, doctor and schoolchild changed. The long, hot summer was over. As he worked away at the new fencing, the young boy pondered his future. With each twist and tightening of wire Tomás considered his heart's point of view, then his head's. Would he follow Finbar to America, or go to London as he and Brendan had always planned; or would he do what was expected of him as the only boy in the family: inherit the farm and keep it in the Steele name. The lure of London, its people and its energy, stirred his imagination. He had always been afraid of the longing he would feel for home, how he would miss his mother, the smell of the hay, Waggy yapping at his heels all the way down to the strand. There would be no strand, no sea, he knew, but there would be life, freedom.

But he had also been thinking about another path in life, one that had come to him only recently while observing Father Nolan. To be married would never be an option, for he had seen what that meant, had borne witness to what would be expected of him, and it repelled him. He could not do such a thing to a person. Father Nolan seemed to have the best life of all in Ballinara. He spent most of his time in his own company, he could read whenever he liked, and he could help and guide people in their lives.

Tomás knew his father was watching him from above in the field. He would be frowning down at him, wondering why the little interaction that had once existed between father and son was now confined to no more than grunted replies to requests and orders. There was no partnership. He would be disappointed, Tomás knew. Disappointed that his son's love for the land, the way of life – a love that made the daily struggle just about bearable – had gone, not to mention baffled by the sudden disappearance of respect.

He knew too that soon Joseph Foley would be along to sit in his odd way to watch Kathleen about her chores – the clothes, or the hens, or the vegetable patch. But none of them could see Tomás noticing them, watching them. They thought him timid, studious. They would not know that he had identified particular times in the day when the family would be busy and he could slip into the cool of the kitchen, remove the too-tight working boots and sit supping a cup of tea by his mother. They could not know how his attentiveness worked its magic as the days unfolded about her.

He had taken up the role of combing her hair, and he checked that her buttons were done up correctly, that both slippers were on properly. Sometimes he noted that a shawl she was wearing was too heavy, or too light, or did not go with the colour of her cheeks on a particular day, and he would change it. He would sit and read aloud by her, little snippets here and there, his own books mainly, but the Bible sometimes, too, which allowed him to think more deeply on the words written there. And the more he sat with her, the more he saw how little the others did. Laura rubbed cream into her hands or kissed her cheek occasionally but was afraid to climb onto her lap any more. Molly would run straight past, oblivious to her, or shout a 'Hi, Mammy!' at her when Kathleen reminded her. Kathleen attended to her, nurse-like, not looking in her eyes or talking to her, and Paddy was never handed to her any more. Where once they were hushed, there now seemed to be something worse, thought Tomás. It was as though she was not there. Life carried on around her. She was less present for Kathleen than Nuala was.

His father would occasionally say, 'Don't forget to kiss your mother goodnight, Molly,' or 'Did you give her her wash yet?' to Kathleen. Nothing was directed at her. To her own husband, she was a set of tasks to be completed, a thing to be attended to. He did not look at her, at her face, any more. Sometimes he stopped by her chair and Tomás willed him to reach out and touch her, or to speak just one husbandly word, but in a sigh's time, he would move on.

And so it was Tomás who saw the first tear one day. The house was quiet, with only the echoes far off of Molly and Laura and the dog intruding on the quietness. He knew they were at the bottom of the boreen, in the field opposite the cattle. They had taken to playing a specific game there after dinner that seemed to involve poor Waggy being a baby. A human baby! He had shaken his head at the notion of it. How long ago it seemed when he and Brendan used to play imaginative games like that, Cowboys and Indians, kings and knights – that had been their favourite, especially as they were sometimes allowed on the real horses up at Reilly's for their games. He felt a pang of loss for those days.

He had been sitting on the windowsill reading from *Huckleberry Finn*, which he had procured from school before the summer break. He was sitting in such a way as to leave her view of the haggard clear but also to keep one eye and ear out for visitors such as Kathleen's Foley man, in case they caught him reading aloud, but then something about his mother distracted him. He paused and looked over at her. At first he thought it was a trick of the light. He hopped down off the sill and knelt before her. There was a shimmering trail that began at the corner of her mouth and ended under her eye. But of course, he had said to himself, if it was really a tear, its course would be the reverse of his observation. He looked at her cheek for a few moments to see if there were any further changes. He even said 'Mam . . .?' but there was no response.

Slowly and with a slightly quavering hand, Tomás placed one finger softly against the trace. Her skin was as cool and smooth as always. He held his finger there and a tear came to his own eye as he felt the sudden need to lay his head upon her knee and feel her arms about him. And when he took his finger away it was moist.

He knelt back, sitting on his heels, abandoning the book. And he watched as tears slowly came rolling down his mother's face. No muscle moved there; she barely blinked. She was otherwise completely still. She must know. He eased his left hand under her own and stayed that way with her until long after his knees on the stone floor had become white numb, until he knew it had stopped. He talked to her of things softly, of their father and Kathleen, trying to banish the image of them behaving like that, like the pigs. She did not respond, but he knew she could hear him.

The next time it happened it was she who squeezed his hand. A secret language was beginning between them. She was beginning to thaw. For a short, elated moment, Tomás wondered if he was Jesus, come again, but then he realized he was witnessing the miracle, not performing it. He urged her daily to speak back to him, to take a walk with him, but he could see it was to be a slow process. He brought her news and gossip from his outings and told her of his confusion about his future. He confided that he did not want to leave her, especially now that he knew she was coming back to them, but he could not stay on the same land as his father. When he spoke of his own anger, sadness or fear, she would squeeze his hand and look in his eye, and that to Tomás was magical.

Some days he sat and watched, waiting for what seemed an age, and there would be nothing. On others it was like a door opening, a sudden glow of light and, not knowing how long it would last, Tomás would encourage her to move around with him, talk to him, even feed herself. She seemed to know when they were alone, for she did not move a muscle when his father or sisters were there. It was in those quiet times, when it was just the two of them, that she began to come back.

*

A soft wind gently lifted some leaves up off the ground, and down. Some it turned in slow, graceful circles before dropping them, as though trying to find its perfect partner for a dance. The lower branches of the willow in the field above waved sadly at her where she stood in the kitchen window. She had been standing there some time, looking, and had forgotten what had brought her to the spot to begin with. If she thought very hard she could almost see Nuala. It occurred to her that this must be how her mother felt to begin with, how mesmeric it was just gazing out at a view you have always known, at a view that was one day transformed into something horrific. Kathleen used to wonder how it must have been for her poor sister – was she scared as she fell from the trailer, so high up for a small girl? Did the descent happen in slow motion or was it so fast she did not even notice what was happening? Did she experience that sudden lurch in her heart that one gets when losing one's balance, and then blackness – or was it the whiteness of heaven? Could she know that a few fields away, Kathleen had cried out at the awful feeling that had swept through her own body? And when Nuala began ceasing to feel did she know that Kathleen would carry on feeling her pain for ever, and that a mother's cry of shock and fear and then the harrowing cries of grief circled still around the four corners of their land, and echoed further still to touch those who knew them?

That day, Kathleen had followed the sound of the mother who bore them both. She ran through the long corn and across the pungent cattle field with a searing pain in her head, and found herself in the haggard, lying on the ground, legs at an unnatural angle. Nuala was lying with her head turned to the left, which was wrong to Kathleen. She always slept with her head to the right, looking at her sister. She was lying in Kathleen's position, and for the first time Kathleen could see why their mother was always told how beautiful they were. She was – and so peaceful-looking, her mouth slightly open as though about to kiss her goodnight. Kathleen had reached to fix her leg – it looked so uncomfortable at that unnatural angle.

'Get off of her!' her mother had yelled. 'Get away, you!' Get away, you. The sentence had wormed its way into her brain and popped up unexpectedly, repeating itself to her over and over for years.

Her head had hurt so much and she was confused. Why wouldn't Nuala open her eyes? Could she not hear their mother's cries? Her father had called out and galloped off on Tom-Boy to get the doctor. It had been a warm day, but Kathleen had felt a sudden chill. No one seemed to notice – why had no one gone in to get Nuala a cardigan? She didn't want to leave her so she removed her own and placed it over her sister's bare arm and neck.

Neighbours came; men, including a younger Mr Reilly, ushering their mother away. No one seemed to see Kathleen. It was hard to control the shivering now, but this was not normal shivering. Even on the coldest day down at the strand it was mainly her arms and legs, and sometimes her chin or teeth chattering. But this was a kind of quiet, violent shaking that seemed to emanate from within her spine, taking over her whole body. She had lain down next to Nuala and placed an arm over her. She shook so badly that Nuala shook also where their bodies

touched – the crooked leg, the shoulder, which was now growing cold, gently shuddering.

From the window, Kathleen could see the image of the two
of them; how heartbreaking it must have been for the men who
found them so. As they approached, Kathleen had opened her
eyes and eventually allowed them to extract her. Her hair was wet,
and the side of her face. And the shoulder strap of her matching
yellow dress. Her father had carried her towards the house, where
they could see Breda O'Brien waiting in the doorway, Tomás
wrapped around one leg and the little girls wrestling against the
unfamiliar body in arms unused to handling two children at once.
Her shivering had begun to subside in her father's arms. She had
looked down at her shoulder, about to wipe it dry. But the strap
was no longer yellow. She touched the purplish, wet material,
frowning. Her finger came away damp and dark, dark pink. She
heard herself gasp. She could not stop herself touching her face
which was covered in the stuff from where her head had lain
against Nuala's. Her scream haunted all her dreams for the next
few nights and the feeling of being constrained by her father's
strong arms as she writhed and fought to get back to her sister,
herself, her love, woke her continually from fretful sleep.

Kathleen's cheeks were wet now as she stood, but wet this
time with tears for Nuala. She reached a hand up and imagined
her sister's blood there again. It did not revolt her, or make her
queasy – even at the time, she had not let them wash it out of
her hair. In the end the doctor had had to give her a calming
solution while Mrs O'Brien brushed the dried blood out onto
newspaper on the floor and then bathed her as if she were a
much younger child, singing lullabies at her.

The kettle began to whistle on the range behind Kathleen, plummeting her back to the present. Her father stood in the doorway.

''Tis all right. I have it. What are you making?'

'I ...' Her voice was thick and woollen. 'Em ... I was just going to do his bottles.'

'Right. Little man ... always hungry what.'

Kathleen looked round and smiled, turning her back on the haggard. Not a foot away her mother sat in her usual position, but her eyes were closed.

'Your mother looks peaceful when she sleeps.' He spoke softly, though the noise of the kettle had not roused her.

'She does. I'll take her out for some air when I have the bottles done.'

'No, no. You'll not be doing any such a thing. Not now that ... not in your ...'

'True. 'Tis best not overdo it, I suppose.'

Kathleen could not bear another silence to hang in the air above them so she stepped away from the window and went about finishing the dusting, having suddenly become aware again of the damp cloth in her hand. The light that she had been blocking illuminated her mother's face. Kathleen turned away, not wanting her father to think she was studying how old-looking she had become, how frail. The kisses she used to leave upon her cheek or forehead or hands were all but forgotten now. Time, and the way of things, Kathleen supposed. Rushing here, running there. It was all she could do to help bathe and dress her.

'Oh, I wanted to say . . . did you notice she's not been taking her food too well? Maybe we should call for Dr Fitz.'

'Is that so?' He was on his way back out again, obviously uncomfortable also. 'Well, all right, I'll send Tom down later.'

'Grand.'

'Grand . . . or you could mention it to him when you next see him.'

Kathleen rubbed hard with the cloth at an invisible stain on the tabletop.

'I mean, you are seeing him regular, like? And eating well . . .'

'Da . . .'

'I know. Sorry.' Her father sighed and looked purposefully for his pipe in his pocket. 'I know. Joseph will be a wonderful father. I wanted to say that. And you . . . you'll be a wonderful mammy.'

'Da . . . please leave me be now.'

'No. If you stop me speaking of it, Kathleen, I might never speak again, and then what would the girls do?' He smiled grimly, with a slight nod towards his wife. 'And they'll be needing reassuring from you of your visiting a least once a week.'

'It's not far. Joseph says it's just outside Duncarrig. Once every week or so, that's my hope. And when they're older, sure they can come down. Joseph insists on it.'

'He's a good man, Kathleen. A better man than me.'

'And me.' It was Kathleen's turn to smile awkwardly, and they both gave a little sad laugh.

'Well, anyway, as there's no knowing when we'll . . . be alone again, I'll say now, for the last time, I'm . . .'

'I know. So am I.'

The sound of Paddy whimpering filtered through the wall, echoing in the chimney.

'Blast it. I'm going to have to get used to timing things properly before long.' She stood up and hurriedly went and put the boiled water into a large saucepan, immersing the bottles.

'I'll go to him. You get on – don't burn yourself.'

'I thought . . .'

'Ah. Yes. Right. I'll leave you to it so. That'll be a hard good-bye, Kathleen.'

Again she said, 'You don't have to. He can stay here with you and Mam . . .'

''Tis for the best. You're his mammy now.' And he left, closing the outside door on the sound of the little boy's tears and her small gasps as the hot water splashed her hurrying hands, both echoing in the silence from his wife. And Kathleen thought, If you know it is the right thing it is easy to close a door, even when the pain is so severe you think it might overwhelm body and soul.

The warmth was leaving the earth underfoot. Soon the rain would come more frequently and steadily and they would be squeezing back into the stiff black shoes that were too small even last winter after a barefoot summer. But he would not complain. He had begun to know he was growing up, now that he knew grown-ups to be fallible, understood that they too needed guidance. He felt special that it was he whom his mother responded to – another secret that gave him a kind of power. He was sure he caught the glimmer of a smile, like a memory, as he kissed her good morning. He would not go to Father

Nolan, for it was not his sin, and he was almost certain you could not ask forgiveness on another's behalf. He had thought of his Miss Ahern, but knew he would feel ashamed and a teacher would probably have to tell someone; he had thought of a policeman, but knew it was unlikely that he would be believed, and besides, he would have to walk all the way into Killnarnan for that. To tell Joseph would be pointless, as he was innocent, a victim, and everyone would know then that Tomás had blabbed. And he had, of course, thought of confronting the man himself. Each time he looked at his father's face he saw a different man now from the one who was there through his upbringing. A stranger. A sinner. And so, each day his resolve grew to love and care for his mother till she was old, whether by making the farm his, or by following in Father Nolan's footsteps. And, above all, he resolved to be a good man, and nothing at all like his father.

'Why's Tom being all funny at the moment?' The two girls had skipped hand in hand on the way down the boreen, but were now walking back up to the house, either side of the thick grassy strip up the middle, yellow dust soft on their toes. On each arm hung a basket overflowing with the last flowers of the season. They held their arms slightly away from their bodies so as not to bang them in case any petals fell off – for they had hand-chosen the perfect ones, which had even involved Molly climbing up on Laura's back to reach ones higher in the hedgerow.

Molly tutted and shifted each basket up her arms, revealing two bracelets of red stripy wicker pattern on her white skin. 'I dunno, is he? Who'd've thought a few flowers could be so heavy?'

'He won't play the donkey game with us any more, and he spends all his time in the fields or God knows where.'

'I dunno. I don't care anyway. 'Tis Brendan who'll be missing him – all the other boys don't like their games.'

'Well, we're lucky so.' Laura glanced over at her sister, checking whether it was safe to make a declaration of their sisterness. 'We'll always have each other to play with.'

Molly tutted again but smiled ahead of her. 'True. But I'll always be faster than you!' She ran ahead slightly, but stopped when a stem leapt from her basket. Laura picked it up, tutting and rolling her eyes in imitation of Molly. They both laughed.

'Can't wait to see the ponies. Come on!'

They hurried along, almost running, while trying to maintain a smooth gait, their small arms beginning to ache with the unaccustomed use of muscles, each giddy with excitement about the day ahead. They had been instructed by Caroline to have the cart decorated by the time she arrived with the spare dress. Laura was to have Kathleen's old First Communion dress, and Molly was to have Caroline's niece's. She was to bring white roses too. The two girls chattered excitedly all the way.

'We must try not to giggle, or Daddy will go mad at us.'

'Yeah, and you'd better not trip me up, 'cause everyone'll be looking at us.'

'No, they won't, they'll be looking at Kathleen, silly ... and Joseph Foley.' Molly said this in a very sing-song big-girl voice and pulled a funny face. She kissed the air and said, 'Mwah mwah ooo will you be my wife?!' The two flower girls spilled into the yard giggling loudly, immediately diffusing the tension of the grown-ups milling about with frowns, organizing the day's events.

Mr Reilly was there with his two horses. One was pure white and perfect for his part in the day's proceedings. The other was old Tom-Boy, who had not been a working horse for a good few years now. Reilly had bought him off the Steeles a few years back for his children's pleasure, enabling Pat Steele to buy another shire, whom Kathleen had named Sandy. Tom-Boy was slightly larger than the white one, with hair so brown it seemed black until you looked closely. He had that doleful look in his eyes that old horses often get, where the corners start to droop and the irises become glassy.

Kathleen watched from her parents' bedroom window as the horses were brought to stand next to each other while their harnesses were measured up. She tried not to feel sad, it being such a merry scene – the girls flitting about the cart, transforming it with an assortment of flowers into a princess's carriage, the haggard busy with people in their best clothes. But the thought of old Tom-Boy always made her feel this way. She had blamed him, when she was a little girl – if only he had galloped faster, maybe the doctor would have come in time.

But he had not been in time. And Tom-Boy had been replaced by a young colt, Sandy, who grew into a stronger horse, able for more and varied work than Tom-Boy. Kathleen had wailed and struck out at Tom-Boy and demanded her father get rid of him. And she thought that maybe she would, once she was dressed, go down and give him a kiss on his nose that once gleamed.

She watched a moment longer as James Reilly lifted Laura up onto Fleck and Molly onto Tom-Boy. Even from the window she could see their faces alive with delight as they set to decorating the bridles with primroses and cowslip, ox-eye daisies and fuchsia. Then she sat down on the edge of the bed to wait for Caroline to come and do her hair. It struck her how big the room seemed in the mid-morning light, and how the space where the cot had been felt empty and, she noted with vague dismay, dusty.

The door opened. 'Knock, knock, Mrs Foley.' It was her father.

'Not quite ... Nearly set?'

'Yes. You? You should get going, miss. You don't want to keep himself waiting.'

'I won't. I was just ... taking time to breathe first.'

'Yes. Always good advice, breathing.'

She caught his smile in the mirror.

'I think the girls might burst with the excitement. You know they wanted to put plaits in the horses' manes?'

Kathleen laughed. 'Poor Tom-Boy. But they're very sweet. They'll be like two angels in their dresses. You'll be very proud.'

'I am, Kathleen. I'm proud of all my girls ... and what they've come through.'

Kathleen looked away.

'Well, I'll leave ye to it so.'

'Thanks.'

'It is right, you know. Having her dress ... She would have wanted ... Well, 'tis traditional, isn't it?'

The dress lay across the bed, behind Kathleen. She had tried it on for size but she hadn't seen herself in it yet. Caroline had let it out slightly around the middle and lengthened the hem. She had her grandmother's silk shawl and a pair of Síle Reilly's shoes. They were white and shiny and a size too small. Kathleen felt like a porcelain doll in them.

She was delaying the moment when she had to look at herself dressed up for her wedding day. It was not how she and Nuala had dreamed it would be as young girls. This was not the great love she had imagined, of course, and she knew it was wrong to wear white. She would be lying to them all, but they would never know unless they looked into her eyes. Even Caroline, measuring her, had commented that she was broader in the hips than her mother. It would not occur to her that Kathleen might be pregnant.

She looked at her face in the mirror, her dress the same blue as the sky outside. And she was sure that she would be beautiful to others in a simple, farm-girl way. But to herself, she would never be beautiful again and that, she deduced, was why she could no longer see Nuala in her. And, as she slowly undressed with leaden fingers, the thought that it wasn't the pregnancy changing her looks, but something deeper, caused her tears to flow ceaselessly. She did not know how she would ever stop.

Her father stepped quietly towards her from his position in the doorway and stood behind her. He reached out an awkward hand towards her shoulder, aching to comfort her. She looked and saw his hand stop in mid-air. And he turned and silently left the room.

Tomás had been given the job of welcoming the guests, which he thought ridiculous as they were all locals with the exception of a few of Kathleen's old school friends who had moved out to Kerry. Father Nolan told him to let people sit anywhere they liked, there being few of Joseph's family coming, 'But keep the first row free for all of ye, of course,' he had said with an excited smile.

'Yes, Father,' Tomás had said politely, but to himself he thought how silly all this fuss was. Since they heard the good news, the whole village had been full of excitement and eagerness to offer their services for the Big Day. It was as if it was the first wedding they had ever seen, the first wedding in all of Ireland. What would their faces look like if they knew the truth of it? What would Joseph Foley do if he knew of the farce? But he did not, and he would do his part. He would smile and welcome everyone.

Tomás meanwhile, was pottering about the church. Father Nolan had gone to prepare and all was quiet. It was the first time he had been in there alone and it was only small so it wasn't long before he had walked each stone flag and grown bored and restless. He lined up the candles on their narrow metal shelves. The spent ones he tossed in the baskets and he wondered briefly what prayers had been sent up in their flames. Tomás hadn't known what to think about God as a child and his prayers had been confined to Mass or those occasions when

Father Nolan came to the house for the rosary and a glass of sherry. Even then the words fell from his mouth with no more thought than breathing and when he found himself really trying to mean them or think of something important that he should be praying about, he found the words themselves became some kind of jumbled and foreign incantation that he could speak but not understand. But reading from the Bible to his mother had brought him a little closer to understanding why men like Father Nolan choose their particular path in life.

Bored with waiting, Tomás sat down on the long bench reserved for their family. He would be next to her, between her and the rest of them, and if she needed to leave, she could squeeze his hand secretly.

Father Nolan's crisp white linen over the altar was patterned here and there with coloured light from the stained glass. He wanted to go up and lay his hand on that invisible space in between the colours of light and the white table to see the effect on his skin. They had never been told it was not allowed but it was assumed by all that the three steps up onto the altar were sacred, for Father Nolan only. But then, the women who cleaned and arranged the flowers were allowed, so why not he? He was there doing a job after all. There was no one in the sacristy and the main door was still shut tight. He opened his ears to the world outside for a moment. There was no sound. The tap of the three steps he took up to the altar rang out in the stone space. Tomás walked cautiously around the table, stepping softly so he would know the moment someone approached the church.

He stood where Father Nolan stood each Sunday and he was struck by how different the place looked from this elevated view. It looked like a different building altogether. While the congregation saw only Father Nolan's face and the backs of the other villagers' heads, Father Nolan himself could, at a glance, see every single one of them, whether they were saying the responses, whether they were bowing their heads in the right places or not – he could probably almost read their minds.

Tomás's body eclipsed some of St Francis's light, casting a shadow across the white cloth. He stood there for some time, marvelling at how the colours played on his fingers as he moved them here and there in the softness of the silence. The hushed atmosphere compelled him to say a prayer, his first real prayer. For once he could concentrate on the words and they flowed out of him as he stood there, back bathed in rainbow-flecked light, and face in shadow, every word a marble dropped on the cool hardness of the floor.

Silently he spoke of his confusion, his secret knowledge of the crime that had occurred in his family. He implored God to understand that it was his own incomprehension that made him unable to act.

'What should I do, Lord? Please tell me what I should do?'

He found himself crying drops of water onto Father Nolan's cloth and childishly wanting his mother's hugs from his childhood. He tried to wipe the spot dry but his fingers left a dark smudge. He thought of Kathleen. And he thought it out loud to God.

'Maybe she forgot how to be a child too. Like me. Maybe

she saw something that grew her up a bit too soon. Maybe she was sick of playing mother to us all. Maybe she thought she was mother . . . but how could he . . . How could he be such an animal? . . . But still . . . I don't understand, Lord. Why have You made this happen? And for whatever we have all done wrong, isn't what You've done to our mother enough? Hasn't she had enough suffering?' The last word echoed in a loud circle around him.

The shock of his voice, amplified and angry, sounded deeper than he thought it really was, like his father's almost. He wished he were a child like Molly and Laura again. He wished he didn't know, and could run off to play Cowboys and Indians with Brendan.

Tomás listened to his coarse breathing, like the breath of one of the cows after it has been pushed and pushed up the hill in the rain. Or a ghostly being that he used to imagine in the dark of night, a monster lurking. He continued aloud, 'Please God, bring the real Mammy back to us. I know she can do it. You've done miracles before. Make her well again, please . . . I'll go in the seminary and be as good as I can be. In the name of the Father, and of the Son, and of the Holy Spirit. Amen.'

'Quick, man. Jesus, you'll be late for your own funeral at this rate!' Joseph Foley glanced with semi-mock contempt at his mentor who was sitting shining his good pair of shoes again while waiting for Joseph. Joseph tutted at this, for what need was there to make the best pair of shoes in the village shine any more brightly?

'Don't use a word like that on a day like this. This is the

best day of my life, remember . . . I don't want anything taint-
ing it.'

The older man smiled at the younger. This little outburst
made him suddenly and acutely mournful for a relationship that
he knew had never been fully realized, despite the intimacy of
their day-to-day life. Even after working hours, young Joseph
was ever the apprentice, always deferent, polite, never speaking
his true opinions for fear of offending or seeming too casual.

And here they were, slightly afluster, both consumed with
the momentousness of the day and the anxious excitement of
it all. A barrier had been let down. They had fussed around each
other all morning, straightening a collar here, fixing a button-
hole there, and generally behaving like two lifelong companions,
brothers almost. Or even father and son, he thought. And on
his last day living there with him, Diarmuid Fitzgerald realized
how much he would miss the boy. And he wanted to tell him
so, to say he was a friend. He wanted to say he wished that
every day they had been as comfortable and as jovial with each
other as they were now. But of course, no, that would be more
than a little silly. He buffed at his toecap one last time and
clipped the tin lid back on to the polish. 'Right then, let's get
going, Mr Foley.'

Joseph looked towards the doctor, but at something much
further away. 'Mrs Foley. Mrs Joseph Foley . . .'

'It has a grand sound to it, Joe.'

Joseph sighed and turned his attention to sorting through a
pile of papers and spare prescription notes on the windowsill.

'Jesus, boy, what is it now? Would you ever hurry up, it's
almost half past.'

'Sorry, I just . . . hang on a minute there, will yeh?'

'I'll be downstairs . . .'

'No. No, wait here, I have something for you. I need you to do something for me.'

The doctor sighed and sat down at the table. 'Hurry. Up.'

'Ah, here we go. This is for you. Well, till twelve o'clock of course. He handed him a handkerchief – his own monogrammed one, the doctor noted – tied into a pouch with a length of string. 'Careful now, when you open it. Don't want it getting lost.'

The doctor tugged at the string, revealing the ring.

'It's Kathleen's grandmother's. I believe she was very close to her.'

'She was. Yes.'

'You did well to come up with this at such short notice.' Joseph scrutinized the doctor's face at this remark for a sign of disapproval. He saw none.

'Anyway, I'd like you to stand up there with me, be the ring-bearer, if you wouldn't mind . . . you know, hold my hand – only metaphorically of course.' The sound of hearty laughter from the two men drifted out of the open window and added to the general atmosphere of village excitement as the neighbours dressed in their Sunday best. Some had begun to make their way down to St Francis's, eager to make the most of this rare occasion.

'Truly, Joseph . . . I am touched.'

'Well, with me not having any family here and . . . well, you're the closest thing . . . I mean, you've been very good to me, taking me under your wing and all.'

'Stop it, you'll have me blubbing before the service has even started. You know I'm soft . . . It's been a pleasure, Joe, having you here. And look at you now . . . it's a different man alto-gether than the one who first set foot in Ballinara.'

Joseph turned to look at himself in the mirror and breathed out slowly to calm his nerves. 'Come on so.' And in their way, they had thanked each other, and knew that each had been as much help and good company as the other since they had met.

They had entered through a side door he had not known existed, like magic, and he had leapt down the steps and into the confession box to hide himself, realizing suddenly that his discovery now would make him appear far more suspicious than had he been found skulking on the altar. He watched them through a crack in the door. Brigid Callaghan, of course, was in charge and began barking orders at her two sisters, who were dressed in the strangest frocks Tomás had ever seen, frocks that in his opinion served only to intensify their ugliness. Moira and Aggie were sent to fuss about the flowers. He had always quite liked Aggie, the youngest one, and thought that if it were not for her annoying eldest sister she might be more popular and outspoken. Brigid attended to the hymn numbers and then the candelabras on the altar.

'What in the name of the Good Lord Himself is this?' Her voice rang out like an old, cracked bell, just as his had done. 'Agatha, did I not tell you to put a fresh cloth on here this morn-ing?'

'I did. You saw me do it, didn't you, Moira?' Tomás could hear Aggie's worried footsteps hurry over to where her sister stood looking aghast at the damp mark on the cloth.

'Sure, 'tis only a bit of water.'

'What? ... there isn't another ready ... Father won't be pleased, especially today of all days. It's his first wedding here in an age.'

'Sure, who would have stained it but him, Bríd?' This time it was the other sister, Moira, and she was standing just the other side of the confession box.

Tomás's heart began to panic. He wouldn't be at all surprised if Brigid Callaghan sent one of them in to check if his hideaway was clean.

Moira continued, 'Don't go changing it now. It'll dry off.'

He was worried his breathing would become uncontrollable again and he would be found out. And what if they did not leave until everyone else started arriving? He would be stuck in there all day.

He heard Brigid tut and then sigh dramatically. 'I don't know. 'Tis best to do a job yourself if it needs doing well. Like mothering.'

'Oh, Brigid Callaghan,' said the voice of Aggie. 'Don't start on that again.'

'Honestly, Agatha, I don't know why you do not agree with me. A child should be with its mother, no matter what the circumstances.'

'But these are such ... exceptional circumstances. And she's the only mother the poor little lamb's ever really known.'

'The poor boy will grow up confused and ... and demented if you ask me. When he finds out his mother's not his mother ... which he will.'

'Well, 'tis none of our business, especially today. And Mr Foley seems such a nice man. A gentleman.'

'Humph. A gentleman with questionable loyalties . . .'

'Well, he's more of a man than any of we three have had the pleasure of meeting.' This was the close-up, loud voice of Moira again.

''Tis true so. A man of any description would do me.' The younger sisters laughed as the third huffed and puffed and clicked her heels down the aisle, commenting brusquely that that was no way to speak in the Lord's house. The main door opened and then closed with a bang.

'Come on. Let's see if Caroline needs a hand quickly.'

'I think poor Kathleen Steele is a living saint, if you ask me.'

'I know. 'Tis about time she had a bit of happiness.'

'And how she dotes on the little one. 'Twas as if he were her own, sure.'

'Bless her. And I bet she'll look a picture today.'

When they too had gone he stepped out and took one last look at the silent, empty church and went to stand by the door to welcome people and hand out songsheets.

When the last guest had arrived he propped the door open for Kathleen to come in and walk up the aisle.

He sat next to his mother and followed her eyes as she looked upon her own wedding dress as her daughter entered, arm in arm with her husband and her two little girls in their special dresses. He wondered what she was feeling, how much she was taking in. All eyes were on the beautiful, good

Kathleen. She watched her husband tread slowly with Kathleen up to the altar.

The girls sat on their stools in front of their pew and Tomás shushed them as the first hymn began. They could not wait to spill their little hankies stuffed with rice, dried lavender and petals all over their big sister. They had not yet been told that she would be going away when it was done, for it would have made it an unhappy day. She looked so sad as she caught the giggling eyes of the girls and, as she looked up at Joseph, he thought, a little afraid. And Tomás understood the enormity of what his sister was doing, had to do, and felt for her. He looked at his father who had sat down beside the girls and bowed his head after delivering her to Joseph, but he could not find it in himself to feel sorry for him.

The bitterness of the cold in the mornings was gradually, gradually lessening. She had begun, over the past couple of months, to settle her own blanket about her, pulling it up, tucking it over her hands when she felt the chill. Under the scratchy woollen material her dry, cracked skin caught. She would use her fingernails to pull at bits of peeling skin, and would rub in little circles to make herself smooth again. She worked away at each knuckle, for that was where it was worst. Tomás would find her some cream no doubt. He was good at noticing these things.

Some days, her ears were full of the noise of the house, and it could come suddenly, like a fright: the children yelling, Kathleen chopping, chair legs scraping – and then the voices would follow their owners outside, or to other parts of the house. And she was left then with the sounds of the house, sounds which never changed, and she was thankful for that.

When there was noise, distraction, she could not see Nuala at all. But she had become less afraid of this and more and more she could not help but engage her mind with what was going on around her. And maybe during the moments that were free of Nuala, her mind felt a little freer too.

Some days she was afraid of opening her eyes and seeing the empty haggard before her, of seeing the faces of her children so much older than she had thought them to be. It would be day when she expected it to be night. She would not have Tomás by her side when she thought he had been there. She did not understand why she was here, every day, life whirling around her as though she were not. It frightened her that a body can be so overcome. And when the memory of that day once more jostled its way rudely to the forefront, she closed down again, for a while. But although the ache within her remained, the despair was less suffocating, and she soon resurfaced.

But Tomás was by her side more often than not. She learned to hear him call to her and they would sit, and he would read and tell of the way things were now in the world, in Ballinara. His presence was comforting, and she was aware that he had been close by for a long time. She listened to her boy, who seemed so grown up to her now. Sometimes his words were as clear as day, other times they filtered dreamily, as if through a haze, a bit like the old priest's long sermons when she was a child. He seemed to understand that it would take time, but he became so excited at the prospect of a walk on the strand with her. He was a good boy, nearly a man. And a good man he was growing into.

She found herself straining to smell, to hear the world outside her.

At night, when the house was quiet, she tried to make sense of things, but it was like a jigsaw puzzle missing too many pieces. Were her recent memories real, or the conjurings of her weary mind? She could not trust it. She did not need much sleep. Her body did so little. The light was usually eking its way through the darkness of night before she nodded off. And in her fretful dreams Nuala was replaced by Kathleen.

She would wriggle her toes, and stretch out her legs. The sight of her feet encased always in slippers made her feel old. She would roll her head on her neck and move her face muscles in little exercises. The stiffness in her every bone ached to be freed. She knew she could do it. She would practise, for deep within her was the urge to trot along the water's edge, her feet free from the heavy woollen socks that had been placed on her for the past five years. She could do it, but she was afraid. How would she make the first step, let it be known to others that she had come back?

And, when she could sense they were all asleep, she would shuffle to sit up in her bed and watch the colour of the dark through the crack in the curtain, the moon painting the sky. She would hum softly. Just notes at first, to test her voice; little melodies of no familiar combination, although when she found a pattern she liked she would repeat it to herself, and to the night.

Sometimes she would hear her husband's singing deep within

her, from somewhere long ago, and would push it aside. She could not abide to recall how this stranger once made her feel. Now his song simply told her of the last lines he would always leave out, that were hauntingly true to her now, 'Our hopes they never have come true, Nora, our dreams were never meant to be . . .'

So she had begun to sing some of the old tunes of her own mother, lullabies handed down, that she had in turn sung once to her own children. She fancied sometimes that, up in her bed, in the dark, Kathleen was singing the same song to Paddy. And at this the notes got stuck in the fug in her throat and she thought that, if she did not swallow, it would choke her and she would die.

He would be big by now, crawling. And she would be big too, of course. Maybe that was why they had not been along in a while, or maybe she had just not noticed. Time was still foggy to her. Days dripped by, but sometimes a week was gone like a puff of smoke.

She remembered that in a drawer of the dresser in the room there were photographs. Two, in little frames that had been given to them on their wedding. She could not bear to look at them and so had hidden them away, but now she knew they were there, the small ceramic handle of the drawer gleamed in the corner of her eye no matter where she looked.

The floor had been swept, the dresser dusted. A small vase of hedgerow flowers sat on a little round mat she had helped Kathleen to crochet when she was small. She must have been in. Had she come and gone while she slept? Maybe it had been Tomás. Nora had to tug at the handle to open it. The thin metal frames were cold on her fingers. The first was of the two of them, before any of the children came along, with her own mother, standing in a line outside the house. The other was of the four of them, Nuala and Kathleen standing in front of their parents, feet together, all smart for the camera. She had spent all morning on their hair. For a moment she could not tell them apart till she remembered – it was Kathleen standing in front of her; she'd had to give her a dig for giggling. She could not bring herself to hide them away again and so set them either side of the vase.

Tomás helped her grow in strength, to be less afraid, encouraging her to walk a little further each day, to carry out small tasks with him. And they began to sit and talk together by the fire in the evenings, only stopping when the latch clicked, signalling his father's return from McCarthy's. She spoke a little falteringly at first, but as the words came back to her, so did the woman behind them, and Tomás thought at times it was as though she'd never been away. He was so patient with her. That support was such a comfort, and she began to feel more like her old self again, with fewer periods when her grief overcame her.

And it was when a message came, via Caroline Walsh's son, that there was a little healthy baby boy that Nora Steele knew it was time. She waited till Colm had left and the two little girls had scurried off to make pictures for their new little nephew, then she said simply, 'Tomás, I want you to take me to Duncarrig.'

He came over to sit by her. 'Are you sure you're ready, Mam? It's a long way.'

'Tomás, I have to. Come on . . . give an old girl a hand up.'

Tomás held out an elbow to his mother. 'There's nothing old about you.'

He helped her as she shuffled towards the mirror, suspicious of what she might find there. Her face was white and saggy and strange. She ran dry fingertips along her cheekbone and pressed them to her pale lips in shock. When she took her fingers away, a dark pink imprint remained. She rubbed at her cheeks to give them a bit of colour. Her coarse, wiry hair was so short and unkempt-looking. She looked like her own mother, just before she died. She teased at her hair with stiff fingers, but the effort made her arms tremble.

Tomás touched her shoulder. 'Let me help . . .' He fetched a comb and rooted around in the basket of ladies' things and found an old stub of half-dried-out lipstick. She applied it shakily, the taste of it on her lip a memory of a life long since past.

Standing up so long had made her feel dizzy but the last thing she wanted to do was to sit down again in that wretched chair. She took a final look at the gaunt painted face staring indifferently back at her. She couldn't see her children in her any more. She suspected there would be little of her in them, also, the small ones especially. One only gets out what one puts in. She tried a smile. 'That'll have to do'.

'You look grand, Mam. Come on . . . Let's get going so.' Tomás pulled her gently away from the mirror.

'Wait . . . I've another job for you first. Go up under my bed

... your father's bed.' She stopped a moment, holding on to the door frame while she gathered herself. 'There's a box. Would you ... go get it for me, would you, love?'

'All right so.' He went to fetch it and then led her outside, helped her onto the cart and tucked her into her shawl. If his father saw him driving the cart out on the road he'd have something to say. But what would he say when he saw who his passenger was? Nothing, probably. He spoke to no one, now Kathleen was gone.

'We should get some bread ... a tart ...'

'But Mam ...'

'They'll see me soon enough, sure. They'll think I'm a ghost. I certainly look like one.' She chuckled and coughed momentarily.

They rode on for some time, Tomás chatting all the way. Nora closed her eyes, the wind fresh on her cheeks, trying to ignore the pain in her hip as the cart bumped and jostled over stones and potholes, until they came to a road she had not seen before, or had never noticed, not having had reason to stop there. Tomás had said he would go in first, so it wasn't such a shock. It would give her a moment to get her breath back. She took in her surroundings. At first she had thought it a grand big house, but then she noticed that none of the curtains matched; there were several bicycles against a wall, and on the scrubby patch of lawn was a broken child's thing, grubby and forgotten about. Facing the building was a street with cramped houses squeezed cheek by jowl, stretching back over a hill. Lines of washing were strung from one house to another, criss-crossing all the way along, upstairs and down. Two children in their nappies sat against a wall playing with a bucket and some balls. How many people lived here? How had Kathleen, who had so loved the freedom and the space of the farm as a child, come to abide in such a place?

Tomás reappeared. 'She said come in. She's a bit weak, like, so just to come in.'

She held the few stems of blossom Tomás had picked for her along the way. They were like a beacon in her hand as they walked, arm in arm, towards the house, a startling pink against the greyness of the place.

The sitting room was quiet. The faint ticking of a clock could be heard from the next room and a little high-pitched yap sounded, far away. Looking about her, she could see that Kathleen had made the best of it, sewing some cream cushions and curtains to try to lift the darkness away from the walls a little. There she sat, in one of her mother's own old nursing smocks, a baby lightly concealed under a blanket. Kathleen's mouth said, 'Hello, Mam,' but no sound came out. The words were choked with tears. Her eyes were all in and her skin was sallow and puffy. A half-hearted plait hung loosely over one shoulder. Nora wanted to go to her, but couldn't somehow. She felt she shouldn't.

'Go on, Mam,' said Tomás, and he awkwardly took the flowers from her, and went into the kitchen to find something to put them in.

She went to sit next to Kathleen. She was sure the armchair had once belonged to Síle Reilly. It was slightly worn on the arms but it suited the little room.

Nora cleared her throat to lose some of the huskiness. 'How are you, love?'

Kathleen could not speak, and only nodded, unable to take her eyes away from her mother's face, which looked somehow more alive and youthful now. There was something there in her tentative half-smile, and in her eyes, that Kathleen had not seen in a long while.

'Sorry . . . it's a shock, I know . . .'

'Mam . . .' Kathleen's voice trailed off, the past few years' confusion and hardship extinguished by this moment. She had dreamed sometimes of this day. She had dreamed of running up to her mother, throwing her arms about her and squeezing and yelping and laughing, but that was sobered by the knowledge of the cursory way she had in recent times attended to her.

'What have you called him?'

'Alfred. Alfred James, after Joseph's father . . .'

'And your Grandda. That's nice, love.' She wanted to reach over and touch her daughter's arm cradling the tiny infant. She could see that he had dark hair already. She stole a look at her daughter. Kathleen's mouth quivered, as if she were holding back a tear. The colour was gone from her cheeks.

'You must let it out, love. You must treasure little Alfred and give him all the love you can muster. You must not forget the living in remembering those who are gone . . . I wanted to say that. I wanted to say that I wish . . .'

Kathleen bowed her head towards her child a little and a big drip appeared on his head, a dark circle on the new downy hair. 'The other one was a girl – she came first.' Kathleen wept aloud now, the baby shaking at her breast. 'I called her Nuala.'

Nora Steele rose from her seat as quickly as her old, stiff bones would let her, and tried her best to cradle them both, sobbing into her daughter's hair. It smelled the same as it ever did.

'I'm sorry, Mam. I don't know—'

'No, Kathleen, I am sorry; 'twas my ... Please don't say you're sorry.'

'No,' she tried to lull her tears, 'but you're here, and that's more than I would have ever hoped for.'

Between both women's breasts the baby Alfred squirmed and cried out. Kathleen settled him. 'Do you think he knows? Can he feel her missing?'

'Love, love ... don't punish yourself so. Those thoughts are not good for you.'

'But I deserve to ... I don't deserve him.' Kathleen gathered the tiny thing into her hands and placed him against her damp cheek.

'Hush now. Here ...' On a side-table, between a bottle of medicine and an overlooked decaying apple core, she noticed a comb. Walking painfully to the back of Kathleen's chair, she untied the plait, and began to work away at the knots and the frizz.

''Twas always stubborn. Both of you had the most stubborn, beautiful hair. 'Twas the envy of all the mothers in Ballinara.'

'Nuala always liked hers down, do you remember, with just a little bit up, like so.' Kathleen pulled a section up to the side with her free hand.

'I do. And when you were both babies, sure I thought 'twould never grow. Two little baldies ye were.'

Kathleen felt herself smile. It was what she had been waiting for all these years, without realizing, to talk about Nuala with her mother. And it comforted her for a moment, and gave her hope for her little boy, to think that there really was nothing like a mother's love. For Nora to come, despite losing one daughter to God and another to sin. How hard it must be to set eyes on the baby before her. But it was like an addiction, feeling her mother's fingers working through her hair. If she closed her eyes she could be a little child again, and that small physical connection made her feel that somehow everything would be all right. She found herself wishing that she would never go, that Tomás would not return to take her away. She had not known till this moment how much she had missed her.

Kathleen turned to look at her mother. 'Mam . . . are you all right now? Are you back to stay?'

Her mother said simply, 'Yes, love. I think I am.' The room was calm now. The baby slept peacefully.

Joseph stepped in from the world outside to find the two of them there. 'Jesus . . .' He was carrying a number of groceries which he almost dropped. The pink flowers shone at him through the gloom.

'Hello, Joseph Foley.' She set the comb down and came towards him a little and tried a smile.

Setting things quickly down, he took her hand in both of his. 'A pleasure to meet you, Mrs Steele. Well, this is good news, what, Kathy? This is good news, two lots in as many days.' He felt the woman wobble a little and offered her a chair.

'Congratulations, Joseph. A happy addition.'

'Oh, the light of my life, Mrs Steele . . . Forgive me . . . it's a bit of a shock.'

'I'm sorry, we should have warned you. Tomás has been so good in helping me feel better.' She gathered her shawl around her. 'I think it's time we should be going. Joseph, could you go find Tomás for me?'

'I think he's just outside with Paddy . . . I'll bring them both in.'

'You're very good, thank you.' Before she left she would remind him to monitor Kathleen's eating and sleeping. She turned back to her. She did not look old enough to be a mother. It had been a long time since she had looked at her daughter closely. She had spent far too long searching her mind for Nuala, too long detached from the family around her. And if she had not abandoned them, her children, Kathleen would not be sitting in this depressing room, would never know what it meant to lose a child.

'Come home, love. This is not where you want to be. You need your family . . . Caroline misses you. And the girls, I'm sure . . .'

Kathleen stood up and went to place the child in his crib. 'No. I can't come back. I can never go back.'

'But 'tis your home, Kathleen. It's where you belong.'

'Joseph's my family now, and he is providing a good home for us. And Molly and Laura, they'll be just fine now they have their mammy back.' She leaned down, wincing slightly, to leave a kiss on the little head. She plucked the two little clenched fists sitting either side of it and tucked them into his blanket.

Nora Steele stepped to the foot of the cradle and steadied

her breathing before looking at the child properly. He was so small, almost too small, and less chubby than her own twins had been. But he was beautiful, perfect. He had his father's nose. She did not know what that made her feel, but she did not resent Kathleen. Nothing she felt would come close to what her daughter was feeling now. At least she had known her Nuala before she died.

A lick of dark hair blemished the child's white, white skin. Not a milky white, but a pure, glowing white. There was a frown on his forehead as he breathed and his thick eyelashes flicked and trembled – what was he dreaming about? His birth, or the memory of being safe and warm and inside? Or was he remembering the presence of his twin, feeling the absence of her, as she knew Kathleen feared? The shock of suddenly realizing how awful that must be, to lose such a part of yourself, made her feel sick all of a sudden. Was it not worse than losing one's own child? Poor Kathleen, to have that grief and then to feel that her own newborn child was experiencing something similar.

She had looked at each of her own children and marvelled at how they could have something to dream about already. Tears welled up in her eyes as she thought of Paddy. Her strength was waning. She could not face seeing him. She wanted to be at home, to be in the sanctuary of her little bed, the room that had kept her safe from the world. But she couldn't leave her daughter in this place, in a life where she didn't fit. And besides, she wanted her nearby, to make up for the lost years. The thought of her sitting in that chair feeding and looking out on the bleak scene outside, nothing but grey and noise and dirt, frightened her. It was her own fault. And Kathleen was only a child. It was her own foolish selfishness that had forced her daughter to grow up so quickly. And now here Kathleen was, mourning her own child and, still, the loss of her sister.

Yet they were united in one sense. They alone, it seemed, knew how grief can come to rule every waking hour. And on that day, with a simple unspoken acknowledgement, the two mothers came to an understanding. And by that, they found a source of comfort within one another, and came to be at last as mother and daughter should be. It was also at this moment, as her baby snuffled noisily in her arms, that Kathleen Steele realized she could come to love the man who called himself the child's father.

Tomás came in carrying the box, followed by Joseph, whose arms had a new bundle in them this time. Paddy had obviously been sleeping as his hair was chaotic and his cheeks were rosy red. He looked about him, his eyes resting on Nora briefly, suspiciously, before squirming to get down. Joseph placed him on the floor which, she noted, had been swept and scrubbed and had a beautiful rug laid on it. It helped lift the room and echoed, she noted, the pattern of the two armchairs. Síle Reilly was a generous woman and Nora knew that it would have been very difficult for Kathleen to accept this kindness. She watched as the boy scrabbled across to a chair and proceeded to wind his way around the room to Kathleen, fat hands grasping each chair until he was near enough to reach up to her. Kathleen sat down, beaming at him.

'He wants up. Would you, Joe? . . . It's hard to give him all the attention he's used to, isn't it, Pad? He doesn't like that I can't lift him.' There was a silence in the room.

'Oh no, you mustn't lift him just yet.' Her mother's voice came quietly as Joseph moved forwards to help, or maybe she spoke only in her head. 'He's a . . . well, he's . . . he's bonny . . .'

Kathleen had not noticed her mother going pale and touching her hand to her head, because something had caught her eye. 'What's that you've got there, lad? What've you got tucked under that arm of yours?' A smile emanated from behind his thumb and he squeezed hard onto his prize. Kathleen tickled him gently under his arm until he let go, and she exclaimed, 'Yellow Ear!! . . . Oh, look, Mam . . . where on earth?!'

But Joseph had noticed and stood holding on to the woman, as though afraid she might break. 'Mrs Steele, are you all right there?'

'I'm grand, thank you . . . it was nothing. Tomás, show Kathleen what we brought. And now, we'll leave ye in peace.'

Then she turned to Kathleen, trying to avoid the little boy's indifferent eyes. 'You'll lay her next to Nuala, won't you . . . and Granny? Father Nolan will come.'

Kathleen nodded and closed her eyes and nose on the soft material of the teddy and breathed in to her soul. Yellow Ear absorbed her tears. Her mother picked up the old stub of apple core and took it with her. She would throw it out in the field when she got home.

'There's more stuff in the box, love,' Joseph said to Kathleen as he lifted Paddy. 'It looks . . . I think it's all Nuala's. You should have it. We'll leave you to it for a minute.'

Kathleen heard the door click and then the murmuring of voices outside. Sounds seemed constrained in this place, closed in; they were not familiar to her yet. She could not love this place. When her strength returned there would be nowhere to walk with the children. Joseph said it was only temporary, and she trusted him in that, but it would not matter where they went. It would not matter if there was an orchard of blossom trees instead of a single vase, because it was not home to her. And although she was married to a good, kind man, she ached inside for the boreen with its sweet scents of honeysuckle and cowslip, and the smell of the hay as she looked down to the sea.

Often, she thought of him, out all on his own in a big field, under a huge pink sky. He would cry out, he would weep sometimes, she knew. He would begin to believe that she had begun to loathe him, as he loathed himself, that she was disgusted by him, and it would eat him up inside. But she did not loathe him, and she wished there was a way to comfort him somehow, to say it was all right. She felt no blame towards anyone but herself. But she could never go back now.

Kathleen sat upon the floor to look through the box. The baby things held no particular significance to her, but there were pictures, letters they had written to each other and posted in paper aeroplanes from one side of the hayloft to the other, or from one tree to another. There were clothes and ribbons, and handwritten prayers and schoolwork, all signed at the top, 'Nuala', and a christening gown. She held it up to the thin light. It was beautiful. At the bottom she found a little tin with a picture of a pink elephant on it. Maybe she had seen it once, long ago, on her mother's washstand. She clicked it open and found two locks of identical hair, tied with string. She picked them up and stroked their smoothness against her lip. Then she replaced them and closed the lid and slid it into the pocket of her cardigan.

She found herself humming the song about the ivy tree to the baby, and in her head the words echoed sadly, 'I left my mother, I left my father, I left all my brothers and sisters too, I left all my friends and my own religion, I left them all for to follow you.'

To the box she added the hospital tag from the day before, the only proof that her baby girl had been there, just for a moment, a breath in this life. She had not even opened her eyes to see her mother's face. She did not cry. She was brave, like her namesake. Kathleen tucked it in under a blanket and whispered to her sister before she closed the lid, 'You look after her now . . .' and she turned towards the baby, who was beginning to snuffle beside her.